Dale Romney currently resides with his wife and children in Utah where he spends every free moment coming up with new story ideas. He enjoys hiking, swimming, spending time with family, and of course writing. *The Lost Order* is his first book series

Follow him on Instagram: @romneydale, or send him an email at author.daleyeiter@gmail.com

This is a work of fiction. Names, characters, businesses, places, events and incidents are either the products of the author's imagination or used in a fictitious manner. Any resemblance to actual persons, living or dead, or actual events is purely coincidental.

THE LOST ORDER: THE BIRTH OF A DRAGOON

DALE ROMNEY

**THE LOST ORDER:
THE BIRTH OF A DRAGOON**

VANGUARD PAPERBACK

© Copyright 2023
Dale Romney

The right of Dale Romney to be identified as author of this work has been asserted by him in accordance with the Copyright, Designs and Patents Act 1988.

All Rights Reserved

No reproduction, copy or transmission of this publication may be made without written permission.
No paragraph of this publication may be reproduced, copied or transmitted save with the written permission of the publisher, or in accordance with the provisions of the Copyright Act 1956 (as amended).

Any person who commits any unauthorised act in relation to this publication may be liable to criminal prosecution and civil claims for damages.

A CIP catalogue record for this title is available from the British Library.

ISBN 978-1-80016-598-4

Vanguard Press is an imprint of
Pegasus Elliot Mackenzie Publishers Ltd.
www.pegasuspublishers.com

First Published in 2023

Vanguard Press
Sheraton House Castle Park
Cambridge England

Printed & Bound in Great Britain

To my wife,
Thank you for believing in me and always encouraging me to keep writing. Without you, none of this would be possible.

Contents

Omen	9
Chapter 1: Albert	14
Chapter 2: The Dream	27
Chapter 3: Marked	42
Chapter 4: Brookshire	54
Chapter 5: Clues	71
Chapter 6: Getting Answers	85
Chapter 7: Preparations	102
Chapter 8: The Adventure Begins	117
Chapter 9: Trouble on the Plains	134
Chapter 10: Ethanan Awaits!	145
Chapter 11: Elves? I Expected More	161
Chapter 12: Prisoners	171
Chapter 13: Escape into the Night	189
Chapter 14: Daratine Mountains	204
Chapter 15: Captured	219
Chapter 16: Secrets Revealed	232
Chapter 17: King Uthael	247
Chapter 18: Ambush	257
Chapter 19: Gruttlik's Weapon	276
Chapter 20: Gerrick	285
Chapter 21: Sunchaser	295
Chapter 22: Long Live the Queen	304
Chapter 23: Journey Back	319

Omen

King Uthael sat on his bed rubbing his aching joints, long pointed ears drooping at the tips, brows long and scraggly, the once elegant and regal face now weathered by the burdens of rule. He grumbled to himself, accepting the pains of old age that bothered him more and more each day. Over two hundred years he had ruled Ethosis, but he felt he still had much to do. His people depended on him, and he would not allow his life's end to interfere with his people's need of him.

Over the past weeks, Uthael's dreams had disturbed him. In them, he watched as a dark shadow enclosed the woodland kingdom where he and his people lived. The darkness encroached on his city as people ran for their lives. The trees decaying became covered with weblike gray moss blocking out the light. Finally, their once beautiful palace was swept up in shadow. Uthael at first discarded the dreams, paying them no mind, but soon they began to feel real. He would awaken in cold sweat calling out in worry. Recognizing these as more than just dreams, he knew he needed to stop his visions from coming true. As king he had the gift of seership, using these visions he saw in his dreams to guide his people.

He pushed himself from the bed, feeling the warmth of the tree soothe his aged feet. With his robes over his sleepwear, the king shuffled over to the water basin on the wall of the tree which formed his palace. The tree supplied the water, bringing it all the way up from the roots that dug deep into the ground. Uthael splashed his face, trying to wash away the images along with his worries. He called for his valet Elu'es who assisted the king in getting ready to receive the day's visitors in the great hall.

Men, dwarves, gnomes, halflings, creatures of the woods, and neighboring kings came seeking visions of their futures. Some traveled hundreds of miles for the opportunity to consult with him.

By day's end, Uthael had grown weary and was glad the hours of receiving visitors were almost through. He watched as the sun shed its last rays through the great hall's windows before deciding he would be done for the day. As he rose his hand to signal Elu'es to help him out of the magnificent wooden throne that the tree itself had created for him, one of the guards announced a visitor. Holding on to his valet's arm he exclaimed, "Send them away. I will take no more visitors today. Tell them to come back tomorrow. I will see them then."

"I ask only a moment of your time, oh wise king," came a pleading voice from the doorway. "I think I have something to say that you will want to hear."

Uthael walking toward the back of his great hall turned as the almost silky voice caressed his ears. A man with bronze eyes in an indigo cloak peered out from beneath the hood. With little more than a cursory glance at the man, he noticed Elu'es shaking his head indicating he should ignore the man and keep going. As Elu'es was about to tell the guard to send away the stranger, Uthael spoke up.

"And what is so important that it cannot wait a day?" he asked, annoyed with the man.

"It is concerning an evil that will befall this land, Your Highness," the hooded man replied earnestly.

Fearing the stranger would harm his king, Elu'es quickly ordered the guards to seize him. Obeying immediately, they took hold of the hooded man, forcing him to his knees.

"That will be enough. Bring him to me," King Uthael ordered. The man was taken to the king and made to bow before him. "Now," said King Uthael, "What can you tell me about this?"

The man pulled back his hood revealing his face. His hair was deep red, his skin a lighter shade which seemed to make his bronze eyes even brighter. "You're a Zydairian," Uthael commented, a look of slight disgust on his face.

"My name is Gerrick, my Lord, and I come to tell you that this shadow you see in your dreams will destroy you and your kingdom."

Elu'es barked at the audacity of this man thinking that something could destroy them. "Nonsense, heathen. No force has ever come close to penetrating our forest.

It is protected not only by our great king but the magic that lives in these woods themselves."

King Uthael patted Elu'es on the arm. "Keep calm, my friend. Let Gerrick finish what he has to say."

"But, my Lord, this man lies. Don't believe this sorcerer's words," Elu'es urged. King Uthael merely patted him again and gestured for Gerrick to continue.

Gerrick bowed. "I understand your valet's concern, but he does not know what you dream and what I have seen. Your kingdom will fall, and I have come to help save it. You are not as strong as you once were, my Lord, if you don't mind me saying." Elu'es and the guards threw Gerrick a look of disgust. How dare he insult their king, but Uthael's head sank at the truth of Gerrick's words.

Still, the king motioned him on, "Continue."

"Age takes its toll on all of us, does it not?" said Gerrick.

Uthael frowned again and nodded his head.

"Without the strength you once had when you were young, you and your people will surely die. There is a power in the Daratrine Mountains that can help you get back your strength and with it, save your people," finished Gerrick.

Uthael could tell his men were getting anxious, he raised his hand to settle them. He stood, staring into Gerrick's eyes skeptically. *How could he possibly know something I do not,* he thought. Uthael was about to turn him away when images of darkness covering his land, destroying his people flashed across his mind. Did he have any other choice? "Take me to this power." He relented.

Gerrick bowed his head in compliance, "Yes, my Lord. you will not regret this. Together we will save your people and perhaps our world."

Chapter 1: Albert

Albert Worthington, twelve years old, and starting his first day of sixth grade, walked down the unpaved country road unconsciously kicking at its rocks. He had on jeans and a green t-shirt with blue and white horizontal stripes, his short hair was spiked up in the front, and his green eyes stared aimlessly at the ground in front of him. His destination was the bus stop several yards down the road where kids gathered for their ride to school. When Albert got within twenty feet of the stop, he raised his head to see who was already there. Just as his eyes began to focus, a dirty plastic grocery bag planted itself on the right side of his head and face.

"Yuck," he said out loud, peeling it from himself and releasing it back into the wind. Wind? There had been no wind before. Not even a slight breeze. He looked around. Nope, no wind anywhere except…where the inflated bag was blowing. Albert stared in wonder as he watched the bag, debris, and other dirt swirl in a ten-foot-diameter circle, a little off the road. Tornados were known to quickly appear in Texas but there wasn't even a cloud in the sky.

That's weird, he thought to himself. *It must be a dust devil.*

The mysterious weather event urged him to investigate. He looked down the road at the bus stop to see how many kids were there. Only a couple more had arrived, and the bus was nowhere in sight. Plenty of time to check out the odd phenomenon.

Albert dropped his pack to the ground and pushed his way through the tall grass closer to the dust devil. The wind grew stronger, pulling him and the grass toward the center. Albert made his way toward the middle as the dust and trash-laden wind swirled around his feet like water down a drain. Each step he took grew more difficult trying to stay on his feet. He stooped down, spreading his arms out for balance. The wind continued to grow in force. He wondered if this was such a great idea. He had turned around, deciding to turn back, when a burst of wind threw him off balance.

Albert rolled over and over, somersaulting toward the center of the dust devil. To his surprise, the wind near the center was calmer, but he could still feel it a few inches above the ground, swirling inward. Cautiously, Albert got to his feet near the center of the swirling winds struggling to maintain his balance. He looked through the long grass in the distance to where the other kids stood and found one of them watching him oddly. With a sheepish grin, Albert waved to him. The boy waved back awkwardly and turned back to his friend.

He shuffled his feet closer to the center. The pull of the wind grew stronger, like hands reaching up from the ground and pulling him inwards. Near the edge of the vortex's center, Albert felt a tug pull him forward. Albert took a step to steady himself only to discover there wasn't ground beneath him. He was about to fall! Circling his arms backward to balance, he realized he wasn't falling, but more frozen in place. Suddenly, the grass was gone, the wind was gone, his classmates were gone; nothingness surrounded him. Yet… he could feel something like a rope tied around his waist pulling him forward. He was moving, but not moving at the same time.

Albert felt himself moving faster and faster, like on a rollercoaster ride at a theme park. He felt nauseous, about to vomit or faint or both! A moment later, he saw brightness heading toward him. Bright white and orange-yellow lights shedding scorching heat streamed past. Where was he? Where were these burning lights coming from? Had he fallen and hit his head? Was this all just some dream? At the split-second Albert expected to melt, the lights dimmed to myriad shades of brown.

A second later, blue lights streaked through the browns. Suddenly, the lights and colors took form in the trees of a forest. The force, now from behind, pulled him backward with a jerk. Like someone slamming on the brakes, throwing him forward in his seat.

Albert shot out of the vortex into the air and came crashing down onto the hard soil, landing flat on his back. He groaned in pain as tingling heat began to radiate from his shoulders and his head began to throb.

What had just happened? Had he just fainted? Or did he just trip and fall? He rubbed the back of his head where he felt swelling forming.

Oh shoot! His classmates probably witnessed the whole thing. He sat up too quickly, his head spinning. He leaned to one side using an arm to brace himself. When his vision cleared, Albert finally viewed the scene around him. No kids. The road was gone too. No tall grass, no plastic bags, no street signs or signs of humanity anywhere. Just forest. Giant trees with bright vibrant green leaves, mixed with luminescent shimmering blues and reds surrounded him. Thick brown trunks planted deep into the ground seemed to hold firm onto their positions.

In front of him, was an odd-looking light-brown bunny whose tail was a giant white puffball larger than itself and long antennae-like ears with fuzzy white tufts. He had never seen such a funny-looking rabbit. Though, the only ones he had seen were at a pet store. It sat several feet away chewing broad blades of grass while staring at him as if watching a scene from a movie. A brown lizard with two tails sunbathed on a nearby rock. Slowly, the bunny moved off into the forest. Albert chuckled to himself as it hopped along, its ears and tail flailing back and forth with every jump.

The distraction of the bunny over, it was now back to figuring out what had happened to him. Had his classmates seen him fall and get knocked out? Had they taken advantage of this opportunity to play a prank on him? Somehow placing him in a forest and leaving him there for fun?

"Okay, guys, this isn't funny," Albert called out.

… No answer.

"Come on, guys." His head was pounding, "I would really like to go home."

… Still no answer.

Getting up his head spun, and he had to catch himself from falling again. If this was some sort of prank, it seemed they had left him to find his way out of the woods. Though he was new to the neighborhood, he did know that the only forest close to town was west of them. Which way was east, though? He looked down, seeing that his shadow was behind him. Then he looked up for the sun. *What? How long was I out?* he thought. It was early morning when he had investigated the dust devil. Now it looked to be past noon.

He needed to double-check and make sure he had his positioning correct. *Moss grows on the north side of trees, right?* Checking the trees nearby, Albert's shadow pointed northeast. He corrected a little more to the right and walked past the rock with the two-tailed lizard, staring at him. *Usually, lizards run when you get close to them,* he thought.

"Do you know the way out of here?" he asked.

The lizard cocked its head as if thinking, then shook it side to side.

Whoa, did that lizard just answer me? He wondered in surprise. Worried the hit to his head might be causing him to see things, Albert sidestepped past the lizard, hurrying away. *Maybe the bunny I saw was a hallucination as well?* He had better get out of this forest fast and home so his parents could take him to see the doctor.

He stumbled along fast as he could. It wasn't long before Albert jumped backward, startled again. Coming around a couple of large trees, he ran into a grazing doe and her fawn. Frightened, the skittish animals took off bounding into the forest. *Now I know I'm hallucinating!* The deer looked like deer; except they had moss-green scales instead of brown fur. Taking a deep breath, he tried to collect himself. Albert found his heading again and continued, this time at a jog.

After what seemed like an eternity, Albert heard the familiar sound of running water. His spirits lifted as he ran toward the sound. He weaved in and out and around the trees, running in whatever direction the sound seemed loudest until he finally arrived at a rushing river carving its way through the woods.

Heaving a huge sigh of relief, he made his way down the grass embankment to the water's edge. Scooping water with cupped hands, Albert took his first sip. He hadn't realized just how thirsty he had been. It was refreshingly cold, its chill soothing his parched throat and pounding chest. Lying on his stomach this time to suck up as much water as he could, he stopped abruptly when a large blue bubble-like shell crept from the water. Frightened, Albert pushed himself away from the water as a crab crept its way out of the river. Now that he could see the entire body, it was the size of a cantaloupe. The creature was colored in different hues of blue. Six legs scurried along the ground with two small claws extended ready to strike, crawling towards Albert.

Albert kept his distance, trying to anticipate the crab's next move. Its claws seemed too small to be of any threat, but he had never seen any crab like this before. Who knew what they could do? Bubbles began to foam out of the creature's mouth. Was that it? Was foaming at the mouth the crab's great attack? Albert huffed out loud, "Oh yeah, you're really scary, aren't you?" He crawled closer to the creature, planning on scaring it back into the water. When he got within a foot, slimy water burst forth from the crab's mouth, hitting Albert square in the face.

"Ughhhhhh," said Albert as he hurriedly wiped mucus water from his lips, nose, and eyes. The water didn't sting but gave off a putrid, boggy smell. One hand flew to his mouth and the other covered his stomach as he tried to hold back the vomit. Quickly he ran to the water's edge far away from the crab. Albert dropped to his hands and knees expelling river water and stomach acid. He dunked his head in the water several times trying to wash off the mucus. Having succeeded in removing most of the smell, Albert went down for one more dunk.

Then he sat on the grass several feet back from the river. He wiped the water from his eyes. He should have guessed that the foaming bubbles were just a sign of things to come. Never again would he get near the river's edge, no matter how thirsty he was. He didn't have much time to relax, however, as several small hands climbed up his back. Frozen in fear of what it might be, he looked over his shoulder coming face to face with two beady little eyes.

"Aaaahhhhh," he screamed aloud. As he jumped to his feet, whatever it was sprung from his back. Whirling around, he found a squirrel the size of a house cat staring up at him. Four arms were held close to its chest as if begging for food and two massive hind legs steadied the creature upright. A long bushy tail helped to counterbalance the grey and white squirrel. Fearing that this furry creature might have ulterior motives, Albert turned and ran as fast as his feet could carry him alongside the river.

When Albert could run no more, he lay against a tree exhausted from his flight. Every part of his body ached, and his legs felt like wet noodles. His thoughts turned to home, wondering if his parents were out looking for him. *How far did they take me into this forest?* He thought to himself. *I don't think I can walk another foot. I guess I will have to find my way home tomorrow unless a rescue team finds me first. Maybe I shouldn't have moved from where I woke up. Isn't that what you are supposed to do when you are lost? Stay in one place?*

He lay on the ground watching the sun move across the sky toward the horizon. As it set, he watched streaks of orange and red blaze across the sky. A battle of colors raged in the clouds as reds and pinks tried to win over grays and whites. Never before had he seen a sunset like it, wishing for a camera to remember it. When the sun finished its descent and darkness encroached, the sights and sounds of the woods began to change.

Mysterious lights appeared in the surrounding trees. Albert watched above him as fluidic lights coursed up the tree trunks and down the branches like veins. Blossoms erupted into turquoise, blue and white flowers and leaves. The entrancing spectacle pulled him farther and farther into its mesmerizing embrace. A high-pitched screech from the other side of the river pulled him out of his hypnosis. His heart pounded and his chest heaved at the thought of what could make such an ear-piercing sound. He didn't know what mad scientists had unleashed such strange creations into this forest, but when he got back he would let the authorities know. If he made it through the night, that is. Tiredness soon overcame him, and he soon drifted to sleep against a large oak.

Albert felt a beam of warm sunshine on his face. He cautiously opened one eyelid. Nothing. No one. He was alone in the forest.

"Ugh, I was hoping yesterday was some sort of nightmare," he whined to himself, tears coming to his eyes. "I just want to go home."

Albert rose to his feet and walked over to the edge of the riverbank. He studied the water carefully, making sure none of those blue crabs lurked beneath the water's surface. Feeling it was safe, he knelt, taking a few sips of water from cupped hands and splashing water on his face, hoping to wash away whatever mucus might be left from yesterday's attack.

He got to his feet and feeling ready for the day, he decided to follow the river downstream. It wasn't long after he had set off that his stomach grumbled and begged for food. He thought his only chance of getting food was to get out of this forest and back to town. Albert wondered if he should try finding berries, but what if he got lost or they were poisonous? What if he couldn't find the river again? Albert decided it was too risky and that his best bet would be to just keep following the river.

Albert's hunger was soon the only thing occupying his mind. He tried to keep his thoughts occupied with school and his homework, but the constant rumbling of his stomach brought him back to food. Every step was a wish of exiting the forest and finding home. At least the river was there whenever he wanted a drink. Walking to the river's bank, he bent to gulp several handfuls of the cold water, always cautious of the blue crabs. Drinking brought much-needed relief and energy to his tired body. When he had his fill, Albert stood and returned to following the downstream flow. But… something had changed. No longer could he hear the birds singing their songs in the trees, the sounds of creatures running around the forest floor silenced, and the blue crabs that had scurried up and down the riverbanks weren't anywhere in sight either. What was going on? Some inner voice told him this wasn't a good sign.

He obeyed a sudden urge to run as fast as he could. From the corner of his eye, he saw something moving with him on a parallel course. A wolf or large dog burst through the bushes barely a few feet away from him! It was a hideous-looking thing, like a dog with stringy, gray fur and black and purple quills protruding from its back along the spine. Even more prominently noticeable were razor-sharp teeth within its bared, gnashing mouth. Fear hastening his pace.

Albert chanced a look at the wolf causing him to trip on a rock. Now face to face with the ground, the animal lunged toward him. Albert somehow managed to roll out of the way, kicking it in defense. Yet, its noxious breath still filled his nostrils. The smell caused him to gag and dry vomit a little, giving the wolf time to turn for another assault. Frantically looking around, Albert found a long, thin branch next to him on the ground. He quickly grabbed it, jumped to his feet, and started flailing it side to side to keep the creature at bay. It emitted a growl that rumbled up from its chest, causing Albert to shake with fear.

Albert's desperation increased, equaling the size of the monster confronting him. He continued swinging the branch back and forth, hoping it would leave him alone, thinking he wasn't worth the effort. The creature was refusing to cooperate. It timed its lunge perfectly, snatching the branch in its jaws, and jerked it from Albert's hand, tossing it to the side, out of Albert's reach.

Albert backed toward a tree, clutching one bleeding hand with the other. He closed his eyes and braced for death. The creature's horrific growling grew closer and closer. Whimpers escaped Albert's lips, wishing he was home safe and sound with his family. Cringing as he expected the creature to lunge for the kill, he heard a sudden crack ring through the air. Albert opened his eyes to see a fiery red ball smash into the side of the creature. Its impact flung the wolf through the air and made the wolf land several feet away. The stark scent of burnt fur filled his nose, causing him to gag, again. The creature lay there yelping in pain. Albert shuddered as he watched it pick itself up from the ground, whining as it ran off into the forest.

What had just happened? Who saved him? The shadow of a creature flew overhead. Albert quickly realized he might be wrong. Whatever it was might not be here to save him but eat him. He tried to hide underneath the nearest tree as a miniature dragon, the size of a medium-sized dog, landed on the ground in front of him. The dragon stood on four legs, its body covered with beautiful jade scales laced with reds and blues. Two small horns crowned its head, a row of spines running down its back, and its tail came to a point like an arrowhead.

The dragon took a couple of steps toward Albert, spread its wings, and lifted itself onto its hind legs, opening its mouth to reveal dozens of small, serrated teeth. Once more it took a deep breath, its eyes focused intently on Albert. Sparks streamed up and out its throat, traveling along the teeth until they formed a focal point in the air before its mouth—another fiery ball was coming. Albert stood paralyzed with fear. His mind told him to run, hide, anything but something held him in place. Why couldn't he move? Was something holding him here? He stood waiting for death. No whimpers. No crying. No sound.

As the dragon unleashed its breath, Albert barely had time to react. Automatically he threw up his arms to protect his face. The fire-streak struck his right arm with a burning sensation that coursed up his arm and through his entire body. Weak and dizzy, his vision blurred, and darkness closed around him. A split second before his eyes shut completely, Albert thought he saw the dragon lift off and head toward the skies.

Chapter 2: The Dream

The pungent smell of ginger and other herbs filled Albert's nose as consciousness returned to him. His body ached, his ears rang, and he was afraid to open his eyes for fear of where he might be. He didn't know how he had survived the dragon's attack, but the strange scents made him think he had been moved somewhere. After a few deep breaths, he gained enough courage to open his eyes. He was in a circular room made of stone and logs. A wood-burning stove opposite him kept the small area warm. The bed he found himself on was made from narrow timbers and had a large animal skin stretched and tethered to the posts in hammock style. Straw piled on the skin made up the mattress and a light cloth sheet acted as a covering. A simple wooden chair sat next to the bed. The clothes he had been wearing had been swapped for a woven white cotton shirt and brown trousers. A table on the other side of his bed held some bottles, a mortar and pestle to grind ingredients, and several bowls containing different dried plants. Was that the source of the smell?

Two doors exited the room: one looked thick and heavy, the other appeared made from simple wood planks. Light entered through an array of curved windows running around the house just below the thatched roof. Where was he? Who was taking care of him?

Albert tried to get out of bed, but his body refused to cooperate. The harder he tried, the worse the pain that shot through him. Apparently, he hadn't yet recovered sufficiently from the dragon's attack. But wait. Dragons don't exist. Then, again, neither do six-legged cat-sized squirrels, crabs with giant blue bubble-like shells, or wolfdog things with huge quills sticking out of their backs. As much as he didn't want to admit it, Albert couldn't stop thinking he might not be on Earth any more. Could that be possible?

Again, he tried to sit up. Pain streaked through his body. Gritting his teeth, he grabbed the timbers of the bed for leverage and pushed. Barely managing to get his head up, he heard a man's voice outside the cottage. He strained to listen to what was being said. But the voice was too muffled from the heavy door and there was still ringing in his ears. Whoever it was stopped speaking as the door opened. Albert quickly lay back down, pretending to still be asleep.

"Confounded elves," the man said annoyed. "They think they rule the entire world." The man turned, seeing Albert fidget in bed. "You can stop pretending. I see that you are awake."

Albert sighed; he could never fool his mother either. He opened his eyes to a middle-aged man standing over him. There was no denying the smirk on his weathered, round face. The man had thinning red hair and bright-green eyes. His white well-worn robes were trimmed with red embroidered symbols around the hood, cuffs, and hem.

"You're not going to hurt me, are you?" Albert whimpered.

The man frowned, "Heavens, no, my dear boy. Whatever gave you that idea?"

"Well, everything else around here has tried to hurt me?"

"Well, I'm not. Where are you from? By the looks of the clothes you were found in, I can tell you're not from around here."

"Uh, Waco."

"Waco? Never heard of it. What part of Thu'hilen is Waco located in?"

Albert looked at him, confused. "Thu'hilen? What is that?" he asked.

It was the man's turn to look baffled. "What is Thu'hilen? Why, it's only the world in which we live," he exclaimed.

Albert lay there, stunned. Thu'hilen? The world they lived in? Yep, he definitely wasn't on Earth any more.

"Wow! I'm in another world?" But… how? He lay on the bed trying to take in what he'd just been told. "I guess they speak English on Thu'hilen as well."

"I don't know what English is, but you are speaking Thulian," the man chuckled.

"No, I'm not. I don't even know how to speak Thulian. You're speaking English."

The as yet unidentified man smiled at Albert, then walked to a strange-looking curved bookcase lining one wall of the man's home—assuming this man owned the 'house' in which Albert currently found himself. Pulling a book from the shelf, he walked back to Albert, opened it, and laid it upon Albert's lap. He helped Albert sit up to look more easily at the words on the indicated page. "Can you read this?" he asked, settling down into the chair next to Albert's bed. The page contained strange symbols, yet to his astonishment, Albert could indeed read them.

"But this doesn't make any sense!" Albert said baffled. "How can I read this? I've never seen nor heard of Thu'hilen before."

"Tell me, my boy. How did you get here from… where did you say you were from again? Waco? Is that what you called it?" the man asked, intrigued.

Albert sighed, taking a moment to gather his thoughts before telling his story. He began with the dust devil and the sudden appearance of the weird vortex and the lights. Albert described his walk through the woods, the bunny, the lizard who could understand him, making special mention of the blue crabs, the six-legged squirrel, the 'wolf' thing, and the miniature 'dragon'. When Albert finished, the man stood and began pacing the small room, contemplating what Albert had just told him.

"Interesting. What concerns me most about your story is the 'vortex' you described. It sounds a lot like a world portal, but a horribly created one, as if whoever created it either didn't know what they were doing or was trying to disguise it."

"Wait. What concerns you the most is some portal thingy?" said Albert dumbfounded. "Not the animals that tried to kill me or the fact that I am from another planet?"

"My dear boy, world portals haven't been in use for a little over three decades now. So yes, that has me concerned. Before then, people used to use them to travel between multiple different worlds on a regular basis. I certainly haven't heard of any bunnies causing trouble. A lizard being able to understand you I can't explain but doesn't seem that important. The Bubble Crab's only defense is a viscous fluid to ward off its predators. To be touched by the Nem Squirrel means you are destined for greatness and that wolf, the Razorback, a simple Keeniss charm will ward it off," responded the man, unsympathetically.

"Whatever. You haven't been living a nightmare for the last two days."

"It's been more like five. You have been asleep for three."

"*Five days!*" replied Albert, shocked. He had already been here five days? His parents must be worried sick about him. He needed to find out about these portals. "Again, whatever. So, why haven't you been able to use these world portal things?"

"No one knows. One day people just stopped being able to create them," answered the man.

"Like you guys forgot how?"

"No, plenty of wizards and magicians still know the magic incantations to create one; they just won't form."

"Magic?"

"Yes, magic. That's what explains your ability to read and speak our language." The robed man looked at Albert's confused face. "You see… by the way, we haven't introduced ourselves. My name is Bernard. I'm this village's local healer. What, may I ask, is your name?"

"Uh… Albert."

"Pleased to meet you, Albert. Now, Albert, when someone creates a world portal that portal becomes part of the worlds they are connected to. When created, the portals have the ability to pass on knowledge to whoever travels through them. Hmm, how else can I explain this? Simply put, whoever created the world portal that you entered wanted you to come through being able to speak and read our language."

Bernard could see confusion still displayed on Albert's face. Trying to make things clearer, he continued. "You see Albert when a portal…"

Albert raised his hand, cutting him off. "I get that part. What I don't get is the part when you said 'magic.' You have magic in your world?"

"Are you saying you *don't* have magic in yours?" Bernard asked skeptically.

"Nope."

"Then how did the person make the world portal that brought you here?"

Albert stared at Bernard confused once again.

"World portals can only connect to worlds with magic, Albert. Either your people have forgotten how to use magic, or they just haven't discovered it yet."

Albert's jaw dropped. "My world has magic?" He thought for a moment and his eyes lit up. "Can I learn to do magic?"

"Certainly, anyone can use magic. Just depends on how adept you are at it. Some learn how to use it rather quickly while others take time."

"I'm going to be the coolest kid when I get back and show them I can do magic," Albert beamed.

Bernard chuckled, patting him on the shoulder. "You have to find someone to teach you magic first, Albert, or get accepted into one of the schools of magic."

"There are schools of magic?"

"Yes, four of them. The College of Nolwenn, the College of Engeram, the College of Atilus, and the College of Haldemar."

Albert looked up at Bernard totally mesmerized. "What are the differences among the four?"

"Well, first is the College of Nolwenn, where I attended." Bernard sat up taller, and straightened his back, obviously proud of the fact. "There we learned all about curative and protective spells as well as other forms of holy magic. At the College of Engeram, they teach students all about the arcane and how to cast elemental spells meant for causing harm and destruction."

"I want to go there," Albert interrupted.

Bernard chuckled again. "Most people do, but Engeram won't just accept anyone—unlike the College of Nolwenn."

"Why not?" Albert frowned, disappointed.

"Because arcane magic can be used to create vast destruction and chaos. Only those tested and proven worthy of wielding such power responsibly are allowed to attend."

"Oh."

"Plus, you have to be accepted by the age of eight."

"Missed it by four years," Albert grumbled. "Guess I'll just have to find someone to teach me."

Bernard laughed, "Good luck. Most, if not all mages of Engeram, refuse to take on apprentices."

"Why is that?"

"If one of their students were to use arcane magic improperly, his master would be held responsible. Then he and his student would both have their magic taken from them."

"Well, that's fine. I didn't want to use um… black magic for anything illegal anyway."

Bernard laughed at Albert's calling it 'black magic'. "'Black magic', that is so archaic. We don't use that term any more, too much of a negative connotation. Now we simply call it Arcane magic."

"Now the College of Atilus," Bernard continued: "There one learns to fight whilst casting minor spells in between strikes or blocks. Their spells are never truly powerful but can help gain them the upper hand in a battle."

"What about the College of Haldemar?"

"Ah yes, the College of Haldemar." Bernard thought for a moment about how he was going to explain the College of Haldemar leaning into the chair. "Well, they study animals."

"Uh, like scientists."

"No, not really. They just kind of sit there and watch them."

Albert gave Bernard a look of complete confusion.

"Well, the whole approach is to observe, to study an animal for its strengths, weaknesses, and defenses, then create a spell that mimics those strengths, weaknesses, and defenses." Bernard could tell by the look on Albert's face that he was still confused. He paused for a minute as a thought came to mind. He clicked his fingers together. "I once met a mage of Haldemar that studied the bubble crab for about a year and a half. He created a spell that would turn his skin into a hard carapace like the bubble crab. He was hideous to look at when he cast the spell… but his skin became so hard that most weapons would bounce right off."

Bernard's story helped Albert understand what he meant. "Ahh, I get it now. That's actually kind of cool!"

Bernard huffed, "Yes, well, it's a new magic and I don't believe it will catch on." He got up from his seat and went to the stove where he picked up a bowl of liquid and handed it to Albert. "Enough chatting for now. Drink this and get some rest. We will continue our discussion later."

Albert took the bowl and put it up to his lips. The sweet aroma had an appeal, pleasant, reminding him of a tea his mother would make for him whenever he was sick. However, the taste was rather uncertain. At first it was kind of earthy, then sweetened slightly, before becoming extremely bitter at the end. Albert wanted to gag, but resisted, not wanting to hurt Bernard's feelings.

"Um, Bernard," he asked shyly.

"Yes?"

"If world portals can't be created any more, how was one created in my world and how am I going to get back home?"

"I'm sorry, Albert, but I do not know the answer," Bernard said sympathetically. He seemed to be trying to understand what Albert is going through. "Right now, there is someone I need to visit," he said as he walked out the room collecting items and throwing them into his knapsack. "Drink all of that potion, then get some sleep. Don't worry, I'll be back by the time you wake again."

"Bernard?" piped Albert.

"Yes," responded Bernard.

"You never said anything about the dragon that attacked me."

Bernard paused at the door as if afraid to answer. "We'll also talk about that when I get back."

Albert watched Bernard leave, then looked back down at the remaining potion in his bowl. "Well guess I'd better just get this over with." For some reason, he thought drinking it all at once seemed like the best way. Chugging the potion, the bitterness intensified, and yet so did the sweetness. It was enough to prevent the urge to gag. Finished, he set the bowl onto the table next to him. Albert laid back down, attempting to fall sleep. He didn't feel the least bit tired. Soon after his eyes closed, yet not fully asleep, he began to daydream.

He pictured himself casting all sorts of spells. Once he got back home, Albert would dazzle all the kids at his school. Maybe he would learn to conjure fireballs or create magic shields that if kids threw things at him, they would just bounce off. Lost in his imagination, a mysterious drowsiness hit him and soon Albert was fast asleep, dreaming.

Albert was high above a small, round cottage with one rectangular room attached to the side. He had never seen Bernard's home from the outside but imagined this is what it probably looked like from an aerial perspective. The view was spectacular from this altitude. A road ran northward past Bernard's house toward a little village with several shops. Farmhouses with spacious fields were laid out around the village. In the east Albert saw a forest with a beautiful blue lake leading upward into enormous mountains. He had never seen mountains in person before. He was shocked how big they could be even from a distance.

He turned to view what lay behind him. Bernard's house sat on the perimeter of a forest that seemed to go on for miles. Giant pines and firs dominated the area, a mixture of other trees splattered the forest, displaying beautiful leaves of dark green, yellow, red, and blue. It reminded Albert of something he'd drawn with watercolors in kindergarten. A river meandered its way along the forest floor, twisting its way south past Bernard's house.

Albert assumed this was the forest he'd been in before arriving at Bernard's. He tried to move forward, wanting to investigate, but this time from a much safer distance high in the sky. Nothing happened, however, as he stood in place. *How do I fly without wings?* He thought. He tried flapping his arms up and down, forward and back, but nothing happened. So, he tried 'swimming' in the air. *Nope, didn't work.* With the failure of both methods, Albert reconsidered his options. *Okay, I'm standing like usual except I'm up in the air. If I were on the ground, I would just walk to move forward.* Albert attempted a few tentative steps forward. But again… nothing!

What was the use of being able to fly if you couldn't move? Sighed Albert. *Well at least I can turn in place.* Looking southward his eyes followed the dirt road leading into the horizon. Folding his arms, he huffed and closed his eyes, *Well, now what am I supposed to do?*

He felt something buzz past him. *What was that and where is it was going?* It looked like a flying lizard about the size of a dog, and it was headed toward the forest.

Hey, it's the dragon that attacked me, he realized with surprise.

He watched as the dragon circled a particular area of the forest and wondered what it was looking for. On one of its passes, something caught the dragon's attention and it turned to a swooping dive. Albert desperately wanted to see what the dragon was going after, but how? All he could do was turn in place. Suddenly, something pushed from behind him. Instantly, Albert was flying rapidly forward. The push was so strong, he was above the diving dragon in an instant. He strained to see what the dragon was stalking, when suddenly a bolt of fire exploded out of the creature's mouth, followed immediately by a flash of light erupting from the prey on the ground. Albert watched, motionless, as an animal soared above the ground, scorch marks on its side. The scorched animal went tumbling into the distance, coming to a stop in a nearby clearing. His mouth agape with surprise, Albert realized it was a razorback that looked just like the one that had attacked him.

Not dead, but obviously in pain, the razorback got to its feet yelping as it hobbled back into the forest. Albert turned his gaze to the dragon. His heart began pounding rapidly, fearing what might happen next. It had pulled out of its dive, swooping around for another pass. Rather gracefully, the dragon landed on the ground and approached the area. Albert tried his hardest once again to move as it skulked under a tree. Looking too familiar, the scene began to confirm his fears; it had played itself out in front of him before. Albert squinted to focus more clearly on the creature's stealthy prowl toward whatever was at the base of the tree. He didn't want to admit he already knew whose back was pressed up against that tree. *His!*

Like a replay, Albert once again saw – but now from above – the dragon slither its way toward him, stop a few feet away, stand on its hind legs, and ready its attack. Desperate to save his other self, he frantically tried again to descend by flapping his arms and legs. He had to stop the dragon, but he couldn't move. The dragon let out its breath and the fire-streak hit his vision's arm, but did not scorch it. He watched as the flame absorbed into the arm and coursed through his body.

Albert saw himself slump to the ground, unconscious. He turned his gaze toward the dragon already disappearing far off into the west. Then came another push from behind, hurling him forward and suddenly he was zooming off after the dragon. His flight was taking him over a vast plain with bright green grass and rolling hills when he came to a stop by another forest at the base of a mountain range wherein a tiny village lay on the outskirts. Albert looked around for the dragon. Where had it gone?

An encroaching darkness began to encircle him. Panic soon took over, leaving Albert desperate to locate the dragon. Where had it gone? He had to know. More darkness crept in. Within scant seconds, the mountains, forest, and village were all lost to his sight, devoured into blackness. Terror filled him. He tried to shout for help. Not a sound came out. The darkness kept coming. Albert tried again to scream; this time even harder. "H-e-l-p!" Still no sound. Overcome with the inevitability that all was lost, and he was going to die alone in the darkness, Albert succumbed to his fate.

Chapter 3: Marked

Albert opened his eyes. He was in bed! The blanket was bunched at his feet, but the dream was gone. Was it a dream? Was it a vision? Maybe it was a bit of both. Did he really watch himself get attacked by that small dragon or was his mind just making things up trying to process what had happened to him? This world, Thu'hilen. Was he really here? What were his parents thinking? What were they doing? They must be worried sick about him. He bet they were probably out searching for him right now with the authorities.

Mustering what strength had returned to him; Albert swung his legs off the bed. He gritted his teeth as he sat up, pain coursing through his body. He took a few long, deep breaths before pushing himself up onto his feet. When he stood, however, he realized his legs were weak. Throwing his arms out, he caught hold of the bed, bracing himself.

He hobbled from one piece of furniture to another as the strength returned to his legs. Soon he was feeling well enough to examine the healer's cottage more closely. He peered at jars full of herbs and other plants he could not identify. In the bookshelf, Albert found a few of the books quite intriguing: one was titled, *Curing the Plague,* another, *Exorcising the Exorcist. Why,* Albert wondered, *would an exorcist need an exorcist?* The one titled, *Ghosts, Ghouls, and Other Undead* sent chills up and down his back. Kids in his world were always trying to scare each other with tales of ghost stories, but it was even more frightening to think that in this world they were real!

Albert was about to pull *The Dragoon Legend* from the shelf when the front door to Bernard's house opened. Albert turned to see a large man enter the room. He had almost shoulder-length dark-brown hair, a stubble-covered face, and hazel eyes looked straight at Albert. He wore metal-plated cloth armor and leather boots. Albert judged him to be about as old as his own dad.

"Well, it's good to see you are up and about," the man said.

Bernard entering behind the man said gruffly, "What are you doing out of bed?"

The man in armor chuckled, rolling his eyes. "Come now, Bernard. He has been lying on his back for three days now. To a boy his age, that's like an eternity."

Albert stood there confused. Who was this man and why was he here?

"Oh, my apologies, Albert," Bernard said, noticing the confusion on the boy's face. "This is Warren. He is the town's Guardian. He also happens to be the man who found you in the forest and brought you here."

"Thank you for saving my life, Mr Warren," Albert responded.

Warren laughed, "Please just call me Warren, and you are more than welcome, Albert. I have a son about your age, and I would hope someone would help him if he were attacked in the woods." They awkwardly stood in silence. "So, Bernard tells me you had been attacked by a wyvern before I found you." Warren looked at Albert in disbelief as he mentioned the word *wyvern*. Albert nodded his head uncertainly in a partial 'yes', wondering what a wyvern was. Warren sat on the bed and motioned for Albert to sit too. Still a little weak, Albert did so slowly.

"Bernard also told me you have a nasty-looking scar that travels up your arm and down your back as a result of that attack."

Confused, Albert looked at Warren and then at Bernard.

"I'm sorry, Albert. I didn't tell you beforehand because I didn't know what it was or meant. I didn't want to startle you," Bernard explained sympathetically.

"Well, anyway, let's have a look at it," said Warren. "Would you mind taking off your shirt, Albert?"

Albert took off his shirt to reveal a scar that started on the front right forearm just below the elbow. Warren traced the scar with his finger, squinting as he investigated its design. It slithered its way up Albert's arm then down his back, stopping just past the shoulder blade, whereupon it branched out on both sides resembling something like wings.

After a few minutes of quiet examination, Warren sat up, rubbing his stubble. "Well it's a mark all right. What it means, though, I don't know."

"A mark?" Albert asked.

"Yup. I've seen something similar in books before. There are many theories, about what a mark like this means, most of them bad."

Albert swallowed hard. Thoughts raced through his mind of all the terrible ways people had died in horror movies he had seen. Or maybe... this mark could turn out to be virus that would kill him slowly. Were demons going to come in the middle of the night to steal his soul? Trying to appear calm, he asked rather shakily, "Bad? What sorts of bad things might happen?"

"Well, Albert," Warren said. "Some scholars believe things like this might mean that you could end up with rotten luck for the rest of your life. Yet others think this type of mark could mean you were going to be a slave to the Dragonkind. One scholar, though, believes this is the mark of the Dragoon."

"What's a Dragoon?" Albert looked over at the book with that word in the title on the shelves.

Bernard followed his gaze and looked back at him with disapproval. Pulling the book from the shelf, he opened it to a certain page and handed it to Albert. "The Dragoon were an ancient order of knights that disappeared over one hundred and fifty years ago."

"What was so special about them?" Albert inquired as he thumbed through the book, his interest now fully piqued.

"Well, Albert, they were said to be 'the dragon's bane'," Bernard answered. "Dragoons were heralded as being the best at killing dragons; it was believed they could actually control the beasts as well."

Albert sat amazed: not only was there magic in this world, but they had dragons too. "This is so cool! You guys have dragons and magic. All that I have wanted ever since I got here was to get back home, but now I want to see what other cool things this world has in it. I would love to see a dragon up close and personal."

"Well, according to you, that already happened!" Warren said with a big grin.

"Are you telling me that's as big as dragons get?" said Albert, disappointed.

Warren laughed heartily. "Oh no, they get bigger, much bigger. Wyverns are just a type of dragonkind. If that is, in fact, what you saw. No one has seen a wyvern in over one hundred years. They started disappearing shortly after the Dragoons did."

Albert's hope and excitement returned at hearing this new information. Once more, his thoughts raced. Maybe he would see more than just dragons! Maybe he would get to see trolls, or giants or other mythical beasts.

"Now that we know that it is a mark, I can release you, Albert. You are free to go," Bernard concluded.

"Um, where am I going to go?" Albert asked, scared of what might happen next.

"You'll come home with me," Warren added.

"With you?" Albert hesitated.

"Yup, we have an extra room; there is no safer place to be. After all, who knows what that mark means? A pack of demons could come after you in the middle of the night for all we know."

Albert's eyes widened.

"I'm only joking, Albert. Demons haven't been seen around these parts for years, or so I'm told."

This didn't calm Albert one bit. It didn't matter that demons never came around. Just the thought of actual demons was scary enough. However, staying with the town's guardian comforted him somewhat. While in Thu'hilen his life had already been threatened multiple times and Warren looked like he could fight off anything. Albert's thoughts were interrupted by Bernard's dropping a knapsack onto his lap.

"Ooph. What's this?" Albert said.

"Those are your clothes and some medicines—just in case," Bernard replied.

"Uh, thanks for taking care of me." Albert grabbed his things and rose from the bed following Warren who headed for the door.

"Don't mind Bernard," he whispered to Albert. "He is one of the most caring and kind people you will ever meet. He just… seems cold."

Outside was a small cart hitched to a single, brown horse. The horse, unlike the cart, was large, making the cart seem more like a chariot.

Albert commented, "That horse seems a little too large for that little cart, don't you think?"

"Blaze here was a gift from the king," said Warren, who stroked and patted the horse's neck. "He was a good warhorse, and I've had him for a long time. I don't go into battle any more and I didn't want to leave him behind, so I gave him a new purpose. It took a while to teach him how to pull a cart, but he eventually got the hang of it... sort of."

Albert and Warren rode in silence for the first few minutes of their trip. There were too many things Albert wanted to know about, but where to start? Albert had been racking his brain for the right question. Without knowing much about this world, what question didn't sound silly? He knew Warren was a Guardian or whatever it was called so why not start there?

"So, what is a Guardian and what do you do?" Albert asked.

Warren's face scrunched a little, thinking of the best way to describe a Guardian. "Well, Albert, a lot of towns, cities, and villages in Thu'hilen have what we call a Guardian. It is their charge to protect that town, city, or village. Guardians tend to have a group of knights who aid them in protecting their respective settlements."

"Do you have knights to help you protect this town?" interrupted Albert.

"No, Brookshire is too small, but my father was Guardian of a town called Winguard with twenty knights under his command. That is where I was born and raised. In fact, from the moment I could hold a weapon, he started training me, whether I wanted to or not. At the age of eight, he made me one of his knights and, at eleven, he was sending me on solo missions or ordering me to lead the others on quests."

As Albert listened, he tried to imagine what life would be like training to be a knight from birth, going out on missions and quests at a young age. He would never have imagined such quests alone at his age, but if there were other knights with him, he figured it might not be as bad as he was thinking. Albert pulled himself out of his daydream to listen to the rest of Warren's tale.

"Now come to think of it, I never really got to know my father; I always thought of him as more of a captain or lord of a county than a father. He never showed any affection toward me. He only taught me how to fight, how to survive, how to lead, and how to take orders," Warren chuckled, staring out ahead. "I guess it worked though. When I was fourteen, I joined the king's army and rose quickly within the ranks. By the time I was seventeen, I was a captain over my own battalion. When there was an uprising or riot, the king would dispatch us to deal with it."

Albert was completely enthralled. Warren gave Albert a big smile, turned his attention back to the road continuing, "The king sent us all over Thu'hilen: aiding allies, fighting wars, discovering new lands. Every day was a new adventure, and I was getting to see all our world had to offer."

"So, what made you quit to become a Guardian?" Albert asked, "I mean, who would give up all that."

"My father actually. He missed so many of my firsts accomplishments and I had missed too many things with my own kids: their first words; their first steps. I started thinking back to how I never had a father who was there or let me know he cared. So, after a mission to the Nazneen Isles, I told the king I was done, that I was leaving the army to be a family man," Warren said this with obvious pride for having made that difficult decision.

"Was he angry?".

"King Altraeus was more disappointed than angry. He tried everything to get me to stay offered me more money, a nice big estate with a large mansion, anything he could think of. He still sends me gifts regularly trying to get me to come back."

"Cool."

Warren thought for a second, confused. "Cool? Ah, a figure of speech your world must use for something that seems pleasing to you."

"Yeah, I guess," Albert shrugged. "So how did you become Guardian of Brookshire?"

"Brookshire's old Guardian had passed away and none of his knights wanted to take up his mantle, so I did. Usually you challenge someone for the right to be a Guardian, but the old Guardian's men were more than willing to forgo my challenge for the post." A huge smirk crept onto Warren's face.

Albert laughed as he imagined grown men in armor shying away from Warren's challenge.

"What about your father? Is he proud that you are a Guardian like him?" Albert wondered.

Warren's face grew grim. "I don't know. We didn't talk much when I was one of his knights, and when I left for the king's army nearly all communication between us stopped. I think he was a little angry that I left his order. Several years later, he died."

"Oh," said Albert, a little guilty he asked.

"Don't feel bad. He died defending Winguard just as he always hoped he would. Ogres attacked the town. I was told he killed three of them before succumbing to his wounds."

"Umm… is that good?" Albert said unsure whether killing three ogres was great or not.

Warren flashed a grin. "Usually it takes two or three men just to take down *one* ogre, so, yeah, I would say that was pretty good. Though I could have taken out five or ten all by myself," he said jokingly, nudging Albert in the side.

Albert laughed at Warren's joke. "Yeah, I bet three ogres are a piece of cake for you," he grinned, playing along. "By the way, what does an ogre look like?"

"Well, Albert, they are really ugly-looking creatures. They stand anywhere from seven and a half feet to eight and a half feet tall, have big, bulbous bodies with light-green, pale, or purplish skin, almost little to no hair on their head and aren't very bright. Except the two-headed ones—but, hey, with two heads, you would expect that they would be a little smarter than the rest."

Warren's description of an ogre fit perfectly with the fairy tales of Albert's world.

"Warren, I was wondering, if Dragoons and wyverns disappeared over one hundred years ago, how come so little is known about them? That doesn't seem like that long ago. Don't you guys keep records of your history?"

"We do, but a great war lasting many years took place in Thu'hilen. During that time, a lot of our history and records were destroyed," Warren informed him. "What we do know of them are mere mentions or images that survived."

"How did it end?" Albert enquired.

"A brave knight named Altraeus rallied a great army and defeated the warlord Geshop, who wanted to destroy all of Thu'hilen. After Geshop was dead and the war over, the people named Altraeus their king and he has ruled ever since."

"Were you part of that battle?" Albert asked.

"No, that was before my time, but my father was. It is how he became the Guardian of Winguard. He was one of Altraeus' commanders."

The sound of pounding hooves speedily coming closer came from behind them. Both turned to see a man on a horse racing up. As he approached, he reined his brown and white paint horse to a stop next to them. The man and his farm clothes were covered in dust, his face and forearms tanned from hours spent working in the sun. "Warren!" called the man, out of breath. "Come quick! Trouble on the road to the fort."

Chapter 4: Brookshire

Warren turned the cart around. Whipping the reins caused Blaze to quickly increase into a gallop, his old warhorse instincts kicking in. The cart bounced and shook as it sped down the dirt road. Albert held on tight, almost flying out of the cart a few times. He was afraid at the speed they were going that the cart would fall apart beneath them.

Albert watched frightened as Warren stared forward focused on the road, continuing to work the reins. Blurred figures on the road, came into focus as they drew closer. From what Albert could see, several men seemed to be attacking a group of well-dressed travelers. Two of the travelers, wielded swords and were trying to fend off the animal-hide-covered ruffians as one of the local farmers burst from his wheat field, a wooden pitchfork in his hands, joined them.

Now several feet away from the ruckus, Warren didn't seem to be slowing. He steered Blaze and the cart directly into the group of attacking men. The men dove out of the way barely in time to not get trampled by the fierce horse or run over by the cart. Warren kicked on the cart-brake and pulled back hard on the reins skidding them to a stop, throwing Albert forward. He caught himself before going head first over the front of the cart and into the back of Blaze.

Before Albert knew what was happening, Warren was off the cart, engaging the first attacker. He easily dodged the man's swing, grabbing the attacker's sword arm in the process. Using the man's momentum, Warren pulled him off his feet and into the ground. The man's sword bounced from his hands. Warren walked over to retrieve it. As he started toward another attacker, Albert watched as Warren pointed to the man, commanding him to 'stay down'.

Warren grabbed the second attacker from behind, pulling him off one of the well-dressed men trying to defend himself. A swift knee to the attacker's stomach caused the man to crumple to the ground. Another freed sword now lay on the ground. Using his foot, Warren kicked the sword up into the air catching it in his free hand, moving onto the next bad guy.

Having overpowered a well-dressed guard, his attacker made a powerful downward stroke. Before he could succeed, Warren blocked the man's sword with his own, stopping the downward motion that would end the man's life. Both men's swords locked together. Warren used the flat of the second sword to smack the attacker's forearm breaking his arm. A third sword now clattered to the ground. The rest of the attackers began to flee at the sight of their friends' being so easily defeated.

Albert watched in horror as the first attacker climbed on the cart, reaching for him. "Not again!" he cried, his life once again in danger. A sudden thud hit the side of the cart forcing both, Albert and the attacker, to turn and see what made the sound. A sword was lodged in the cart through the trousers of attacker's leg.

"I don't have to miss," said Warren, walking toward the cart the other sword ready to be hurled through the air. "Out of the cart." The attacker slowly pulled his pants from the sword's edge and got down from the cart, then took off at a sprint, running down the road. Warren pulled the stuck sword from the cart, seeing Albert frozen in place and in shock. "Albert, are you all right?"

"Uhh," was all that managed to escape his lips.

"There is no need to be frightened. I promised that I wouldn't let any harm come to you," said Warren. Albert reassured, yet still a little scared, nodded. "Good, now stay here while I go make sure everything is all right."

Albert sat in the cart trying to relax. The whole experience had been amazing until the point where one of the men tried to steal Warren's cart. He now knew why Brookshire only needed Warren to protect them and why their king desired to have him return so badly. He had made three professional bad guys look like beginners and scared off the others. A couple minutes later, Warren was back on the cart and turning around to head back to Brookshire.

"Elves," exclaimed Warren. "Always overconfident. They should have known to bring more guards. Oh well, those bandits shouldn't be bothering them any more."

"Elves?" said Albert, excited. "Those were elves?" He turned to try and get a better look, but with all the clothes they were wearing they looked like normal people.

"Yep, heading to Ethanan," replied Warren. "Trying to see if their elvan cousins will let them in. Good luck, to them too. They are going to need it."

Albert and Warren passed the first building on the main street of Brookshire about fifteen minutes later. Albert watched as people darted in and out of shops, finishing their business before the last rays of sun disappeared from the sky. A farmer was struggling with his donkey who sat stubbornly in the middle of the street. Other kids around Albert's age ran around with wooden swords playing some sort of game. Albert assumed it was their version of cops and robbers.

The road eventually forked to go around a large pub that had lights welcoming the night's customers. As they drove by, Albert watched people enter to relax after a hard day's work in the fields. Warren steered Blaze down the right fork toward the other edge of town. More shops and little houses lined the street, with a road here and there shooting off toward other parts of town. Brookshire was a quarter the size of where his family had just moved to but seemed a lot busier. Albert was beginning to wonder if Warren and his family lived somewhere on the outskirts just like Bernard.

At the edge of town, they stopped before a large, two-story-house set back from the road. On top of the pitched wooden roof flew a flag on a pole. It was too dark to make out its design though he could distinguish red-and-white stripes.

The house was of brick with a bay window to the right of the door and a porch that ran along the front. A small stone wall about four-feet-tall enclosed the property. Three evenly spaced, large, rectangular windows looked out from the second floor. A warm light glowed through the bay window draperies, extending a warm welcome.

Albert grabbed his knapsack and followed Warren through the gate into the front yard. The path to the front door was paved with smooth stones, the lawn on both sides was dark green and neatly cut. A flower garden ran the full length of the front of the house. In the dim light Albert couldn't determine what types of flowers they were but did recognize rose bushes in the garden.

"Who takes care of your yard?" Albert asked, adding an approving nod. "It looks very nice."

"Thank you." Warren graciously accepted the compliment. "I take care of it."

"How do you have time to do all this?"

Warren paused and looked around. "There's not much protecting or guarding needed in this small farm town. So, I took up gardening as a hobby."

Albert followed Warren up the stairs and into his house. The front door entered into a large front room. A blue couch with matching armchairs sat perfectly positioned upon a beautiful red handwoven rug covering most of the hardwood floors. Oil-burning lamps sat atop the decorative end tables which separated the couch and chairs. The rest of the room was lit by a fireplace in the wall separating the two rooms. Faint whiffs of smoke filled the air, mixed with a mild scent of fresh flowers, giving the room a homey feel. Mounted above the hearth, Albert noticed a wicked-looking double-bladed great axe and two smaller war axes. The beards of the axe pointed outward, looking as if they could slice through someone with ease. The two war axes had the same beard with a sharp spike on the other side.

Warren's wife and daughter sat together on the couch reading a book while his son sat in an armchair playing with a dagger. As Warren and his young guest entered the house, the family arose.

"It's about time you got back," Luke said, grabbing the sheath from the end table. He slid the dagger in and placed it back on the table.

"Everyone, this is Albert. He will be staying with us for a while. Albert, this is my son, Luke." Luke had short, dark hair and blue eyes, was just a hair shorter than Albert. His face lean like his father's. He wore a plain white cotton shirt and brown woolen pants. At the introduction, Luke brought his hand to his brow flashing a salute.

Ignoring his son, Warren continued, "This is my wife, Nicolet."

Nicolet had long black hair pulled back and kept in place with a decorative barrette. She, too, had blue eyes, and was just a few inches shorter than Warren. She seemed several years younger than Albert's mother. She wore a plain green dress that just missed the floor when she stood. She smiled at him, when introduced, then walked over to give Albert a hug.

"It is a pleasure to meet you, Albert. You are more than welcome to stay with us as long as you need." Nicolet's warm welcome reminded Albert of his mom and tears welled up in his eyes.

"*Why* is he crying?" Luke shot out.

Nicolet gave her son a glare at his outburst. "He's probably homesick. You would be too if you were so far away from your family."

"No I wouldn't," Luke looked away with a scowl.

Warren then introduced his daughter. "Last and certainly not least is my lovely daughter, Gemma."

Gemma was several inches shorter than Albert and Luke and even shorter than his own sister. She had dark brown, shoulder-length hair, green eyes, in a round face, and was a couple years younger than the boys were. She also wore a shoe-length red dress. When introduced, Gemma curtsied, informing Albert it was a pleasure to meet him. Luke rolled his eyes at her manners.

"Well, now that we all know each other," Warren continued. "Luke, will you please, take Albert up and show him where he will be staying while the rest of us get dinner ready?"

Luke shot his dad a salute then grabbed the dagger from the table and headed toward the stairs left of the front door. "Come on, Albert. I'll show you where your room is. You mind if I call you Al?" Luke asked.

"You mind if I call you Lou?" Albert retorted.

Luke gave a quick, short laugh. "I like you, Al."

The upper level had three doors and a sitting area with a bookcase along the far wall. The sitting area was decorated with a brown sofa, an armchair, and a blue rug. The three doors, Albert assumed, led into the bedrooms. Luke went to the first door and opened it.

"This is my room," he said plainly.

Inside, was a bed with a trunk at its foot and a desk against one wall. Weapons lined the rest of the walls in the room.

"Wow, are all of these yours?" Albert asked.

"Yup." Luke walked around the room, casually showing Albert all the different swords, axes, and maces. "My dad gave me them."

"These are so cool."

"They're all right. Most of them were gifts from the king that my dad didn't want." Luke shrugged. "He always wanted me to take up the sword or axe as he had, but I prefer something a little… subtler."

Luke walked to the desk and opened the main drawer. Inside, neatly organized, were dozens of knives, daggers, and throwing blades. Luke pulled a couple of small daggers and twirled them around in his hands. As he twirled the gleaming weapons, Luke said, "One day, I'm going to become one of the king's spies, or maybe even an assassin!"

He put the knives back and the boys left his room to continue the tour of the upstairs. The next door had a 'No Boys Allowed' sign tacked to it. Albert said, snidely, "All little sisters must be brats no matter what world you come from." The two laughed as they walked to the last room.

Luke opened the door to reveal a simple room with a bed, writing desk, and a trunk for clothes. "And this is your room. It's not much but…" Luke trailed off.

"That's okay. I don't have much," Albert said, holding up his knapsack.

Albert entered and opened the trunk. Inside was a quilt and a tray which could slide from side to side. He set his clothes on top of the blanket and the items from Bernard on top of the tray. Closing the trunk, Albert looked up to find Luke rummaging through the writing desk. He walked over, where Luke said, sympathetically, "The desk has parchment, a penknife, ink, and a quill. You know in case you want to keep a journal while you are here or something."

Just then the two boys heard Warren call upstairs telling them to come down for dinner. The smells coming from the kitchen made Albert's mouth water. Albert followed Luke down and through the door, left of the fireplace, into the kitchen and dining room. Wooden cabinets and counters lined the walls and a small, wood-burning oven and stove sat in a corner. A sink stood under a large kitchen window. In the dining room were a wooden table, four chairs and a bench for sitting. A door leading outside, separated the kitchen from the dining room. Another large window looked out from the dining room out to the back yard.

While Nicolet was busy spooning food from the pan, Warren and Gemma set the table with plates, cups, knives, forks, and spoons. As Albert reached the table, Gemma quickly ran over to pull out a chair, instructing him to sit. When Luke stepped to take the seat beside Albert, Gemma quickly stood in his way, glaring. Luke looked at Albert annoyed; Albert just shrugged. Luke moved to the other side of the table sliding onto the bench.

Finally, Warren and Nicolet took their seats at each end of the table. Albert stared at all the delicious food before him: a roasted chicken surrounded by dishes of mashed potatoes, gravy, rolls, and salad. He lifted his fork, but Warren stopped him.

"Hold on a second, Albert. We need to thank someone first."

Albert felt embarrassed and awkward. He had forgotten about dinner prayer. His family used to have it before their lives got too busy. He watched as Warren looked at Nicolet with thankful eyes.

"Nicolet, thank you for this lovely meal. As always, it looks and smells delicious."

Luke and Gemma echoed their father. Nicolet smiled and nodded motioning for everyone to dug in.

Warren started off the conversation, "So, Luke and Gemma, what did they teach you in school today?"

Hope they don't make me go to school, he thought. *I wonder what they learn? If it is something about mythical creatures, I'm going to be in trouble.*

"Well, first we learned how to add numbers together," Luke said.

"Then we moved on to subtraction," Gemma finished for him. "I don't know why we have to learn this stuff. We are never going to have to use it."

"Enough about school," Nicolet interrupted them. "I think we would all like to hear about Albert and how he got here."

Albert almost dropped his fork, stopped eating, frozen with fear. He wasn't prepared to talk, and Nicolet had just put the spotlight right onto him. Nervously, Albert reached for his glass of water. Swallowing a huge gulp, he wiped his mouth with the back of his hand.

"Um," began Albert nervously. Caught off guard, he didn't know where to start. "I guess my family is a lot like yours. There is my dad, James, my mom, Amber and my little sister, Sarah. We just moved to a small town outside of a place called Waco, Texas. I was on my way to school when I fell through the world thingy, or whatever Bernard called it."

"World portal," said Nicolet, politely correcting him. "Was your family with you when you entered the world portal?"

"No, I was alone," replied Albert. "My parents were getting ready for work and my sister stayed home sick." Albert moved onto the events after going through the world portal and being in Thu'hilen. When he got to the bubble crab and how it sprayed him in the face, Luke burst out laughing.

"You got sprayed by a bubble crab?" asked Luke. "Did you vomit? Oh, I so would have vomited. That stuff is nasty." He continued to laugh.

"Hey, it wasn't funny," Albert said. "How was I supposed to know it would spray me with the most foul-smelling liquid I've ever smelled in my life? It was my first day here in your world."

"All right Luke, you've had your laugh," said Warren glaring at his son. "Now apologize and let's hear the rest of your story, Albert."

Luke cleared his throat fighting back more laughter. "I'm sorry Al, I'm not trying to be mean, and I forgot you aren't from our world."

Albert calmed then continued, telling them about the events of the previous days: how the forest went quiet suddenly and he felt as if something were watching him. He told about the scary wolf-looking thing that chased him.

"We call those Razorbacks," Gemma said.

Albert mentioned that the name suited it and they all agreed.

A kind of reverent awe descended upon the room when he told them about his encounter with the wyvern. Luke and Gemma began leaning in closer, both, eyes wide, glistening with excitement, mouths hanging open. Nicolet, arms folded across her chest, a dull look on her face, leaning back in her chair, was doubtful of Albert's story. When he finished, Luke and Gemma assailed him with all sorts of questions of what the wyvern was like. Nicolet calmly held a finger in the air. Albert watched as Luke and Gemma obediently calmed down and sat quietly in their chairs.

"Are you sure of what you saw, Albert?" asked Nicolet, politely. "Wyverns haven't been seen for over one hundred years and you say you saw one just the other day and that it attacked you? You had been in the forest a couple days without food and very little water, this could have *all* been a bad dream."

"Nicolet, dear, I'm sure if you saw the mark along his arm and back you would believe it," said Warren, motioning for Albert to uncover the mark on his arm.

Albert revealed as much of the mark as he could on his arm by pushing up his sleeve. Nicolet's eyes grew wide, her pupils dilating, her face glowing with excitement. Jumping out of her chair, she rushed to Albert. She nearly choked him as she pulled down the back of his shirt to see as much of the mark as possible.

Nicolet immediately burst out with a flurry of questions. "How long was it? What was its wing span? How much did it weigh? How many spines did it have down its body?" She stopped for a second to take a very quick breath before continuing, "How many horns did it have and how long were they? Did it have a scale pattern and if so, what were the colors? How fast do you think it flew?"

Albert sat overwhelmed, trying to answer as many of her questions as he could. Finally, Nicolet leaned back in her chair obviously taking a breath to calm herself. She interlocked her hands and rested on her stomach. "I can only imagine what meeting a wyvern would be like. It must have been exhilarating!"

"More like frightening," said Albert, remembering his terrifying experience.

Dinner finished, Albert was about to head upstairs when Warren put a hand on his shoulder walking him toward the door leading outside, "Come on, Albert. Let's get some fresh air." Outside it was cool and crisp, instead of humid and heavy like back home. Looking up, he saw numerous stars in the sky and wondered if any of them was Earth.

"Nicolet is that *one* scholar I told you about earlier. She wants to know everything about anything and can get a little carried away. I'm giving you a break from questions."

"It's okay. Your family makes me miss my own. Even my little sister, Sarah," responded Albert.

"I never had a little sister growing up, but I can imagine they can be a pain to an older brother. Especially when I see what Gemma puts Luke through," Warren laughed.

"You have no idea," Albert joked back.

"Don't worry, Albert. We'll get you home," Warren again put a hand on Albert's shoulder.

"But how?" Albert asked skeptically. "What is so great about you two that makes you so confident?"

Warren smiled at Albert. "We've been through a lot of amazing things together. Completed missions that not even King Altraeus thought possible. Figuring out how to get world portals working again should be a breeze."

Albert took several deep breaths. "Well, you don't have to hurry too quickly. I still need to learn some magic and see a proper dragon up close."

Warren chuckled. "We'll see what we can do about that. Just don't hold your breath."

When they had gotten their fill of the cool night air, they headed inside and to the front room were Nicolet was waiting. She had him sit down beside her and handed him a book. Its cover read, *The History of Thu'hilen*.

"Take some time to learn about our world," she encouraged. "It's all that we have managed to recover since the great war."

"And if you need anything, don't be afraid to knock," added Warren pointing to the door behind them as he left.

Albert was excited. No one had ever let him stay up as late before. He didn't feel tired, especially after that big dinner and three days of sleeping at Bernard's. He opened the book and flipped through the pages, looking at the chapter headings. Some were long, going on for dozens of pages, while others were extremely short, only a few paragraphs. Some of the chapter titles that stuck out to him were, 'The Rising and Falling of Nations', 'How the Continent was Settled', 'The Ancient Order of Magi', and 'The Best Places to Eat in Thu'hilen'. The chapter that caught his eye more than the rest was 'The Seclusion of the Ethanan Elves.'

He decided to start there. Albert read how the elves were a proud and noble people. Their knowledge and wisdom brought people from all over Thu'hilen to seek their advice. Wanting to know how or why they became secluded, he decided to skip a few pages to the end of the chapter. Albert found how the elves, for some reason, stopped travelling out of their forests and letting people in. No one knew why the Elvan king called all his people back to the woods and refused any outsiders from coming in. But what about the elves Albert had heard Bernard talking to when he first woke in the healer's cottage? Did they come from a different group of elves? Albert finished the chapter with more questions than he had started with.

He read until halfway through the next chapter. His eyes grew heavy and was having a hard time staying awake. Glancing toward the clock, he decided one o'clock in the morning was late enough to stay up. Albert closed the book, set it on the end table, and headed off to bed.

Chapter 5: Clues

Albert had the dream, again. It had to mean something, didn't it? Waking drenched in sweat, he wiped the wetness from his forehead with his hand, trying to calm his breathing. Though he knew it was only a dream, it had felt real. Looking out the window of his room it was still dark. Going to it, he reached for the latch. A gust of cool air washed over him. Albert took a deep breath, it was crisp, invigorating, and calmed his nerves. He sat in the window for a minute until he finished calming down. He peered over at an old barracks in the back yard trying to picture three or four guards getting the rest they would need to protect the village another day. When he felt ready, he took in one more deep breath and then went back to bed.

A knock at the door woke him the next morning. The sun was shining through the window as he groggily rubbed his eyes and asked who it was. "Sorry to wake you, Albert," said Nicolet from the other side, apologetically. "I just wanted to let you know breakfast is downstairs when you are ready."

He sat up stretching his arms wide to loosen up his body. Going to the chest at the end of the bed he put on the clothes he was wearing when he fell through the portal. Stretching one more time, he rubbed sleep from off his eyes, opened the bedroom door and headed downstairs. Warren was in the front room sitting in one of the armchairs reading a piece of parchment.

Warren welcomed him looking up from his parchment. "Good Morning."

"Good morning," Albert said. "What are you reading?" he asked.

"Oh, it's just a list of things the townspeople want me to look into. Most of it is ridiculous, if you ask me, but it keeps me busy."

"Hmm, so am I going with you today or…"

"Nicolet and I thought to send you with Luke and Gemma today, if that's all right with you," Warren asked.

Albert nodded his head, expecting to spend another day in school just like he would back home. "Sure. That sounds fine to me." He took a couple steps towards the kitchen, but quickly turned back remembering he was going to ask Warren something. "Can I ask you something really quick?"

Warren looked up from his paper. "Sure, what is it?"

"Last night I read something about elves and disappearing into some forest, but I overheard Bernard saying something about elves yesterday. Was the book not updated? Did they make it out of that forest by now?"

"You must be referring to the Elves of Ethosis," replied Warren. "Nope they are still there, holed up in their little world. The elves Bernard spoke to the other day are from another group. They are on a quest to see if they can bring their woodland brothers out of their little hole and back into the real world."

"Oh, okay," said Albert a little disappointed.

"Don't feel bad for them, Albert," Warren responded consolingly. "They chose the life they wanted to live."

"I'll try. When I read that chapter, I just felt like they were in trouble, and someone should help them is all. Where is Ethosis anyway?"

"It's actually west of here, across The Great Plains," answered Warren. "Now, stop worrying about them and go get something to eat."

Albert nodded and turned back toward the kitchen. Wait! The forest from his dream or vision was west of here. Maybe that's why those elves felt so important to him? But should he tell Warren about it? He thought a moment more. *Better not disturb him. Warren has enough concerns.*

In the kitchen, breakfast was sitting on the table with Luke and Gemma finishing their meals. Albert found plates of bacon, scrambled eggs, chopped fried potatoes, and a bowl of strange-looking fruit. He filled his plate, warily grabbing something that looked like a purple apple with warts and a blue banana in the shape of an elongated 'S'. They were the only safe-looking fruit in the bowl. When they finished, Albert, Luke, and Gemma emptied their plates into the waste basket next to the sink, set their plates and silverware in the sink basin and headed out the back.

In the daytime he found that the backdoor exited into a tiny courtyard. An old, dried-up fountain sat in the middle, hinting at its past beauty. The courtyard had two curved stone benches facing the fountain and was paved in smooth stones. On the other side of the courtyard was the old barracks, now being used as the schoolhouse. Another separate path met up with the pavers leading down the side of the house and around front.

The barracks had been emptied out beside a desk on one side of the long building, a half circle of chairs, and a blackboard with chalk and an eraser. There were four other children in the classroom already waiting for the day's instruction. As they walked to the sitting area, Luke introduced the other kids. The first was a stout, short, round-faced dwarf with curly, auburn hair and pudgy hands known as Darwin. He was the blacksmith's son. Second was Oscar, a gnome with wavy blond hair who was no bigger than a toddler. Next came the governor's son, Rupert who had short brown hair and wore nicer clothes. Last was Rachel, the girl Albert could tell Luke obviously had a crush on by the way he introduced her. Unfortunately, so did Rupert. He made sure that Rachel was always near him. She had long, wavy brown hair that framed her face and was wearing a silken blue dress.

The newcomers took the three open seats closest to the door shortly before Nicolet entered the room, arms filled with books and papers. *Of course, Nicolet is the teacher,* Albert thought to himself. *Warren did say she was a scholar, making her the perfect person to teach the kids in the town.*

Nicolet walked to the middle of the room in front of her desk. "Good morning, everyone. Today we have someone new in the class. This is Albert. He will be staying with our family until we can find a way to get him back home. I hope all of you make him feel welcome. Now on to today's lesson."

Her lesson was on goblins, what they looked like and how to deal with them. By the end of her lesson, they all knew how to spot one of their cons and how money and precious gems mean everything to a goblin. As Luke and Albert got up to leave, Rachel rushed over to introduce herself to Albert. Following close behind, Rupert swooped in, placing himself between Rachel and Albert.

He puffed out his chest, introducing himself, "I'm Rupert. The governor's son."

Albert merely stepped around Rupert, sticking out his hand to introduce himself to Rachel. Rupert fumed angrily with Albert's clear ignorance of who he was and how he was the only one that got to talk to Rachel. Rachel, realizing Rupert was losing his temper, told

Albert it was a pleasure to meet him and then excused herself.

Rupert turned to Luke, saying loud enough for Albert to hear, "Your new friend should watch who he's talking to. Wouldn't want something bad happening to him."

Luke smirked, "You know Rupert anytime you want to have a go, I'm ready and waiting." Fear flashed quickly over Rupert's eyes, who turned on his heels hurrying out the room.

"Don't worry Luke, I'm not afraid of that momma's boy." Albert said loud enough for Rupert to hear him. "What that was all about?" He turned to Luke.

"Ah it's nothing," said Luke. "Every time Rupert tries to bully or threaten someone, I try to remind him that he isn't the biggest fish in the pond."

Albert laughed and asked what they were going to do next. An excited smile came over Luke's face. "How about I teach you how to use a sword?"

Albert waited out back just beyond the courtyard. Luke came out of the house with two wooden swords. A nervous smile crossed Albert's face as he was handed a sword. Luke took a couple steps away, turning to face him.

"Okay, now what?" Albert asked hesitantly.

"Wait for my instruction," Luke laughed, shaking his head. "Okay, now, Albert, stand with feet shoulder width apart, firmly planted, both hands gripping the hilt of the sword, like this."

Luke demonstrated to Albert what he had just told him. Albert did as he said, copying Luke's stance as best he could.

"Okay, Albert, now I'm going to swing at you from the right and I want you to try and block it," Luke warned him.

Albert nodded. Luke performed a middle blow attacking Albert's right side He moved his sword to block Luke's swing but didn't block well enough. The stroke broke through pushing Albert's sword aside colliding with his arm. Albert winced in pain as the wooden sword struck him.

"Albert, you have to put a little more muscle into it than that," Luke sighed.

Albert rubbed his arm then squared up his stance, this time with more determination. Luke informed him he was going to do the same thing then performed another middle blow. Albert moved to block, bracing harder this time for the impact, stopping Luke's blow.

"Good," Luke said approvingly. "This time from the other side."

Luke performed another middle blow this time from Albert's left. Albert moved the sword to block his attack.

"Great," Luke said, encouragingly. "Now I'm going to alternate between the two blows getting faster and faster. Are you ready?"

Albert nodded. Luke began swinging his wooden sword back and forth, allowing Albert to block each blow, each time increasing in speed. When Albert had gotten used to blows, Luke changed up his attack pattern. Albert hadn't anticipated the change and missed a block, getting knocked on the side of the head. Pain seared through his skull and his head throbbed. He dropped his sword and began rubbing the side of his head, trying to ease the pain. Just then Luke smacked him across the ribs.

"Ouch! What are you doing Luke? Didn't you see me throw my sword down?" Albert yelled.

"Yep, and it left you wide open for another attack," Luke replied with a smirk.

"What?" Albert said confused.

"One of the first things my dad taught me was never let your guard down, even if you sustain severe injury. It only leads to more injury."

Albert sputtered unable to think of a reply. "Well, it's my first time. Can't you go a little easy on me?"

"Why?" Luke laughed. "My dad didn't go easy on me. He said the more aggressive the teacher the faster you learn."

Albert, a little flustered picked up his sword and began swinging it wildly at him. Luke deflected and parried all the attacks, eventually disarming him and tripping him to the ground.

"Not bad, Al," he said encouragingly. "See just after a few minutes, you already figured out how to properly swing a sword. Needs a little work but you will get better. Now get back up and let's try again." Luke held out his hand, helping Albert to his feet.

By the end of the day, Albert was bruised and sore from head to toe. Luke had been relentless. When Warren saw Albert, he gave Luke a concerned look. "You teaching Albert how to use a sword or just giving him a good beating?"

Luke smiled, "I'm only teaching him the way you taught me."

Warren remembered how battered and bruised Luke had been and thought maybe he should have gone a little easier on him. "So how is it going?" Warren asked.

Luke continued to smile. "Not too bad, Al is a quick learner. Plus his thicker build seemed to help soften the blows."

The latter comment offended Albert a little. He wasn't fat by any means, and he had always been one of the thinnest of his friends. Though compared to Luke's trim and fit physique he guessed he did seem a little 'thick'.

Over dinner, Warren told them a story of how he had been captured by goblins on one of his missions and had to get himself free by fighting their champion. The problem was the champion was an ogre with a goblin mask on and Warren wouldn't be given a weapon. Warren admitted that he felt foolish for thinking goblins would use one of their own men as their champion.

After several minutes of dodging the ogre's attacks, he tricked the ogre into believing it wasn't a *fair fight* unless he had a weapon. After thinking it over for a second, the ogre walked over to one of the goblins onlookers, clobbered him over the head and then took his weapon giving it to Warren who slayed the ogre and won his freedom. Albert and Luke were mesmerized by his tale, while Gemma worried, glad her father never went on adventures any more. The story over, they cleared the table and headed up to bed, Albert complaining about his lumps.

"You know, Al, you did really well for your first time handling a sword, even if it was only made of wood." Luke reassured him. Albert began to feel a little better about himself, until Luke threw in the jab about the sword being wooden.

"You even got me once," Luke added. "See, right here." Luke pointed to a tiny bruise on his elbow.

"I did that?" Albert asked surprised.

"No," replied Luke. "I got that swatting at Gemma during breakfast this morning, but I made you feel better for a second, didn't I?"

It did make Albert feel better, or at least it did until Luke had told the truth. Now he just felt more hopeless than before and swore his pains ached even worse.

"Thanks Luke, that made me feel *so* much better," Albert said sarcastically.

"Anytime, Al." Luke smiled back. "Goodnight."

Gemma stopped Albert at her door, "I thought he did wonderful today."

Albert awkwardly thanked her and said good night. She waited till he was at his room before returning the gesture with a sweet innocent smile. Albert crawled into bed, finding it difficult to find a comfortable position to lie in.

He had the same dream again that night. He awoke breathing heavily and drenched in sweat. The dream didn't get any less intense. Getting up, he felt his bruises from yesterday still hurting him, especially the bump on his head. He moved to the window for some fresh air. The first rays of light were making their appearance. He realized that he probably wasn't going to get back to sleep and decided to go downstairs.

Albert lit the desk lamp in his room and made his way downstairs. He found the book of Thu'hilen's history on the end table, and sitting on the sofa, thumbed through it. The sun had just come up when Warren came out of his room dressed in his armor.

"Good morning, Albert," he said. "Anything wrong?"

"Oh nothing," Albert replied. "I just keep having this dream or vision that keeps waking me."

"Oh? What is it about?" Warren asked.

"Nothing really, but I've had it every time I go to sleep since the wyvern attack."

Warren positioned one of the armchairs to face Albert on the sofa and sat down. "Tell me about it."

Albert recounted his dream. Afterwards, Warren sat still contemplating for a moment. Then he went back into his room. A moment later, Warren and Nicolet returned together. She sat next to Albert with Warren in the armchair.

She took Albert by the hands, looking at him solemnly, "Albert, Warren has just given me a brief account of your dream and I want you to tell me how you felt at the end of your dream when the darkness started to surround you."

"Like my life was about to end," replied Albert.

"Where did it feel like the darkness was coming from?"

Albert thought for a second, replaying the dream in his head. A feeling of fear raced over him as he pictured the woods that lay beyond the little village that sat at the border.

"The forest," he told her.

"Did the wyvern fly into the forest in your dream?" she asked.

"I don't know, maybe," he replied. "The wyvern was gone by the time I got to the edge of the forest."

Nicolet patted Albert's hand, getting up from the couch, she silently walked to the center of the room deep in thought.

"What do you think is going on, Nicky?" Warren asked.

"I don't know. Albert, that forest you saw in your dream is the forest of Ethanan. It's home to a group of elves and sits at the base of the Daratrine Mountains. Many years ago, it is said that a colony of wyverns lived in those mountains but one day they vanished. Not long after, the Elvan king, Uthael, called his people back into the woods. We haven't heard from them since."

So those elves were the one from his dream. "The Ethosis Elves?" asked Albert.

"Do you know about them?" Nicolet asked.

"I may have told him about them yesterday," said Warren, jumping into the conversation. "Albert asked a question about them from the book we gave him, plus he heard Bernard talking to some elves. Also, we helped some on our way back from Bernard's house. Albert asked if they were the same elves. I didn't think it had any relevance, but now it seems it might."

"You mean you told him about the Ethosis Elves, and you didn't think it had any bearing on what's going on?" Nicolet responded with a frown.

"In his defense," said Albert, coming to his rescue. "When I asked about the elves, Warren had no idea about my dream."

Nicolet sat, calmed herself, and collected her thoughts. "Okay, first I don't think that was a dream you had Albert, but a vision. Second, the disappearing of the wyverns, the seclusion of the elves, your arriving, and getting marked by a wyvern can't all be a coincidence. Something is happening here," Nicolet said confidently then headed for the bedroom. "Warren, tell the kids there will be no school today. I need to go talk to Dannon."

Albert looked at Warren, "Um, what's going on?"

Warren straightened up in his chair. "Many mages and scholars including Nicolet have spent years trying to figure out the mystery behind the disappearance of the wyverns and the seclusion of the Ethanan elves. You have either brought us a new clue or a new question to the dilemma."

"Oh… Who's Dannon?"

"He's an old wizard who lives outside of town. Dannon has spent more time than most trying to solve this mystery."

"Cool. Can I go see him?"

"Most likely not. He hates children and can't stand to be around them."

"Bummer. Not even me?"

Warren chuckled at Albert's word choice. "Your people do have some strange sayings." Warren stood. "Well, I guess that leaves me for breakfast. Is bacon, eggs, and toast good enough for you?"

"Yessir, that's my favorite breakfast."

"Good because it's all I know how to make."

Chapter 6: Getting Answers

Since school had been cancelled, Albert and Luke went out back for more sword practice. Albert parried one attack, then another and dodged one before, *wham*! Luke made a surprise attack, striking him in his thigh. A jolt of pain coursed through his leg. Instinctively, he went to grab for it. As he did, he remembered what had happened last time and what Luke said about not letting his guard down and pulled his thoughts back into the lesson. Luke attacked with a mid-blow that was intended to connect with his upper arm. He rolled out of the way and landed on his feet with his sword in a defensive position.

"Excellent, Al," commented Luke. "You remembered to keep your guard up after that cheap shot I pulled." Albert grinned, pleased with himself. "It would seem that you are ready for me to teach you how to attack after having just defended yourself."

For the next hour, Luke instructed Albert how to properly go from attacking to defense and then fluidly back to attack. He demonstrated how to parry one attack, strike with his own, then back to defending. Albert was beginning to find that practicing with the swords was possibly the most enjoyable activity he had ever done. Not only was Luke an excellent teacher, but he and Luke had lots in common and it felt like they were becoming best friends.

Luke eventually called for a break, which Albert welcomed graciously. The two sat down on a bench in the courtyard drinking from their waterskins. Albert had blocked or parried a lot of Luke's attacks but had missed even more. He watched as welts and bruises formed.

"So, I wonder why we didn't have school today," Luke said, slyly.

Albert felt there was no harm in telling him why. "The reason is because I had some sort of vision about that wyvern and some elvan forest. So, your mom rushed off to talk to some guy named Dannon."

"Oh really?" Luke gave an evil grin. "Shall we go see what about?"

Albert felt a lump rise in his throat. *Maybe I shouldn't have told Luke,* he thought to himself.

"I don't know. Your dad said Mr Dannon doesn't like children."

"Pfft," Luke got up and pulled Albert to his feet. "Come on. This will be fun. Plus, I've always wanted to see into that old codger's house."

Albert reluctantly followed Luke to the front onto the street, following the road east out of town. They traveled past several farms and finally coming to an old red rectangular wood house with a pitched roof and a circular stone tower attached at one end. The house was small, yet with the tower having added a couple more floors than the main house. A dilapidated wooden fence enclosed the perimeter of the yard of tall grass. A decrepit gate swung freely on two loose hinges with a dirt path led up to the front door. Luke motioned for Albert to follow him around to the side of the house with the tower. He pointed to a window a few feet off the ground that was cracked open.

"See that window there, Al?" he asked.

"Yeah," Albert said, worried.

"That's how we are going to get in," Luke smiled.

Quieter than a mouse, Luke climbed through the broken fence, headed for the window. Albert followed close behind heaving and grunting. *How in the world did Luke do that so quietly?* he thought to himself.

Below the window, Luke asked Albert to give him a boost. Albert intertwined his fingers, making a step for Luke who put a foot in Albert's hand then pushed himself up and climbed into the window. Once in, Luke turned around, grabbing Albert's hands, and helped him up. Turning, they found themselves in a large circular room with twelve doors lining the walls. The room baffled the two as it was too large to fit in the tower.

"So," said Albert. "What next?"

"Well, honestly, I didn't know what we would see in this house, but I did not expect this." Luke scratched his head. "I guess we just try a door."

He walked over to the closest one on their left. Opening the door introduced them to a giant rooster, except instead it had a lizard's tail and bat-like wings.

The creature screeched loudly at them, charging. Luke slammed the door just in time for the creature to slam into it, throwing Luke to the ground.

"What in the world was that?" Albert asked, terrified.

"A cockatrice," Luke shakily replied. "Shall we try another?" he said enthusiastically.

"Maybe we should just head back." Albert headed for the window. When he got back though the scenery outside had changed. Instead of the wizard's yard he now looked over a barren frozen tundra. "Well, I guess we aren't getting out the way we came in."

"What do you mean?" asked Luke heading over to see. "Oh," he exclaimed.

"So, another door?" asked Albert.

"You know it."

Albert opened the door on their right. This time, they saw a dock overlooking a vast cove. The two looked at each other, shrugged, and ventured out. There was nothing to see out there but water, rocky cliffs, sandy beaches, palm trees, and long grass. Albert walked to the end of the dock and looked into the water. Far below the surface, he could see a dark figure. Hunching down to get a better look at what it was, he noticed the figure enlarging. It continued to grow as it grew nearer. A pit in his gut formed and he had a feeling that it was time to leave. Albert turned. "Run!" he shouted at Luke.

The boys got halfway to the door when enormous tentacles came bursting out of the water causing the dock to sway side to side. Both lost their footing and went sprawling, hanging on to the planks so that they wouldn't fall off the side.

Tentacles searched wildly as Albert and Luke crawled as fast as they could. They got tossed back and forth as the tentacles wrapped around the dock searching for them. They barely made it through the door as a tentacle crashed against the frame. The two went sprawling to the floor as another tentacle suckered its way across the open door. Luke quickly crawled on all fours and slammed it shut. Dripping with water, the two boys sat on the floor trying to catch their breath.

"How on Thu'hilen did Dannon get that thing into that room?" Luke heaved a huge breath.

"What do you mean? That had to have been a portal to somewhere else." Albert could barely speak.

"Nope, I'm pretty sure that was a room of the tower. My mom told me mages can make rooms a lot bigger or smaller than they actually are."

"Okay so, what's up with the window then?"

"That might actually be a portal."

After catching their breath, they decided that when trying a room, they were only going to peek inside and not enter. One by one, they opened the doors only enough to see what it looked like inside. Every door had some sort of odd creature in it with its own habitat. Some of the creatures charged upon seeing the door open while others looked to see who it was and then lost interest. One of the rooms they opened had a colony of lizards with long needle-like horns at the end of their snouts. They clamored around Albert staring at him in fascination.

"Why are they just standing there looking at you?" wondered Luke.

"I don't know," said Albert. "But I met a lizard in the forest when I first got here that seemed to understand what I was saying." As he spoke, the lizards began swaying back and forth excited to hear him speak.

"Whoa," said Luke amazed. "How did you do that?"

"I don't know," replied Albert. "But I don't think we have time to figure that out. Who knows how long your mom will be here talking to Dannon and we have to find out what is going on."

"Right," said Luke. "Um, how do we get them back into the room now?"

"Hmm," said Albert looking around for something to corral them back into the room. "Maybe I can just ask them to go back in."

"Sure, why not?" said Luke interested in what would happen if Albert did.

Albert leaned forward with his hands on his knees, "Go back in your room please." Accepting his request, the little horned lizards turned around and scurried back into the room, allowing Luke to shut the door as the last lizard entered.

"Can you talk to lizards in your world?" asked Luke.

"Nope," replied Albert still shocked that that had worked.

Hmm, thought Luke. "Well, I guess we will have to ask my mom and Dannon about that as well."

Going back to their search, they finally got to the last door at the back of the room.

"This has to be the way out. If not, well I guess we are stuck here till Dannon shows up to do whatever it is that he does with all these creatures," said Luke.

They slowly and cautiously opened the door hoping that it wouldn't be just another room. To their relief, behind the door was a stairway leading up. The boys sighed and entered passing the threshold of the door, shutting behind them. Turning around, Luke grabbed the door handle only to find it was locked. Albert sighed with annoyance.

"Well, I guess there is nowhere to go but up," said Luke, innocently.

Albert groaned and the two boys climbed the staircase that was lined with windows. Every window they passed was a different scene to their disappointment. One window was of a nice beach with palm trees and gentle ocean waves while another was a jungle during monsoon season with hurricane winds and rain. Eventually, they came upon a window that overlooked a thriving city.

The two stared in wonder as people swarmed the streets darting in and out of shops. People on horseback and carriages hurried along the brick paved roads. Sweet smells of baked goods filled the air and sounds of chatter and music permeated their ears and nose.

"I think this is Tiranos," Luke said excitedly.

"What?" questioned Albert.

"You know the capital city of Thu'hilen, where the king lives," Luke replied, nonchalantly.

"Ahh, cool," Albert responded.

Luke looked at Albert oddly, wondering what he meant by 'cool'.

"It's just something my people say when they like something."

"Oh, cool."

They laughed, closed the window, and continued up the endless flight of stairs. After passing a half a dozen more windows they finally came to a landing. Tired and sore from climbing so many stairs, they stopped to rest. The landing had another window, a door and more stairs that continued upwards.

Looking out the window, Luke was surprised to see Brookshire once again. Albert cheered with joy to see familiar scenery. The problem was that the window was at the top of the tower. The two boys groaned with disappointment when they realized they couldn't simply climb out and be free. What scared them more was that the tower kept going up when logically it shouldn't. Quickly Albert checked the door behind them to see what was on the other side. Inside was a circular room lined with doors. The window to the outside world looked upon a snowy landscape. Disappointed he closed the door.

"What's behind the door?" Luke was almost too afraid to ask.

"Another room with doors and a snowy window," Albert depressingly replied.

"Ugh," Luke groaned.

"Okay, Luke, we got three options. One, we try and climb down the side of the tower. Two, we continue up the stairs. Or three we take our chances with the door room."

Luke slumped to the floor and grumbled.

"Option number three it is," Albert said, trying to be enthusiastic.

"*Why* would you choose number three?"

"Because, I'm sick of climbing steps and I don't really feel like falling to my death. Who knows, maybe there will be food behind one of these doors or something."

Luke looked hopelessly up at Albert. "Fine." He got up off the floor and followed Albert through the door that shut and locked behind them.

"Guess we aren't going back that way," said Luke upset with how things were turning out.

They looked around at each door then, giving up, Luke bowed to Albert. "Be my guest." Albert walked up to the third door on his right, grabbed the handle and turned it. Taking a deep breath, he pulled it open to an aisle of bookshelves. Relief washed over them. Apprehensively, Albert called out to see if anyone would answer. When no one answered, they ventured down the aisle to the main thorough fair reading the titles of the books as they went.

Near the end of the aisle, one book caught Luke's eye. Reaching up he pulled it off the shelf. When the book was moved, a low growling sound emanated from somewhere in the distance. Luke slowly put the book back on the shelf hoping that the sound would stop. To his disappointment the growl was coming closer. The sound of large paws scraped along the wooden floor as it moved. Albert peered out of the aisle to see what was coming their way.

A large dog the size of a brown bear was skulking down the library headed towards them. Albert quickly ducked back in the aisle. "Luke, are you afraid of dogs?"

"No?" he replied, cautiously.

"You might be soon."

Luke looked out of the aisle to see the massive dog sniffing his way to them. Quickly, he ducked back into the aisle. Looking around for somewhere to go, they noticed the door behind them had disappeared. Looking up, Luke saw that the bookshelves did not go all the way to the ceiling. "Quick, climb the bookshelves."

Albert saw the open space above the shelves and climbed onto the shelves behind Luke. Just as they reached the top, the dog rounded the corner. It growled in disgust not finding its prey. The dog sniffed around following the scent up the bookshelves finding the intruders. Albert and Luke looked guiltily at the dog as it curled its upper lip in satisfaction. The dog's bark shook the shelves almost knocking the boys from their perch. Rising on its hind legs, it tried its best to snatch them in its massive jaws to pull them down. Lucky for Albert and Luke, its head came several inches short of the top shelf.

They had to decide fast what they were going to do. Together, Albert and Luke came to the same conclusion. They would have to jump from one shelf to the next in the direction of the front of the library. Taking a deep breath, they leapt from the shelf they were on to the next. Landing, they flung their arms out, balancing, to keep themselves from falling into the aisle. They readied themselves for the next jump and sprang forward, trying to get ahead of the barking dog.

Watching his prey get away, the dog tried to follow them. Leaping into the air, it managed to get its front paws over the top of the shelf. Its back legs kicked and scraped against the bookshelves as it pulled itself up. The boys looked back to see what was happening, but it was too late. The shelf teetered back and forth under the dog's weight, finally tumbling toward the shelf they were on. They quickly jumped to the next shelf before the first crashed into theirs. The force of the blow began a chain reaction! Fast as they could, the two jumped from shelf to shelf while the bookshelves behind them tumbled over.

Growing closer to the front shelf, they didn't know what to do. Climbing down would take too long. Even if they did make it down, could they get out of the way before the shelf fell on them? They only had seconds to look around before the next shelf would crash into them. At the end of the aisle to their left was a door that hopefully exited the library.

"The door," both said in unison and pointing.

The two sprinted along the shelf toward the door. As they got close, Luke shouted for Albert to jump and roll when he hit the ground. Albert leapt off with Luke close behind him. Doing as Luke said, he went into a roll as he hit the ground, then was back on his feet. Bursting through the door at the last moment they collapsed onto the ground sprawling out onto the floor exhausted from their flight.

"Uhum!" came a voice from above them.

Albert and Luke looked around to find themselves in a sitting room with a coffee table and a couple of sitting chairs. An old man with short white hair and a short beard wearing an elegant maroon mage robe glared down at them from his chairs. His brown eyes burrowed into them making them shrink back in fear.

"*What are you two doing here?*" came a very stern, familiar-sounding voice from behind them.

They turned their heads. Nicolet stared at them furiously. The old man looked to where they had come from. His eyes widened at the sight of a mound of books flowing through the door. The mage raised himself to his feet, strode past Albert and Luke, unbelief on his face, and leaned into his library the best he could, putting his hands on the doorframe for brace.

"What have you done to my library?" he roared. "This is why I don't let children into my house."

"I am so sorry, Dannon," said Nicolet apologetically. "I should have guessed Albert would have said something to Luke and that they would come investigating."

Dannon waved his hand while speaking a word Albert had never heard. Instantly the bookshelves moved back into position with all the books arranging themselves back on the shelves. The giant dog whimpered down the aisle shrinking as it neared the door to the size of a German shepherd. Dannon bent down petting it on the head asking if it was all right.

Dannon then whipped around, finger pointed, marching towards Luke and Albert who were still on the floor. "You two little…" he said, getting ready to cast a spell.

"Dannon!" Nicolet interrupted, standing with her hands on her hips, a fierce look in her eyes. "Are you planning on cursing two small children?"

Dannon stopped in his tracks, "Well… uhh… I was… umm… thinking of maybe…"

Nicolet cocked an eyebrow, daring him to finish his sentence.

Dannon calmed down, straightened his robes, "Well then..." He trailed, off clearing his throat. "I know your son, but who is the other?"

"This is Albert," introduced Nicolet helping them from the floor. "He is the boy I have been telling you about."

"Hmm, fascinating," replied Dannon as if unimpressed. "He doesn't seem all that special to me. How did you get into my house anyway?"

"The window at the base of the tower," Albert offered. "By the way, you have some weird pets."

"What do you mean 'weird'?"

"Like that giant octopus thing," Luke said as if accusing Dannon of doing something illegal.

"Sasha? What about her?" Dannon asked.

"She tried crushing us against the dock," Albert said, flabbergasted.

"Oh nonsense. She's harmless. She was just trying to give you a hug," Dannon replied.

"A hug?" burst out Albert. "Then there was that Cockadoodle thingy."

"Anna Marie?" Dannon rubbed his head. "Well... yeah, she might try and take a limb or two."

"Try to take a limb?" Luke said aghast. "And, Albert is special. He can talk to lizards."

A loud whistle rang throughout the room. "Boys!" said Nicolet sternly. Albert, Luke and Dannon immediately went silent. "Albert, you never said anything about being able to talk to lizards."

"Well, I didn't really know I could till now," replied Albert innocently.

"Well, we will discuss that later, but for right now I want you two to go home," she said, pointing to the door.

"Um... how? This place is a maze?" Luke retorted.

Nicolet rolled her eyes with a sigh, "When you come out of that door, take the third door on your right and then the next two doors on your left."

Albert and Luke hurried out of the room heads hung low. With instructions, it was easy finding their way back outside. Returning to Luke's house, they found Warren standing on the front porch, arms folded, with a stern look on his face. "So, you snuck into Dannon's house, did you?" he said gruffly.

Albert wondered how he knew what they had done. Neither of them answered, staring at the ground. Warren stepped aside to let them inside. Luke walked immediately to the stairs heading for his room. Albert guessed he should do the same when Warren stopped him. Warren waited for a moment until Luke was in his room and then motioned Albert over to the sofa.

"So, what was it like inside Dannon's home?" Warren asked, intrigued.

Warren's question and demeanor caught Albert off guard. He had thought he was going to get a lecture or something. Instead, Warren was excited, like a little kid wondering how a ride at a theme park was. "Come on, Albert, you have to tell me. I've only seen that silly sitting room. I've always wondered what the rest of the house was like."

Albert relaxed. "If I tell you, does that mean I'm not in trouble?"

"Nice try," replied Warren. "You still snuck into someone's house. So, tell me."

Albert half smiled and described their adventure in the house. Warren was enthralled by every word. By the time Albert had finished recounting his adventure, Nicolet had gotten home. Seeing her enter, Warren immediately changed his attitude. "Albert, I know our world is new and exciting to you, but you can't let Luke talk you into going places you don't belong." Nicolet rolled her eyes as she walked past. She knew better than to believe he was lecturing Albert. Warren was itching to get out and go off on an adventure himself. He advised Albert it would probably be best if he went up to his room.

As he climbed the last stair, head hung low, he could hear Warren and Nicolet talking and ducked behind the railing trying to hear what they were saying.

"So, what did the old wizard say?" asked Warren.

"He wasn't certain what any of this meant," replied Nicolet. "He did mention, though, that a trip to the Ethanan forest might not be a waste of time."

Albert wanted to desperately eavesdrop longer, but thought if they didn't hear his door shut, they would come to investigate. Left hanging, he entered his room and pressed his ear against the door wishing he could hear how it ended.

Chapter 7: Preparations

Albert didn't see much of Luke after school the next day. Without him, it was Warren's turn to teach him how to use a sword instead. He was worried when Warren brought out real swords to practice instead of wooden. Albert was shocked at the weight of the small, short sword he had been given. It felt as if it was five times heavier than the one made of wood. Almost instantly, Albert understood why Luke was so great at sword fighting. Warren patiently and carefully went over every little aspect of the sword, all its parts and how it should be respected. Carefully he showed him where to place his feet and how he should step while swinging or defending. The first attack of Warren's shook Albert's hand and he nearly dropped the sword.

"Metal isn't as forgiving as wood, is it," said Warren, with a chuckle. "Don't worry, you will get used to it. Try deflecting the blade away from you, instead of stopping it coming at you."

By the end of the lesson, Albert felt more confident with the sword. He hadn't been hit the entire time and wondered if his skill was increasing, or if Warren was just taking it easy on him.

Inside the house, Albert plopped down on the couch, exhausted, his limbs feeling like wet noodles. "I'm sorry Albert, but it is now time for *your* punishment," said Warren, arms folded towering over him. "Come on, get up." He reached down grabbing Albert by the arm pulling him to his feet.

"Ugh," Albert groaned. "Okay, what is it that I have to do?"

"Your punishment will be accompanying me on some errands."

The blacksmith was the first place they visited. When they entered, a short man with a long, blond curly mustache and grease-stained coveralls greeted them. The man only stood about three and a half feet tall, and his face was worn from age and hard work. From a distance, though, you would mistake him for a child.

"Why, Warren, what brings you in today?" asked the man politely.

"Very businessman-like Brom, I like it," replied Warren with a nod of approval.

Brom laughed, "Thanks, I'm trying. Bowen says *one* of us needs to be likable for the customers. Who do you have with you?"

"Brom, I would like you to meet Albert," said Warren introducing him.

The small man's eyes lit up. "So, you're Albert. I've heard so much about you from my son, Oscar. You go to school with him." He held out a childlike leathered hand. Albert smiled, reciprocating the gesture. Much to his surprise the man's hand grasped his firmly with more strength than his size let on. "I'm Brom, as Warren said, co-owner of this here establishment. Give me one second and I'll go get the big man in back. He will want to meet you." Before Albert could say anything Brom had disappeared to the back room.

"Gnomes. Always in a hurry," commented Warren. "Go ahead and look around. I need to talk with those two in private anyway."

Albert walked the shop, inspecting dozens of tools, weapons, and armor pieces, noticing the differences in qualities. A small counter with an ancient looking register had been placed several feet opposite the entrance door. Some items appeared to be junk, others of the most ornate design. The amount of detail that went into the armor was astounding to Albert. These two, undoubtedly had spent many years honing their craft. As Albert stared at all the swords, axes, bows, lances, spears (and many other weapons he couldn't identify), he wondered why a small farming town needed so many different types of weapons.

He wanted to touch them all and, since no one was around, why not? Swords were always his favorite. Albert walked to the large assortment of swords from longswords and cutlasses to broadswords and rapiers. One particular sword caught his eye. It was a longsword with a golden pummel that came to a conal point. Its grip was made of leather dyed blue with silver stitching and a cross guard made of silver. The bright steel of the blade had gold flakes molten into it and was polished to a mirror finish, allowing him to see his reflection. A scabbard with a golden locket wrapped in the same blue leather as the grip hung on the wall below it. Albert was reaching for it when a voice from behind made him jump.

"Like that one do ye?"

Albert turned to find a different man standing behind him. The dwarf's hair and beard a mess, sweat beading his face. He stood almost a foot shorter than Albert. He had on his leather apron and a tool belt.

"Sorry to frighten you, I'm Bowen," he said in his deep, raspy voice holding out a hand. Bowen's hand was firm and strong.

"Where's Warren?" asked Albert, still a little jumpy.

"He and Brom will be a long shortly. They have some… uh…" He scratched his beard thinking of the proper words, "Business to attend to. So, you like the sword?"

"Yeah, a lot. Can I touch it?" asked Albert.

"I would let you if I could, but unfortunately that sword is a little finicky," replied Brom.

"Finicky?" replied Albert, confused.

"Lunastus, is a magical blade," answered Brom. "The man who gave it to me said that it chooses its master instead of the person choosing it."

"So, no one can touch it?" asked Albert.

"No one, but me," replied Bowen.

"So, it chose you?"

"Not exactly. The blade only lets me handle it. I have never been able to use it in battle," corrected Bowen.

"What would happen if I were to touch it?" asked Albert.

"Don't know," replied Bowen. "Why don't you go ahead and give it a go."

Albert thought for a moment, "Okay, I will." He reached out his hand to grab the hilt. Goosebumps formed on his arms as he nervously got closer. Curious whether he would be chosen or not. His fingertips grazed the leather handle as sparks shot from the grip. Albert recoiled from the shock, waving the pain from his hand and flexing his finger to return the feeling to them. "Ouch, it shocked me."

"Yeah it did," laughed Bowen.

"You knew that would happen," accused Albert.

"Sorry, lad, I did, but understand I knew it wouldn't seriously hurt you," said Bowen, apologetically.

"Are you tricking people into touching Lunastus again, Bowen," said Warren entering from the back room, a disgruntled look on his face with Brom in tow. Brom was smiling happily a shiny new coin purse in his hand.

"Anytime you want to try your luck again, Warren, you come right on back," informed the little gnome.

Warren ignored Brom walking over by Albert and Bowen. "Let's just get what we came for, Albert. Is it ready, Bowen?"

The dwarf nodded and retrieved a short sword from the counter. He handed it to Warren who handed it to Albert. Taking the sword in his hands, Albert investigated it. The sheath was made of polished dark mahogany. Its handle had no pommel, just a long hilt wrapped in smooth, crimson-red leather. The guard was a simple bar made from dark, almost black steel.

"Well go on. Take it out of the scabbard," Bowen said excited.

Pulling it from its sheath, Albert found the blade was just under two feet long with a magnificent, straight, single edge. What mesmerized Albert was the color, it was a dark blue, almost black with red diagonal striations. He had never seen anything more amazing in his life.

"Wow it's," he paused. "Not to sound girly, but beautiful."

Both Bowen and Brom laughed, Bowen's deep and hearty, while Brom's was light almost like a cackle.

"You betcha it's beautiful. One of my finest works," Bowen said with pride, showing him how to lash it to his belt.

"Is this one magical as well?" Albert wondered.

"Indeed it is, lad. That sword will grow with you," replied Bowen, his face showing how pleased he was with his work.

Albert didn't know what he meant by *grow with him*, but he assumed he would figure it out sooner or later. "Warren, did you buy this for me?" asked Albert surprised.

"Well, Nicolet and I decided you might be needing it," said Warren, innocently. Albert was confused by Warren's words. He assumed he would find that out later, as well. "Well, on to our next stop, shall we."

The next shop they entered was a bakery. The sign that hung on the door read, 'Myrtle's Paradise'. Inside, the aroma of fine baked breads and pastries filled Albert's nose. It really did smell like paradise as the sign had read. No one tended the front counter of the shop, but he could hear someone humming and the thud of a rolling pin in the back room. A flood of memories rushed to Albert's mind of his mom baking goodies for when his sister and he would get home from school. He had to stop, taking a few deep breaths to keep from getting homesick.

A chime had sounded, signaling their entry. "Be with you in a moment," came a spirited voice from the back room. Albert sauntered around the bakery while Warren walked to the front counter and waited. The sights and smells of all the different breads, rolls, and other pastries in the shop made Albert's stomach rumble. Never before had he seen so many different types.

Albert was about to ask Warren what they were doing here when a six-and-a-half-foot tall woman with a thick, muscular build, in her early thirties stepped out of the back room. She had brown hair with streaks of gold pulled back into twin braids running down her back. Though her stature was menacing, her face was kind and soft with bright-green eyes. She had on a bright-blue dress and a white apron spotted with different colors of frosting.

"Good morning, Warren and his little friend," she announced. Her voice was kind but quite loud. "Odd seeing you in here two days in a row. Did you not get enough goods yesterday?"

"I, uhh, forgot some things yesterday, Myrtle," said Warren. "By the way, this is Albert. He will be staying with my family for a while."

"Oh, well, it is a pleasure to meet you, Albert," said Myrtle holding out a hand.

Albert stood there staring at the large woman and the peach fuzz like fur that lightly grew on the back of her hands. He had cautiously stuck out his hand to shake hers when he noticed a catlike tail tipped with bushy golden fur swishing from behind her body. Stunned, he could only stand and stare.

"Oops, I forgot," said Warren, embarrassed. "You probably have never met a Mauran."

Albert shook his head, no.

"Probably haven't seen a Gygan either, have ya?" added Myrtle with a laugh.

Again, he shook his head.

"Well, my dear, I am part of both. My father, a Gygan, is a sort of giant and my mother was a Mauran. They are a people who resemble a feline or cat." Myrtle pulled up her hair on the side of her head to reveal ears that resembled a cat's. They were also covered in fine short hairs.

"Okay, cool," said Albert. "It is, umm, a pleasure to meet you."

Myrtle laughed once again at his uneasiness. Albert didn't know how she could be so easy-going. Where he came from, if someone had acted the way he did that person probably would have been offended. Myrtle, on the other hand, seemed as if it didn't matter.

"Great. Now that introductions are finished, how about we purchase a few things?" said Warren, trying to hurry things along.

"All right, then, what do you need," asked Myrtle.

"I just need two loaves of Kelsney bread," Warren said.

"Kelsney bread?" said Myrtle, confused. "Are you going on a trip? You know these things stay good for weeks?"

"No, we just don't want to have to come visit you again, so soon," replied Warren. "Extra mouth to feed and all."

Albert could see that his eyes were wide and that he was looking intently at her, trying to telepathically send her a message. *But, why was he being so secretive? Was he going on a trip? What would happen to him? Was this why Warren had purchased him a sword?*

"Okay. Well give me a minute," said Myrtle, confused, heading for the back room. She reappeared with two loaves of bread in her arms wrapped in brown paper. She set them on the counter and slid them to Warren with a smile. "Here you are, Warren. Though I don't know why you want Kelsney bread for eating at home. It doesn't taste as good as fresh but, oh well. Don't worry about paying me now. I'll just put it on your account."

"Thank you, Myrtle," replied Warren. "I'll see you nex…" He looked at Albert suspiciously. "Next time I come in." Warren finished obviously trying to recover.

All right, something must be going on, thought Albert. It also had to be about him. Otherwise, why was Warren being so cryptic? And, why would he not tell Albert what was going on. It looked like he would have to eavesdrop in on Warren and Nicolet's conversations a little more.

Having said their goodbyes to Myrtle, the next store they visited was a meat shop. Here they again purchased supplies that would last a couple weeks or more before heading on to the next store for supplies. Warren was definitely preparing for something like a trip. Albert desperately wanted to know why was he acting so strange. Did it have to do with Albert's dream or the elves? He wanted to ask, but it seemed all he did since getting to Thu'hilen was ask questions. Everyone must be getting tired of them by now. Still he had to know, he just needed the courage to ask.

By the time they were at the gate to Warren's house Albert was ready. It was now or never he told himself. Albert took a breath to settle his nerves, "Warren, can I ask why all the food?"

Warren paused, hand on the iron latch of the gate, pondering his answer. "I would like to tell you, Albert, but I'm just going to have to ask you to trust me. You'll find out soon enough."

Warren's answer did not satisfy him. It seemed that if he wanted to find out what was going on, eavesdropping was the only way he was going to find out. "All right," he replied. "I guess I can wait until then."

"Thank you, Albert. I promise it will be worth it," Warren said, gratefully.

Inside the house, everything was covered in sheets and all the windows were open, allowing for air circulation. At the back of the room Luke could be heard cleaning out the fireplace, complaining as he went along. Albert's new best friend was covered in soot from head to toe making it hard for Albert to recognize him. The only thing that clued Albert that it was Luke was his blue eyes pleading to his father as they walked in.

"Don't look at me like that," said Warren, unsympathetically. "You are the one who snuck into Dannon's and got yourself into this mess." Obviously, his misery ploy hadn't worked. Luke went back to cleaning. "Come on, Albert, let's go see what's for dinner," said Warren ushering him to the kitchen.

"What is that?" asked Luke coming up to them, seeing the sword at Albert's side. Albert immediately reached down guiltily attempting to hide his gift from Luke's sight.

"Nothing that concerns you, Luke. Now get back to your chores," responded Warren.

"Well this isn't fair. *We* break into Dannon's, and I have to clean the fireplace while Albert gets a brand-new sword," said Luke angrily.

"Listen, Luke, I know it may seem that way, but it's not," Warren calmly replied. "There is a reason your mother and I got Albert this sword, a reason you don't need to know yet." Luke stared at his father defiantly, arms folded across his chest, as if saying to his father that his answer wasn't good enough. Warren put his hands on his shoulders, looking down at him caringly. "Luke, Albert has been wondering the same thing and all I told him was to have patience and soon enough he would get his answer. All I ask is that you do the same thing."

Luke looked to Albert, who nodded to him with a wink. Ahh, Albert was already coming up with a plan to figure out what. "Okay, Dad," responded Luke, acting apologetic. "But whatever it is, it had better be good."

"Thank you, Luke. Now please go back to cleaning out the fireplace, so *I* don't get in trouble."

The next day was much the same. After school, Warren gave Albert another lesson, this time using his new sword. Warren focused more on attack and how to move fluidly from a defensive position to an offensive one. Albert mimicked his movements, paying close attention to the proper footwork. It only took him a few swings to get familiar with the new sword. He discovered that Bowen had put a long hilt on it, making it perfectly balanced and easier to use. Plus, it allowed him to handle it with two hands. This way he had a little more strength behind it.

"Good job, Albert," said Warren, encouraging him. "Remember, though, always make sure you have your feet spread properly apart. Watch those foot positions, and don't hesitate in your swings and thrusts. The follow through is important. That way you can break an opponent's block."

"Right," nodded Albert. "I just don't want to hurt you is all."

Warren laughed, "Trust me, you aren't going to hurt me. These basics will save your life in a fight, but against an experienced fighter, you would be lucky to land a blow. There are still dozens of techniques and little tricks you need to learn to even think about going up against a veteran fighter."

"So, you are saying I can go all-out against you?" asked Albert eyes excited.

"Be my guest," replied Warren, confidently.

"Sweet!" Albert attacked Warren with everything he had. The match didn't last long. After a couple swings that Warren easily parried, he disarmed Albert with a quick flick of the wrist. Albert's sword clattered against the ground a few feet away, the edge of Warren's blade at his neck.

"Well that was fun," said Warren stepping backward and tapping Albert on the head with the flat of his blade. Albert rubbed the slight sting away where the blade hit. "For you, maybe."

"Don't take it too hard, Albert, you have only been using the sword a few days," reminded Warren, sitting on a bench overlooking the fountain. "Now go have fun. No punishment today."

Albert picked up his sword, sheathing it. He looked up to see Nicolet watching from the kitchen window, an anxious look on her face. *I wonder what's going on with her.* He left Warren to enjoy himself in the warm sun and headed for the back door of the house. As he was about to reach for the latch the door swung open, Nicolet holding it for him.

"So, how was practice," she asked.

"Great," replied Albert. "Just wish I were as good as Warren."

"Don't worry, you'll get there," she smiled.

After he entered the house, she exited and shut the door behind him. Albert snuck to the window to catch a peek of what was going on. He watched Nicolet hurry over to Warren, sit, and began speaking. Now was his chance. Albert ran to the front of the house, out the door, around the corner and stopped. He leaned against the house, concealing himself, trying to hear what was being said.

"Everything is prepared then?" asked Nicolet.

"Yes, I'll write to Captain Reno at Fort Valdrum tomorrow, letting him know of our intentions of taking Albert to the Ethanan Forest in three days," replied Warren.

"Good,' said Nicolet. "Albert's appearance and his visions about the forest can't be mere coincidence. Generations of questions will soon be answered."

"We hope," corrected Warren.

"No, my dear husband," said Nicolet confidently. "Events are beginning to take place and Albert is the key to them."

Albert turned away, head spinning with questions. All this was about him. Still he didn't know what it meant. Why was he so important? What made him the key? What events were beginning to take place? All he knew was that he couldn't wait a few days. He needed to know now, but didn't know where Fort Valdrum was, let alone Sanoran or the Ethanan forest, but he knew who did.

Chapter 8: The Adventure Begins

Later that afternoon, Albert found Luke mucking the barn. Now was his chance. If he had learned anything about Luke, it was that he wanted to be like his father. Warren had spent most of his childhood adventuring and Luke wanted the same. Albert just had to tell him what the big secret was and since everything was ready, they should just go by themselves instead.

"Hey Luke," said Albert, announcing himself.

"Oh, hello, Al," replied Luke. "You shouldn't be here. If Mom and Dad find you, they are going to add *another* lifetime to my sentence."

"I'll be quick, Luke. So, I overheard your dad and mom talking this morning and I found out what the big secret was," said Albert to pique Luke's interest.

Luke paused, a pitchfork of hay and manure in his hands. "Oh," he said feigning interest. "So, what is this big secret, then?"

"Your parents are going to take me to Ethanan forest."

"What?" said Luke incredulously. "I've been begging them to take me somewhere my whole life. You are here a week and it's off they go."

Albert could tell Luke was upset at the bomb he had just dropped. Now was his chance. "You know, Luke, they don't plan on leaving for three days. All the supplies are sitting there in the kitchen. We could wake up early tomorrow, before anyone else, and head for Ethanan without them."

He saw a spark of fire glimmer in Luke's eyes but quickly fade. "I don't know, Al. We would get into a lot of trouble. *I* would get into a lot of trouble. My punishment is almost over, I don't want to be stuck doing these disgusting chores for the rest of my life."

"Okay, Luke," replied Albert, acting as if giving up. "Maybe when they officially tell us the plan in a few days, I'll ask if you can come along." He slowly headed to exit the barn, giving Luke plenty of time to stew over the thought.

"Al," Luke called out to him. Albert turned around. He could tell Luke was fighting with himself what decision to make. "Let's do it," he finally decided. "Tomorrow morning, early, before dawn I will come get you."

"Yes!" cheered Albert. "We are going to be just like your dad when he was our age," he added to solidify Luke's decision.

"Yeah, except we won't have a bunch of knights tagging along," replied Luke.

The next morning, Albert awoke to a light rapping on his door. He wearily opened his eyes, wondering why someone had woken him up so early. Suddenly, he sat up, remembering. Getting out of bed, Albert threw on the clothes he had laid out last night, attached his sword to his belt, and grabbed the knapsack he had prepared the night before.

He opened the door to find Luke waiting for him, practically bouncing up and down with excitement as if he had been waiting his whole life for this moment. Luke had on a pack that bulged heavily, two daggers on his belt, and a set of throwing knives strapped to his leg. "Is this journey really going to be that dangerous?" whispered Albert, nervous that he only had his sword.

"It shouldn't be," replied Luke softly. "We will be traveling along roads the entire way there, but my dad always told me to be prepared for anything. Mainly, I just brought most of this stuff along for practice."

"Well should I grab anything else?"

"Nah, you should be fine. Let's go. I've already gone downstairs and grabbed the food."

Albert's heart began to pound. It was time. They were hopefully going to find some answers. Why he was brought here if it was indeed purposeful instead of accidental. He didn't like sneaking out with Luke and getting him into more trouble. He didn't like going behind Warren and Nicolet's backs. Albert had to get this solved, though. He had to get back to his family, let them know he was all right. A few calming breaths, "Okay, let's go." He nodded.

Luke, a big grin on his face, snuck them out the front door, across the front lawn and down the road.

***

"It's about time they left," said Nicolet. She and Warren were in bed, quietly listening to everything taking place outside their room. "I got tired of acting secretive and ominous."

"You and me both," replied Warren. "I didn't think I could be more obvious, but tell me, why are we letting them go off alone again?"

"You know how much Luke looks up to and idolizes you," reminded Nicolet. "He has been dying to go on a journey like this one. Besides, this is the safest part, and you will meet up with them in Valdrum for the rest of the way."

"True," said Warren. "Well, I guess I better get up and go see Bernard."

"Yes, you shall, and I shall go back to sleep." Nicolet turned over, bundling up in the blankets.

***

A little before noon on the third day of their journey they saw the walls and eastern gate of Fort Valdrum. Albert and Luke were grateful that tonight they would get to sleep in a real bed instead once again on the hard ground. The trip so far had been uneventful. They had passed merchants and other people traveling from the fort to Brookshire. Albert did have the vision once again, but this time it was slightly different. This time, when he reached the Ethanan Forest, he noticed the Daratine Mountains looming in the distance. He watched as darkness crept out of a large tree in the forest, moving rapidly in the direction of the mountains and spreading upwards into the air. Now airborne, the darkness covered everything he could see. Soon it began encircling him, the fear began to overcome him. Shutting his eyes, he wished he would just wake up.

Much to Albert's surprise, he didn't wake up drenched in sweat, heart pounding. He must be getting used to the dream's ending. Had that already happened or is it yet to happen? Was this world already covered in darkness? Or is Albert having this vision, so he could stop it from happening?

When Luke awoke that morning, Albert explained to him the new ending. Afterward, Luke had the same question. The rest of their trip, the boys talked of things they liked to do in their worlds. When Albert mentioned baseball, Luke's face lit up. "I like the idea of trying to hit a ball thrown at you and stealing bases." Albert could tell he didn't really catch on to how the game was played, but it was fun talking about something that he liked to do anyway.

As they got closer to the gate, Luke drew Albert near to give him a little advice, "Okay now, Al, as we go through the gate, act like we do this all the time. It is just another day."

The guards at the gate wore green uniforms with the symbol of a silver rose embroidered on the chest. People freely entered and exited the fort town, going about their business. Upon proceeding through the gate, Albert watched the guard examining them from head to toe. He tried to act casual, hoping not to draw too much attention. Eventually, the guard turned his gaze toward others, assessing whether they were trouble or not.

Through the gate, they saw a sign reading, 'The Eagle District'. It was a jam-packed corridor full of homes on either side of the street with little shops on the main floor. People roamed the main road, some on horses, others pulling carts, some walking with baskets full of goodies. Seeing a man riding what looked like a giant golden chicken, Albert stared in amazement.

"What's that?" he asked.

Luke looked where Albert pointed. "Oh that? That's a Cuckooloo."

"A what?" Albert responded dumbfounded.

"An exotic bird from a country in the east. A lot of rich people own them. They run fast, but that's about it. You can't really use them to pull a cart or carry anything."

Albert could tell Luke wasn't very impressed by the Cuckooloo, but he thought they were awesome. The city seemed almost militarily organized with all the houses looking the same. Made of brick, mortar and wood, every building was uniform. There were soldiers everywhere, either standing guard or patrolling the area.

From a side street to Albert's right, he could see the river and a coliseum on the other side.

"Hey Luke, what's over there?" He gestured, full of wonder.

Luke looked across the river at the coliseum. "That's the battle arena," he replied, eyes wide with excitement. "They hold matches and tournaments there. Fighters from all around come to compete against each other."

"Do they kill each other?" Albert asked, frightened.

"No," Luke replied.

"What happens if someone does kill an opponent?"

Luke paused for a moment, "I'd rather not say."

Two rivers ran through the fort and converged below a large platform made from stone and marble, making up the center of the city. A beautiful white stone arch read, *Ordellia's Court,* welcoming them to the main place of commerce. In the middle of the platform was a magnificent fountain carved in the shape of a great serpent. The giant snake twisted and turned in the air as it rose from the fountain's base. Water being fed from the rivers sprayed out in all directions, showcasing its majesty and elegance.

Little shops sat along the water wall of the platform, selling wares. Albert was amazed by the many different items being sold. Jewelry, furs, food, trinkets, lined the streets. One shop even had a sign that read, 'Magic Scrolls'.

"Are those real?"

Luke nodded his head, "They only work once, though. That's if you have the willpower to cast the spell in the first place. After incanting the words on them, the scroll turns to ash."

After searching some of the shops, Albert wished he had money to buy something. When they were finished browsing the shops, Albert asked where they were headed next. Luke suggested they go to the fort and Captain Reno. A short walk led them to the garrison. Along the way to the right of the road was a field full of catapults and ballista. To the left was a cathedral.

The garrison was a three-story building with towers at each corner. Each standing taller than the garrison wall, giving a perfect bird's-eye view of the surrounding countryside. Guards could be seen patrolling the towers and along the wall. At the gate, a solider stopped them.

"State your purpose," he commanded.

"We have come to see Captain Reno. We would like his permission to venture through the West Gate," Luke announced.

The guard studied the two boys. "All right, you seem harmless enough. Leon," he shouted, and a soldier looked their way.

Leon sprinted over to them. "What do you need of me, Sir?"

"These two young men have asked to speak with Captain Reno. I need you to take them to him," The gate guard replied.

"Yes, Sir," Leon replied with a salute. "This way, please."

Albert and Luke followed Leon across the yard to the Garrison. Leon was only a few years older than they were. He had short, wavy, brown hair parted on one side. It bounced as he walked. His uniform was new, a sign that he had only been in the king's army a short time. A single bronze bar on his sleeve signified his rank as a private.

Inside the building, imposing granite floors and walls reminded them that it was solidly built for war. Weapon and armor stands were positioned by every door for quick access if the call to battle rang out. Leon led them down a side hall to the back of the building, stopping at a thick wooden door. A woman stood there; arms folded. She wore a dark-brown outfit that reminded Albert of a Shaolin monk. Her sash was red embroidered with golden thread. Hard pieces of leather armor had been sown onto the shoulders, elbows and knees of the garment. The shoes she wore had a sheet of bark attached to the tops as did the gloves that hung from her waist. A piece of cloth with the image of an eagle and an olive branch in its beak covered the lower half of her face, obscuring her identity. The woman's brown eyes examined them quickly as they approached, then stared straight ahead.

"Captain Reno's personal guard, maybe," whispered Luke.

Albert and Luke cautiously approached the door as Leon knocked, waiting for a reply. The boys continued to stare at the woman in fear and awe. Her golden-brown skin had hints of freckles on her cheeks. Dark-brown hair was carefully gathered into a bun on top of her head.

"Who is it?" came a voice on the other side.

"Private Leon, Sir. I have two boys here who wish to speak with you."

"Let them in," came the voice.

Leon opened the door and ushered them in, shutting the door behind them. Captain Reno was in his late forties with peppered black-and-white, short hair. His square face was rough from years of combat, and he sported a neatly trimmed mustache. His armor was more regal than the rest of the soldiers', but still had the same green tabard with the silver rose on it. He stood behind a large wooden desk urging them to come forward with his hand. Waist-high bookshelves lined the walls. Behind him, a large window overlooked the training grounds. Tactical maps of the country were pinned to the walls above the bookcases. Two chairs sat in front of his desk for his guests.

"Hello, I am Captain Reno. Why have you two young gentlemen come to speak with me today?" he asked.

Luke bowed. "Hello, Captain Reno. I am Luke, son of Warren."

All three of them stood in silence. Finally, Luke elbowed Albert, clearing his throat. Albert stood a second before realizing that he was supposed to introduce himself.

"Oh... I'm Albert Worthington... um son of James Worthington," he said, bowing seconds later as he realized he had forgotten.

"Ahh, so you are Luke, Warren's son. Your father has told much about you. It is a pleasure to finally meet you, and it is a pleasure to meet you Albert Worthington, son of James Worthington. Do have a seat," said Captain Reno, motioning to the chairs in front of him.

Luke thanked Captain Reno and sat down, Albert following his lead.

"Captain Reno, we have come here to ask you permission to pass through the West Gate," Luke said.

"And what reason do you have for venturing into the Great Plains?"

"We are on a quest, Sir."

"Oh... and what is the nature of this quest may I ask?"

Luke didn't know if Captain Reno would believe that they were on a mission to see the elves and the Daratrine Mountains. Or, he could believe them, in which case Luke knew he wouldn't let them pass through the gate. So, he decided that the captain didn't need to know.

"I'm sorry Captain Reno, but I cannot tell you," Luke replied.

"Then, I'm afraid I can't let you go through the gate."

"Why not?" argued Luke.

"Because, I simply cannot allow two children to venture forth into the Great Plains alone, even if one is the son of the Great Warren. They are no place for children. Bandits and thieves roam around unchecked. Then there are the nomadic tribes, who are completely unpredictable."

"I'm not afraid. I can handle myself," Luke burst out. "And Albert has received some training and can handle a sword."

Captain Reno looked at Luke fiercely, forcing him to shrink away slowly. "I'm sorry Luke, but I can't allow two twelve-year-old boys to venture forth out into the Great Plains alone."

Luke was about to burst out again, but Albert grabbed his arm, restraining him.

"Captain Reno, sir," Albert said, meekly. "Please, Sir, we need to get to Sanoran and the Ethanan Forest. Ever since I arrived here. I've had this horrible vision about the forest, and it keeps getting worse. We need to get there and figure out what's going on."

Luke looked at Albert upset that he had told him why they were on their quest.

"You know, you two are the second group that has requested access to the gate on their way to Ethanan. A company of elves it was, and I was reluctant to let them pass as well. I'm sorry, Albert. I just can't let you two go out there alone," Captain Reno said sympathetically.

Albert was about to plead more with Captain Reno when a door to the left of the captain opened, interrupting the conversation. A man in a light-brown cloak entered the room. His hood pulled up, hiding his face so they could not tell who he was. The man walked over to Captain Reno and whispered into his ear.

"Are you sure about this?" Captain Reno asked the man.

He nodded. Sighing, Captain Reno picked up a quill from his desk and wrote a letter on a piece of parchment. The hooded man then turned and left the room. Having finished writing, Captain Reno rolled up the parchment and set it aside. Albert and Luke were confused about what had just happened and what was on that piece of paper. The captain picked up an opened letter from off his desk. "Do you know what this is?" he asked Albert and Luke. They shook their heads, no.

"It is a letter from your father, Luke. In it he has asked me to let him pass through West Gate with his son and a special guest on their journey to the very same forest. He also tells me that he should arrive a couple of days from now," Captain Reno looked back and forth between Albert and Luke assertively. The two grew nervous, knowing the ending of this speech wasn't going to end in their favor. "Seeing as how Warren is not here, my only assumption would be that you two couldn't wait and ran off ahead of him. I feel it would be best if you two waited here patiently for Luke's father to arrive. We have comfortable accommodations here at the fort. It is only a couple more days, boys."

Rallying his courage, Albert spoke up. "I'm sorry, Sir, but I just can't wait. This darkness needs to be stopped."

A scoff came from Captain Reno's lips, "And why do you think two twelve-year-old boys can stop such darkness? What can you do?"

Albert stood boldly, staring back at Captain Reno, "I don't know, but something inside tells me I have to do this and there isn't much time."

Captain Reno sat in his chair, hands together, staring at his desk, contemplating. He looked up to Albert. "Destiny and fate are interesting things, and no man knows their workings. If it is your destiny to travel to the elvan forest, then I have no power to stop you. The stars will find some way to get you there. I know of the darkening of the forest and Sanoran. It was once the great entry into those woods, teeming with all sorts of life. Now Sanoran is but a shadow of its former self, a place for bandits, thieves, and other surly folks to hide and take refuge. I wish I could send a troop with you or even an escort, but I cannot afford any of my men to go with you."

Reno stood, grabbing the rolled-up parchment. "Tonight you will stay here in the barracks. Get some food and rest. First thing tomorrow, take this to Gerard at the West Gate. He will open it for you and let you pass."

Albert and Luke jumped out of their seats excited. Luke quickly grabbed the rolled-up letter and the two bolted for the door. Before they could leave the room, Captain Reno cleared his throat loudly to get their attention. The two stopped, realizing that in their excitement they had forgotten to thank him. They spun around and, bowing, thanked him several times. Captain Reno shook his head with a chuckle. "Be careful, boys. Many dangers lurk on your road ahead. You can leave tomorrow, but I really think it would be wise to wait for your father."

"We will be careful," Albert and Luke replied together and hurried out the door.

Leaving Captain Reno's office, Albert noticed that the scary looking monk woman was gone. Wasn't she supposed to be the captain's guard? Oh well, who could think about that now that they had permission to head to Ethanan. Leon stood waiting to show them to their rooms.

The next morning, Albert and Luke didn't bother following the road back to Ordellia's Court and on to the West Gate. Instead, they followed the Garrison wall around, cutting through the field with the catapults and ballistae. As they darted in and out of the rows, a guard shouted at them to get out of there. Albert and Luke shouted sorry as they ran back to the road.

Two men stood watch on either side as they approached the West Gate. Albert and Luke came to a skidding halt before the one closest to the guard house door, out of breath.

"Are you Gerard?" Luke heaved.

"Sorry Sir, I am not. He is inside the gatehouse if you would like to speak with him."

Inside the gatehouse, they found an elderly man sitting at a desk. He had thinning grey hair and wore a worn suit of armor. He stared out a window, daydreaming.

"Excuse me, Sir," Luke interrupted.

Gerard slowly came back to reality, blinking his eyes and smiling. "Well hello, what can I do for you two young fellas today?"

"Are you Gerard?" they asked together.

"I am," he responded.

Albert and Luke smiled at each other and handed the letter to Gerard. He carefully looked it over, smacking his lips.

"So, you two want to venture to Sanoran, huh?" Gerard asked rhetorically. "And you have Captain Reno's approval? Well, I guess we can open the gate for you two."

Gerard got up from his desk heading for the door. Albert and Luke followed him outside where he signaled the guards to open the gates. Both guards turned and pulled levers on the wall behind them. Mechanisms in the wall could be heard as the gate started to lift into the lintel above. When the gate had finished opening, Gerard gave them permission to proceed. They thanked the man and the other knights, then hurried off down the road to Sanoran.

Chapter 9: Trouble on the Plains

"All right, Albert, this is it. The last stretch of road until Sanoran and Ethanan," said Luke excitedly.

"Stop there," came a feminine voice from the road.

Albert and Luke watched the woman who had been standing outside of Reno's office step from behind a tree onto the road, followed by the cloaked man who had spoken to the captain.

"You two are coming with us," she said, her accent reminding Albert of someone from eastern Europe.

Confusion raced through Albert and Luke's minds. What was going on? Aren't these two working for Captain Reno? They had gotten permission. So why were they hassling them? Is it all some sort of trap?

"We're not going anywhere with you," said Luke, defiantly going for his daggers.

"Luke, what are you doing?" asked Albert, scared.

"I'm not letting these two creeps take us," replied Luke. "Come on, Al. We can take them."

Nervously, Albert drew his sword. Luke shouted a war cry and ran straight for the woman. She easily swatted away his attack. Grabbing one of his arms, she twisted it behind his back. Luke screamed in frustration, trying to break free. Albert stood frozen in place. Just like the razorback and wyvern attack, he was going to die.

"*Run, Al,*" Luke shouted.

Run? How could he run? What was the purpose of running? Besides, he couldn't leave Luke behind.

"*Run, Albert,*" Luke shouted again.

Breaking free of his fear, Albert followed Luke's advice. He ran. He didn't make two steps before an axe sliced through the air, planting itself in his path. *Wait! I know that axe,* realized Albert, staring at its design. He turned to the hooded man who had thrown it at him.

"Warren?"

Luke turned his head to the hooded man, "Dad?"

Warren pulled back the hood, revealing himself. "Let this be a lesson to the both of you," Warren said, reprimanding them. "You two should have waited for me as Captain Reno suggested. These plains are crawling with all sorts of fiends who would use you two for target practice." The woman let Luke go.

"I'm not afraid!" said Luke, rubbing his arm. "I'm brave, like you."

"I'm sorry, Warren," said Albert, bringing him his axe. "I just wanted to find out what was going on and didn't want to have to wait."

"It's all right, you two," said Warren placing a hand on their shoulders. "I just hope Anyia's and my lesson has taught you something."

"Yeah, don't fight someone who's far better than you," said Luke, flatly.

"And be patient and wait," added Albert.

"Well, truthfully, Nicolet and I planned on you two doing the first half of the journey alone," informed Warren. "Though, you two running off without telling anyone probably wasn't the greatest idea."

They both hung their head in shame.

"Hold on. How did you get here so fast?" asked Luke, trying to put the pieces together.

"Well, Luke and Albert, here is another lesson for you," replied Warren. "When traveling, don't just run off heading for your destination on your own two feet. Find a quicker way. Now before we head for Sanoran, introductions are in order. Luke, Albert, this is Anyia. Anyia, this is my son Luke and his friend, Albert."

"It is a pleasure to meet you," she said removing her mask, revealing herself to be in her early twenties. "Now, Warren, if you don't mind, I will go fetch the horses."

Yes! thought Albert. *Finally, no more walking!*

Anyia returned moments later with two horses, one a white thoroughbred and the other a brown paint.

"Okay," said Warren. "Luke, you will ride with me. Albert," he looked over to him. "You, will ride with Anyia."

Albert was excited, nervous, and scared all at the same time. He had only ridden a horse once before with his dad. He remembered sitting close to him and holding on tight. Albert had never sat close to a girl before, let alone held on to one, especially one as beautiful as Anyia.

Warren and Luke mounted the paint and Anyia the thoroughbred. She held out her hand to help Albert up. Nervously, he took hold and climbed onto the horse behind her. Sitting as close as he dared, Albert lightly put his arms around her. Anyia, chuckling at Albert's shyness, spurred the horse forward, forcing Albert to tighten his grip.

"That's better," she smiled. "You don't have to be so gentle. I don't break easily."

"Question, Dad? How do you two know each other?" Luke asked.

"Oh, about eight years ago there was a small revolt," said Warren casually. "Anyia here was their leader. In the end, she surrendered to me."

"Need I remind you, that the last time we fought, I had my hands around your throat ready to snap your neck," she replied shortly.

Warred huffed, "I only let you get your hands on me so I could get close to you. You wouldn't stop dancing around. Go ahead boys, ask her who came out with a scar and who didn't."

Anyia looked away embarrassed. "I admit, I did not see the dagger in your hand." She looked at Luke. "Your father stabbed me right below the heart, ending our fight and the rebellion." Anyia touched her shirt on the left side of her stomach.

"What happened after that?" Albert asked enthralled.

"Well, fearing for my life, Warren said if I were to surrender, he would spare my life," she said solemnly, thinking back to the moment. "So, I did. He removed the dagger, bound my wound, and used what little magic he knows to stop the bleeding. The next day, my people gave up and went home."

"Wow," said Luke. "How old were you?"

"I was thirteen."

Albert and Luke were awed that someone a year older than them almost defeated his dad.

"Why didn't you kill her?" asked Albert.

Warren smiled. "She was a kid and fighting for what she believed was right. Anyia is one of the best fighters I've seen, I couldn't deprive our world of her skill. Besides, she makes a far better ally than an enemy."

Anyia smiled and bowed in her saddle, "And you, make a great friend and mentor."

Albert and Luke spent most of the ride asking Anyia all sorts of questions: where she was born, who taught her to fight, and why her people started a revolt in the kingdom. Anyia explained she was born in a small northern village called Lentiel. At the age of three, her family sent her to the Juko Monastery to become a monk. There she studied under Master Kai who was the Grand Master of Juko. "The reason my people started the *revolt* was to take back the land *your kingdom* had stolen from us," stated Anyia firmly.

"Your people had given the land to us as a gesture of peace many years back," retorted Warren.

"My people were tricked into giving the land away." Anyia hurled the words.

Warren, not wanting to start the same argument again, bowed out and let Anyia win. At the end of the day, they were more than halfway to Sanoran. Tomorrow, they would make it there well before nightfall. They chose a small group of trees to make camp for the night. After unloading the horses, Anyia lashed them to a tree while Warren started a fire. Albert and Luke set up the beds. After a small meal, Warren, Albert, and Luke went to bed as Anyia took first watch.

She climbed one of the trees for a better view of the landscape at night. From her perch she could see back to the road and across the river. Several hours had passed and two of the four moons now high in the sky increased her visibility. Anyia had finished scanning across the river and was now looking toward the road when she saw two figures darting through the long grass. Stealthily, she dropped down from her perch and without a sound she woke Warren.

"Warren," she said calmly. "Get the boys up. We have company."

Springing out of bed, he grabbed his battle axe.

"I'm going to sneak behind whoever it is," Anyia whispered.

He nodded. Waking Luke, a hand over his mouth so he wouldn't make a sound. "Shhhh, we have company."

Luke nodded grabbing his daggers. He crept over to a nearby tree. Warren moved to Albert with the same procedure. "What do I do?" asked Albert, scared.

"Okay, Albert, I want you to grab your sword and go hide behind that tree." Warren pointed to a tree that was two down from Luke's. "I'm going to be behind the one in the middle. I want you to stay down and try to stay hidden."

"Okay," Albert whispered crawling over to the tree Warren had pointed to.

"Dad?" Luke said quietly. "Where is Anyia?"

Warren, in position, answered. "She is sneaking behind them."

"Are they bandits?" Luke asked.

"Don't think so. The only bandit camps I know of are across the river."

The intruders grew closer. Warren put his finger to his lips, signaling them to be quiet. He stood, back to the tree, battle-ax ready, while Albert and Luke crouched down trying to stay hidden. Warren ready to jump out and attack when an arrow sank into the tree he was hiding behind. Seconds later, a barrage of arrows came flying between the trees. Albert and Luke tightened up against their trees trying not to get hit. Warren stayed calmly against the tree often sneaking a look to see which direction the arrows were coming from.

The barrage of arrows ceased. Warren chanced another glance. "Get ready. We have five of them closing in," Warren whispered.

Warren, roaring, leaped from behind the tree to get the nomads' attention. Three of them charged him, clubs and crude axes prepared to strike. He batted them away, striking them with the shaft of his battle-ax hoping to frighten them away. One sank and crawled off after a solid blow. Warren was ready to face down the last attackers when an arrow sank deeply into his upper arm. Grunting, he now began swinging his axe in wide arcs to fend off the other two.

Albert watched as Luke scurried off into the darkness. *Great,* he thought to himself. *Now it's just me.* Keeping behind the tree, he hoped everything would be over before he had to do anything. He was trying to muster up some courage to venture a peek when a creature covered in fur stepped into view. Albert couldn't tell whether it was a man or a beast. It stood half a foot taller than he did and had small antlers coming out the side of its head. Standing up nervously, Albert held up his sword to defend himself.

The nomad raised his crude scimitar into the air, bringing it down in an arcing motion. Albert timidly blocked the strike, barely staying on his feet. The man-beast kept swinging at him wildly. Albert managed to somehow avoid all the attacks. His fear abated and the paralysis that froze him in the past was leaving.

Confidence growing, he took a deep breath trying to remember what Warren and Luke had taught him. He soon gained some ground by forcing the nomad back. The man-beast made another downward strike which Albert parried, moving to the side and forcing the beast's blade into the ground. Albert slid his blade up the nomad's sword and smacked his pummel into the man-beast's face. The nomad shrieked in pain, leaving himself wide open. Albert, taking the advantage, stabbed the creature in the thigh.

The man-beast howled. He grabbed his wounded leg and retreated from the fight. Albert was shocked, amazed, and proud to have won his first sword fight. A horn blew in the distance and the nomads retreated. When Warren and Luke came back into sight, Luke was covered in dirt. Warren had the arrow still sticking through his arm.

"What happened to you two?" Albert asked amused that he had not received any injures.

"This?" Warren stated. "A lucky shot is all."

"Nothing!" replied Luke. "It's dusty out here, Al. I was staying low to the ground and got some dirt on me is all."

"What were they?" asked Albert.

"They're nomads," replied Warren.

"What did they want?" asked Luke.

"We are probably too close to their camp, so they were trying to either scare us off or kill us."

"Why didn't we run?" asked Albert.

"Best thing to do with nomads is defend our camp. Let them know that this is our territory for the night. Once they realize that, they will leave us alone."

"You've dealt with nomads like these before, haven't you Dad," asked Luke, sarcastically. "Is this what real adventures are like?"

Warren chuckled. "Fun isn't it, Luke?"

Luke huffed while Albert looked scared and worried.

Moments later, Anyia made it back to camp with a large red mark underneath her right eye. They looked at her questioningly. Five archers had ganged up on her. When Warren chortled that Anyia had been wounded, she went over and grabbed the arrow sticking out of his arm moving it around. He howled in pain, begging her to stop. Satisfied, she broke off one end and quickly pulled the other through. Warren inhaled sharply, fighting through the pain. Grabbing some bandages, she wrapped the wound. Then Anyia hovered her hand over Warren's arm casting a spell.

"At least I didn't get shot," Anyia boasted.

"Well, if someone had been a little quicker at her job, I wouldn't have," Warren shot back.

Anyia rolled her eyes. "I'm going to go check and see if any more are coming."

Warren offered to go with her and the two disappeared into the night. Several nervous minutes passed before Luke and Albert heard back from them. They were surprised to find Warren and Anyia dripping wet, slightly shivering.

"We followed them across the river," stated Warren. "When they got back to camp, they moved into defensive positions, assuming we would retaliate. Our plan succeeded; they won't be bothering us any more tonight. You guys get some sleep. I'll stand watch the rest of the night." When first signs of light crept over the horizon, he began waking everyone. Luke and Albert complained, begging him to let them sleep.

"If you two want to go on any more adventures, you'd better get used to not getting much sleep. Now come on. The forest of Ethanan awaits," Warren announced, pointing to a forest that loomed in the distance. Anxiety mixed with excitement washed over Albert. Hopefully, he was one step closer to getting home.

Chapter 10: Ethanan Awaits!

By the time the sun had risen, they were on the road progressing at a much faster pace than yesterday. With the rest of the nomad tribes possibly close by, Warren thought it best to reach Sanoran by day's end. "So, if we only wanted to scare the nomads off? Why didn't we try and talk to them?" asked Albert, still confused about the attack last night.

"Nomads aren't the easiest people to communicate with, Albert," Warren informed him. "First, no one has ever been able to decipher or translate their language and second, they are more like animals than men. Their intellectual capacity is limited, and they lean towards brute force, like attacking to scare off people."

"But Dad, I thought nomads usually kept to themselves," Luke wondered.

"They do, unless they feel threatened, like we witnessed last night," Warren replied.

"So, we were threatening," Luke said, proudly.

"I doubt it," responded Warren deflating Luke's ego a little. "I think something else has riled up the nomads. They usually try spook tactics first, then move to attack if that doesn't work. I wonder if some of the bandit troops have been warring with them and they thought we might be a scout party. Either way, we will have to report it to Captain Reno on our way back."

"Well, at first I was scared when they attacked," said Albert, wanting to bring up the fact that he had fought off a nomad by himself. "But, when I was able to dodge and parry the nomads' attacks, it became a lot easier to fight back."

"That is what happens when you practice hard and have great teachers," Anyia told him.

"Thank you," said Luke proudly.

"It wasn't all us," Warren said, humbly. "Albert is a good student."

Albert blushed.

By midday, they had reached Sanoran and, from what Albert could see it looked in disrepair. The wall that surrounded the town was a mixture of polished stone patched with dilapidated wood panels. No gate guarded the entrance, just two disinterested guards. The main road through town was littered with garbage and riddled with deep, muddy potholes. The tiny wood homes and stone shops that lined the street were in disarray. Their thatched roofs had caved in, all the windows and shutters were broken, holes in walls were poorly patched with mud. Most of the homes looked as if they were barely holding up.

"This towns a pile," stated Luke.

"Shh," shushed Warren. "It is believed that this town is our only way into the forest, and if we want them to let us through, we can't afford to offend them. Let's head for the town hall up ahead."

As they continued, they noticed the townsfolk were skittish giving them a wide berth. The town hall seemed to be the only building in the town kept in good condition. It had polished stone steps with hand carved wood columns surrounding its porch and entry. Large wooden double doors were locked and the drapes in the windows had been drawn shut as well. *Is the place closed for some reason? Why keep it looking nice if it isn't used? Maybe they are just out for lunch,* thought Albert.

Warren asked a passerby why the townhall wasn't open. The man looked at Warren in fright and hurried back in the direction he had come.

"Maybe there is someplace we can get some information? A shop, maybe?" said Anyia. She asked a woman who was walking past. "Excuse me, miss, is there a place we can get some supplies?"

The woman raised a shaking hand to point to a street on their left then walked speedily away from them. Making their way down the road, they found a small cobblestone building, its sign above the heavy wooden door reading 'Leegahr's'. This must be the place. The building had loose stones bulging from its walls with mortar missing. They could see through cracks into the little, poorly lit shop.

A man with greasy black hair dressed in worn nobleman's clothes that looked two sizes too small sat on a wobbly chair inside waiting for customers. His round, chubby face looked as if it hadn't been washed in weeks and a pungent odor filled the air around him. He introduced himself as Leegahr and asked what they were looking for.

"Nothing in particular," said Warren. "We just had some questions and we're hoping you could help us out?"

Leegahr studied them cautiously as if worried they might be there to harm him. "About what?'

"You don't need to worry, my friend," replied Warren, trying to calm the man down. "We aren't going to harm you. We just needed to see this town's magistrate, but your town hall seems to be closed."

Leegahr wrung his hands together, looking back and forth among the well-armed group. "Well, there have been suspicious people about lately," he replied, timidly. "So, the-ugh-town hall has been closed for security reasons."

The man's eyes kept darting to the weapons at their sides. "Leegahr is it?" The man nodded his shaking head. "There is no need to be afraid. I am Warren, the guardian of Brookshire, east of here. I promise you we aren't here to harm you. And if bandits or thieves have been attacking your town, we can help. It's kind of my job."

Leegahr's fright seemed to disappear, "The town hall should be open tomorrow morning. You should be able to see the magistrate then." He held out his hand, evidently hoping for some reward for his information.

Warren gave a fake smile and handed him a few coins. They thanked Leegahr for the information and turned to leave.

"Oh, and if you are still in need of supplies? You could try the shop next to the town hall," informed Leegahr as they exited.

"You shouldn't have given him the money," said Anyia, once they were back on their horses.

"Yes, but these people are poor and if we want to get into the forest, we need to make friends," replied Warren.

"You mean you," Anyia corrected him. "I will not be going into the forest. I have my own quest, if you will remember, but I will stay with you until we can talk with the magistrate." Warren nodded in thanks while Albert and Luke looked disappointed. They enjoyed hearing the stories she told about the places she had traveled on her adventures.

"Well, there is still sunlight left. We should go check out that shop as Leegahr suggested," said Warren.

"Agreed," said Anyia.

The shop's sign was broken, hanging from one chain. It only had one legible word, 'The'. Inside, the shop was in even worse condition than the sign. One corner of the building had fallen away, the roof sagging. One of the windows was boarded up and the other was so dirty, if there was any light outside the building, you wouldn't be able to tell. Upon entering, they saw a boy about ten sitting on the counter swinging his legs back and forth. His clothes were covered in mud and his long blond hair was unkept. He greeted them in broken Thu'hilen and asked what they needed.

Again, they found nothing of interest in the store. All the supplies were either spoiled or about to be and the shop was a mess. Nothing was organized, vegetables, fruits, and cheeses in the same baskets, different sorts of meat hanging from wherever they could find a place. It all smelled slightly of mold and decay. Thanking the boy for letting them look around, Warren gave him six copper pieces and they left the store.

"So, that was a waste of our time," Warren said, quietly. "I wonder why Leegahr sent us there?"

Night was now making its appearance. Investigating multiple different side streets, they decided to get a room at the nicest looking inn they could find. It was called 'The Snoring Troll' and looked to have more than two rooms. When they took their horses around back, they found that the barn was big enough to fit both horses, but just barely. They tended and fed them before going back upfront. Inside the inn, an old woman with a crooked nose and several warts on her face sat knitting a sweater. Warren greeted her and asked if she had two rooms available.

"Thirty-five copper a night for each room," said the old woman without looking up.

Thirty-five? That seemed kind of pricey. Warren was about to haggle down the price, but thought of the reception they had received from the rest of the townspeople. Graciously, he pulled out the money and set it on the counter. The woman slid the money into a drawer, "Take any two keys from the board."

Four keys hung on the wall, none of them having numbers indicating which room they went to. Warren grabbed two keys that were next to each other, hoping that the rooms were adjacent. Trying the keys in all the doors, they found they opened rooms that were across the hall from one another. Each room barely fit two beds, a chair, and a wood stove in them with shuttered windows.

"Luke, Albert, and I will take one room and you can have the other Anyia. One of us will just have to sleep on the floor," said Warren.

"No need Warren. I am fine with either Albert or Luke sharing a room with me," she responded.

"Thanks, but we'll be fine. I've spent many nights sleeping on a hard, wooden floor."

Albert and Luke both reassured Warren they would be fine staying with Anyia. Warren rolled his eyes, shoving them into the room they would be staying in. Anyia giggled and wished them all goodnight, entering her room. Inside their room, Warren moved around fidgeting with objects around the room.

"Dad? What's going on?" Luke asked, bewildered.

"Just placing some alarms. In case someone tries to sneak in at night. I don't trust these people... yet," said Warren.

Albert didn't know whether to feel secure or worried. He decided to take his sword to bed with him, just to be on the safe side. After Warren was done, Albert and Luke got into the two beds while Warren grabbed a blanket from his pack and slouched down in the chair, axes at his side. Exhausted, they quickly ate whatever food rolled out of their packs. After the short night they had had before, it didn't take long for them to fall asleep.

Beams of light pierced through the cracks in the shutters waking the boys. *Guess this meant that no one tried breaking in during the night,* thought Albert. Several moments later, they heard a knock at their door, Anyia's pleasant voice announcing herself. Obviously, nothing had happened to her as well. Breakfast eaten and ready to leave, they headed for the main foyer. The old woman who tended the counter last night was nowhere to be seen. Assuming guests just left their keys when they were ready to leave, they put their keys back on their rings and exited 'The Snoring Troll'.

They were relieved to find that their horses were still in their stalls. Leaving them there watered and fed, they walked to the main street to find the town hall now open. The people on the streets greeted them more politely this time. Bakers seeing them pass their shops ran out with goods asking if they wanted anything.

Albert found it strange that yesterday no one would talk to them and now today they were acting as if they had always lived there.

Once at the stone steps of the town hall, Albert and his friends hoped it would be open. Slowly they took the steps one at a time. When they reached the top step, the large double doors swung open. Inside, two well-dressed men held the doors open for them. Fine carpets covered the floors, silk drapes adorned the windows, antique suits of armor decorated the walls and magnificent chandeliers hung from the ceiling. Albert saw a fat little man sitting at the far end of the hall on a large wooden chair. Town people swarmed him asking what his opinion was on anything and everything.

"That must be Sanoran's magistrate," guessed Warren.

When they got to the man in the chair, they noticed he looked a lot like Leegahr from the shop. This time, though, his clothes fit, and his hair was clean and tidy. They also noticed a boy standing next to him that looked like the one from the second shop they had visited. Only he was clean as well.

"Hello my friends," said Leegahr. "What can I do for you this fine morning?"

Warren was about to greet him, but Albert interrupted. "Aren't you two the shop keepers from yesterday?" Warren frowned at Albert.

Leegahr laughed. "Ahh, good eye, my boy, good eye. Why, yes, we are."

"So, are you Sanoran's magistrate as well?" he asked, confused.

"Hahaha," he laughed again. "My dear boy you are a clever one. I am sorry about yesterday's charade. We aren't very trusting of outsiders, so we wanted to see what kind of people you are."

"And?" Warren jumped in.

Leegahr looked up at him with a smile. "Pleasant people. Good folk who mean us no harm, unlike that bloke who showed up a few days ago."

His comment caught Anyia's attention. "Magistrate?" she asked.

"Yes, my dear?"

"This man that showed up the other day. Did he have a beard, a scar on his forehead and a wooden club for a left hand?"

"Why yes, and what an awful man he was. I had to hire those mercenaries you see out there to remove him from our town."

"When was this, and what direction did he head, may I ask?"

"It was yesterday, right before you arrived. He was headed north through the Great Plains. Why would a nice girl like yourself would be looking for a ruffian like that?"

Anyia smiled, fiercely. "That man stole something precious from my village and I've been trying to get it back. Thank you, Magistrate. Now, I will take my leave."

"You are very welcome, my dear," replied Leegahr.

Anyia bowed to Leegahr. She turned to Albert, Luke, and Warren, thanking them for their companionship while they travelled. Warren reciprocated while Albert and Luke were bummed to see her go.

"I told you, my friends, I had a quest of my own," she reminded them. "And, now, I must leave. When next we meet, I want to hear all about how your adventure ends, Albert and Luke."

"And you will tell us about yours?" asked Luke.

"Of course, I will," she smiled. "Now, I must go. Farewell." Anyia embraced each of the boys then hurried on her way.

"My dear, what a sweet girl and now that we have solved her dilemma," said Leegahr pleased. "What can I do for you three?"

Warren cleared his throat. "We request to enter the Ethanan Forest, Sir. We want to speak with the elves."

Leegahr scowled. "I'm afraid I can't do that. Only elves are allowed into the forest, except on permission of King Uthael's Emissary."

"Well, may we speak with him?"

"I'm sure Gorduin would love to speak with you, but it is not possible at the moment. For, you see, he will not be back for another two weeks."

Albert's heart sank. Would he really have to wait for two weeks before he would be allowed to continue?

He was already worried enough about this supposed darkness.

"Is there anything we can do to get into the forest any sooner?" Warren asked.

"I'm afraid not," Leegahr responded, sympathetically.

Warren bowed in submission. "Very well. We would be more than honored to enjoy your lovely hospitality for two weeks."

Leegahr bowed his head. Warren grabbed both Albert and Luke, turned and headed for the door. Albert wasn't ready to give up yet, though, and fought to break free of Warren's grasp. "Don't worry," Warren whispered. "We aren't waiting here two weeks. Just play along." Albert obeyed and followed Warren out the door.

When they were outside, Warren asked the nearest person the way to Ethanan Forest. The young blonde woman looked at him with a raised brow and pointed down the street. He thanked her and they hurried off in the direction she pointed. The road twisted back and forth and ended at a gate with a single guard. Warren pulled Albert and Luke into an alleyway a few buildings away before the guard could see them.

"Okay, you two, here's the plan," he said, pulling them in close. "You are going to head to the alley across the street and make your way to the wall from behind those homes. I'll distract the guard, while you two sneak into the forest."

"Dad, why don't we just exit Sanoran and enter the forest from outside?" Luke asked.

"Normally that would be my first choice, but rumors say that the elves put a spell on the forest, so you can only enter and exit at a certain point. Elvan magic can be powerful and I'm not ready to see if that rumor is true."

Albert and Luke nodded in understanding. "So, what do you think happens if you try and enter the forest anywhere else but here?" Luke asked.

"I don't know, and I don't want to find out. I'm leaving this up to you two now. This is your adventure. Now go."

Luke led Albert to the corner of the building. Peeking out, he waited for the guard to look the other way. When he did, the two ran across the street to the other alley. Quickly, they made their way to the backside of the house. Luckily, the way to the city wall was clear: with no fences in their way. Albert and Luke hurried to the building next to the wall of the town. Down the alleyway they saw a stack of crates close to the gate.

They made their way to the crates as quietly as possible. Luke peeked out to see Warren walking up to the guard to start a conversation. The guard had no interest in talking and asked him to move along. Warren just ignored the man and kept trying to converse with him. The guard began to get annoyed and told Warren if he didn't leave soon, he would have to force him to.

Warren merely changed the subject to the Battle Arena in Fort Valdrum and asked the guard if he had seen the mysterious fighter from the other day.

By now, the guard had had enough of Warren and grabbed him, trying to escort him away from the gate. Warren barely fought back, trying to make it look real, mouthing to Albert and Luke to 'go now'. Signal received, they quickly snuck out from behind the crates, through the gate and into the forest. Thankfully, there was a trail. The gate was soon well out of sight, and they slowed to a walk, assuming they were safe. Albert looked at the forest around him. It wasn't magical or whimsical like he imagined an elvan forest would be. The treetop canopy blocked out most of the sun and thick layers of greenish-grey moss seemed to be growing on every tree. The air was humid and heavy, making it hard to breathe. An eerie feeling surrounded them as if something or someone were watching them.

As they proceeded farther into the forest, the path dwindled and disappeared. Soon nothing could be seen of it, and they began to wonder if they were going in the right direction. Strange sounds echoed in their ears, sending shivers up their spines. Worse, the disturbing sounds seemed to be getting closer. One sound, louder than the rest, seemed almost right next to them. It was a deep wheezing noise that sounded like a broken bassoon.

Albert and Luke drew their weapons, searching the forest. Cautiously, they moved forward checking in every direction as the sound grew ever louder. A screeching noise pierced the air from above. Looking up, Albert and Luke saw a mushroomlike creature jump down from out of one of the trees. They dove out of its way, barely escaping being crushed against the forest floor. They sprang to their feet, preparing for the next attack.

"Albert, it's an Enoki," Luke shouted at him. "Watch out for the spores it sprays at you."

Albert was completely perplexed at the creature that stood between them. It was their height with a multicolored mushroom cap. The head and body were off-white color covered in boils. Four bulbous legs jutted out of its body. A mouth large enough to swallow a head opened wide. He didn't see any eyes, but the Enoki seemed to know exactly where they were.

As it turned to face Albert, Luke jumped behind it and stabbed it with his dagger. The Enoki screeched and turned around on him, using its bulbous head to smack him to the ground. Now that the creature was not facing him, Albert moved in slashing it with his sword. Spores came spraying out of the wound immediately, almost hitting him.

"Stab, don't slash," said Luke getting back to his feet.

"What?"

"If you slash, spores will spray from its wound."

Keeping it between them, they switched off attacking and defending making sure to only stab the

Enoki. Soon the creature started to stumble and miss its attacks. As it fell to the ground, it gave off a high-pitched squeal. Albert and Luke panted, sweating as they watched the creature take its final breath. They looked at each other and laughed, proud that they had taken down their first enemy together. Their celebration was cut short as screeches could be heard in the forest all around them.

Dozens of Enoki raced towards them. Albert and Luke turned and ran deeper into the forest. Albert grunted in disbelief at the speed of the creatures. For large, bulbous mushrooms they moved extremely fast. Deeper and deeper they continued to run into the woods, the creatures constantly gaining on them. The farther they ventured into the forest, the more light pierced through the treetops. Soon Albert noticed the Enokis falling behind. A few more yards and they were completely gone. Both boys fell to the forest floor, chests heaving, relieved that the danger was over.

"Oh, man, I thought we were dead for sure. Those things were fast!" Luke puffed.

"You're telling me! And running in these boots made it worse," gasped Albert.

"Well at least we're out of trouble," sighed Luke.

"For now," came a silky voice.

Chapter 11: Elves? I Expected More

Albert and Luke looked up to see several tall, muscular men with pointed ears in light armor. Their weapons pointed at the boys. A small lithe woman with long amber hair and an oblong, golden-eyed face stood behind the warriors, arms folded. She wore a fitted white dress embroidered with emerald and golden leaves. With a signal, two of the men picked the boys off the forest floor by the arms, taking their weapons. The elvan woman circled, investigating them. Her steps were so light, she seemed to hover off the ground.

"What are two humans doing in our forest?" she asked sharply, her voice piercing them to their core.

"We have come to see the elves," Albert answered, shakily.

"Well, then you have seen them," she said, with a hiss, glaring at them.

"Please ma'am," Albert pleaded. The elvan woman turned her gaze upon him. Albert swallowed hard. "Ma'am, I have come to see the elves because of a vision I keep having."

"Oh! Do tell us what this vision is about," she said, with a roll of her eyes.

"Well, it has to do with a wyvern, the forest, and a darkness engulfing it."

The woman raised her hand, cutting him off. She studied two of them carefully. "Leave us," she instructed the guards.

When they hesitated, she smiled, turning to an elf whose garb was more intricate than the rest, "Captain, I will take them from here. You can leave their weapons with me. They pose no threat."

The captain nodded. His men handed the woman Albert and Luke's things. When they were out of sight, she handed Albert and Luke back their weapons, "Follow me, quickly." They hurried along a hidden path through the forest that seemed only to be visible to the elvan woman. "You may not be able to see it, but the road we travel leads directly to Ethosis." As they grew closer, the forest continued to open, allowing golden sunlight to pierce the treetops and illuminating the ground below. Green-scaled deer pranced around playing in meadows. Puffy-tailed rabbits bounded across the grass. Everywhere he looked, Albert noticed forest animals converging on the elvan city seeking their protection.

Soon their path intersected a marble path leading the way to the center of the city. Albert was amazed at the construction of their homes. The trees seemed to have grown themselves into homes where elves could live. They were as wide around as a house with a door and windows made from the trunk. Lights of blue, green, and white shimmered on trees that had fashioned themselves in poles along cobblestone walkways. Magnificent columns and pillars of gold and silver decorated the homes and streets. At the center of the city stood a gigantic tree whose base looked like it had been shaped into a temple. Spire-like limbs stretched high into the sky breaking through the treetops.

"Is our city not beautiful?" asked the woman with a smile.

Enthralled, Albert and Luke could only nod in agreement. She took them to a tree with an elegantly hand carved door set in its base. Looking up, Albert saw circular bulges protruding from the trunk. He assumed that they must be rooms the tree had created for its inhabitants, by the windows peering out of them. The woman opened the door and ushered them in.

Inside the home, it was warm and comforting. Peace washed over them as they stood in the room taking in the beautiful, hand-crafted wooden chairs, sofas and couches. Silver sconces lined the inside of the trunk giving the room a soothing glow.

"Mother are you home?" came a voice, from within a doorway.

Down a set of stairs came a young elvan girl around Albert and Luke's age. She had wavy, golden blonde hair that sat loosely on her shoulders. Her bright-green eyes contrasted with a blue and tan dress flowing from her shoulders.

"Yes, Lily, I'm home."

When the girl entered the room, she stopped, looking nervously between her mother and the boys. "Mother? Who are they?"

The woman walked over to her daughter and put her arm around her. "I think some introductions are in order. I am Ashearah, high priestess to King Uthael, and this is my daughter, Lilious."

"I am Luke, son of Warren," said Luke, as he bowed.

Albert stood there, again forgetting to introduce himself. Luke rolled his eyes and cleared his throat.

"Oh, umm, I'm Albert Worthington," he stuttered, trying to regain his composure.

"Well, now that we know who each other are, let's hear about this vision," urged Ashearah, directing Luke and Albert to sit on the chairs. She and Lilious elegantly walked over to sit with perfect posture on the sofa. He decided to start by telling her he wasn't from Thu'hilen and on his second day here, a wyvern had marked him. He pulled up his sleeve to show her. Ashearah held up a hand to stop him. She contemplated what he had just told her, sitting for several minutes staring off into space.

"Did I do something wrong?" Albert whispered to Luke.

"How should I know? I've never met an elf like this before," he whispered back.

Lilious shushed them. "Please be quiet. My mother is trying to look through time and see these events."

Several more minutes of silence went by before Ashearah's face contorted into disappointment. "Interesting."

Albert and Luke looked at each other. "What is interesting?" Albert asked.

"I cannot see these events. It's as if something is clouding them from me," she said continuing to frown. "Will you continue, Albert?"

After telling Ashearah and Lilious about meeting Bernard, he began to recount his vision. Albert described flying in the air, the wyvern soaring past him, its attack and the mark it left on him. Then he told how the wyvern flew west across the Great Plains and into Ethanan. He hesitated before telling her about the end of his vision when the darkness takes over. Taking a deep breath, he continued to tell her how the vision ended.

"So, you say that this darkness comes from the forest and covers all that you can see?" she asked.

"Yes, Ma'am," he replied.

"You may call me, Ashearah, Albert," she said.

"Yes, Ashearah, but the last time I had the vision, it changed."

"How so?"

"Well, last time, I actually saw where the wyvern went. It flew to the Daratrine Mountains." He paused. "And the darkness, it was coming from somewhere in this forest, from a big tree, I think. Like the one at the center of town. Then like a mist it crept up into the mountains and, from there spread everywhere."

Ashearah elegantly stood and paced the room. From the look on her face, Albert could tell she was trying to decipher what the vision meant. Ashearah walked back and forth for several more minutes before she turned and faced Albert.

"Now, Albert, as you may or may not know, there used to be a colony of wyverns in the Daratrine Mountains. Every time I try to look at those mountains in my mind, a fog is covering them." She sighed. "You said you were marked? May I see it all, please?"

Albert turned around and pulled up his shirt to show Ashearah the mark on his back. As she looked at it, her expression turned into sheer joy. Ashearah's eyes lit up and a smile covered her face.

"Do you know what this means?" Ashearah chirped.

Albert, Luke, and Lilious looked at each other puzzled.

"It means that the wyverns are still alive," she said cheerfully. "And if they return, our once-beautiful forest might be itself again."

Albert pulled down his shirt. "You mean it wasn't always so creepy and filled with those mushroom creatures?"

"No, it used to be full of light and wonderful animals," Ashearah replied.

"How long ago was that?" asked Luke.

"Nearly one hundred and fifty years ago."

Albert's jaw dropped. Embarrassed, he tried to compose himself. "I uhh... can't believe you are one hundred and fifty years old."

Ashearah chuckled. "We elves live very long lives. Our king has seen more than seven hundred years in his lifetime, though the usual life span of an elf is four or maybe five hundred years."

"So, how has he lived so long?" Luke asked.

"No one knows," Ashearah sighed. "When I was a child, I remember him being a very old elf, but one morning he was young again and since then it seems he hasn't aged a day."

Albert and Luke looked at each other confused. How can someone never age?

"By the looks on your faces I can see you are wondering the same thing I am. King Uthael said he had discovered a new power that would protect our kingdom from a coming darkness. Many doubted that any sort of evil could touch these lands so our trust in our king began to waver. One of those who doubted was my father. Soon, we no longer saw the wyverns of Daratrine in the forest, the trees started to become dark and overgrown. Dangerous creatures began to appear. Everyone that had doubted the king started to believe what he had been saying."

"Is that why the Elves of Ethanan retreated into their city and sealed off the forest?" asked Luke.

"Yes, our king feared that the outside world had been overrun and to save our people, we had to use magic and create a barrier around the forest. We left the town of Sanoran as the only entrance into our woods and a legion of men there to secure it."

Luke laughed. "*The Outside World*, as you call it, hasn't been overrun. It's the same as it always has been since you disappeared. And Sanoran? The only people who live there are a bunch of wimps who had to hire mercenaries to protect their city."

Shock overcame Ashearah, forcing her to brace herself against the sofa. "Hearing this has made my fears come true. I have come to believe that our king has been lying to us and has something to do with the shadow covering the forest."

"Are you all right Mother?" Lilious cried, rushing to her mother's side.

"I am all right, my dear," Ashearah reassured her. "My father was right all along."

"About what?" asked Luke.

"About the king," she replied. "My father was a powerful sorcerer and it always bothered him that the king was able to regain his youth overnight. He studied and researched every spell and power he could for the rest of his life to try and find how the king had done it. You see, elves value and treasure life, and though our lives are long, some feel we don't get enough of it. All elves believe they have a set mission in life and if accomplished will travel to Vaerdunia when this life is over."

"Vaerdunia?" Albert wondered.

"Yes, it is said to be a place of peace and serenity where one can find eternal rest and live a life of joy."

"Oh, like heaven," said Albert.

"If that is what you wish to call it," Ashearah responded. "Now, some elves feel at the end of their life they have not yet completed their mission. Hence their want and need for a longer life."

Albert and Luke nodded in comprehension.

"In the end, my father was never able to find out how the king regained his youth. Before he died, he made me promise him that I would find the truth and dispel the shadow that hung over our kingdom. Shortly after, he passed on into the afterlife. Ever since, I've dedicated my life to becoming Uthael's high priestess so, I could get close to him and discover the truth behind his returned youth. Now, I must get you to the king. The news of your arrival will have reached his ears and he will want to question you."

"Hold on second," said Luke. "Why are you telling us all of this? And if this king of yours is such a bad guy, why are you taking us to him? I mean, from what you told us, it doesn't sound like you are on his side, so why would you aid him? And another thing, how do you know we aren't spies for your king, hmm? Sent to discover people who might be plotting against him."

"Yeah," interjected Albert. "How do we know we can trust you? The king's story could be true, and you could be the person that brought this evil upon your people."

Ashearah sat back on the couch. "You two are right. You have no reason to believe me. And I know of no way of proving my tale to you. I do know one thing, though. You two are not the king's spies. That mark on your back proves it. No magic or fabrication could replicate the mark of the Dragoon."

Albert sat stunned. So, Nicolet was right. It is the mark of the Dragoon.

"As for what side I am on or whether or not my king is a *bad guy*," continued Ashearah. "There are no sides, and King Uthael is a good man who has done great things for his people. Sometimes, though, good people can make bad choices. It doesn't mean they are a bad guy. It just means they followed the wrong path. What I'm trying to discover is how the king got his youth back and why this darkness is attacking our forest."

"We're sorry for accusing you," said Luke lowering his head.

"It is all right, boys," she assured them. "I would have been more worried if you hadn't questioned me. Now let's go. His Highness is probably waiting."

Chapter 12: Prisoners

Ashearah spent a few minutes instructing how they should act before the king, making mention not to say anything of how Albert got here or the wyvern. Albert and Luke followed Ashearah out of the house heading for the great tree at the center of the city. As they walked along the streets, Albert noticed the elvan men were tall, muscular, and dressed regally, while the women were short, delicate, and lithe wearing elegant dresses. Their hair was amber, golden-blonde, platinum or straight black.

As they neared their destination, Ashearah informed them the tree was called the Tree of Anora and stood as their palace for thousands of years. Its craftsmanship was beautiful with soft gold, silver, and brass inlays. The enormous double doors made from a bright oak. On them was an engraving of the tree itself with a kingly figure, arms stretched wide, welcoming his guests at the base. Inside, a dark-green rug ran along a polished wooden floor up to a throne made of oak. Pillars formed by the tree twisted around themselves and stretched to the vaulted ceilings. The same mysterious blue, green, and white lights lit the room. Guards stood at the door and lined the hall as a young elvan man sat on the throne, a smile on his face, delighted to greet his visitors. The man looked far too young to be in his later years with long golden-blond hair, bright-blue eyes, and smooth skin adorning his regal face.

"My king, these are the two humans that were found in our forest. I have interrogated them and found them harmless," bowed Ashearah.

Both Albert and Luke felt a little offended to be referred to as harmless.

"Humans? In our woods?" King Uthael asked, intrigued. "Tell me, how is it outside of our forest? Has the darkness destroyed everything?"

"Everything's fine," said Luke. "No darkness to be seen."

"Really?" he said, eyes wide open. King Uthael looked at them suspiciously.

Albert and Luke stood before him awkwardly smiling up at him.

The king returned the smile and stood throwing his arms into the air. "This is wonderful news. In honor of these two young gentlemen bringing us such great tidings, we shall have a feast. Two days from now, we shall have a celebration unlike one our city has seen in many years."

"Your Highness," Ashearah exclaimed. "I don't think this is the time for a feast. These boys have wandered into our forest."

"Come, come, High Priestess, this is good news," King Uthael consoled her. "Our allies outside of our forest are alive, which means that soon we can conquer this darkness once and for all."

Ashearah snuck Albert and Luke an unsure look. She hadn't anticipated this kind of reception.

"Now, Ashearah if you would escort our guests to their chambers. I am sure they are exhausted from their long journey. Get them a bath and more appropriate attire," King Uthael ordered.

Obeying her king, Ashearah bowed and escorted them to a door off from the throne. As they left the room, Albert turned to see King Uthael walk to his valet stating how wonderful it was to see humans again. Ashearah ushered them down a hall to a set of doors with two guards at the back of the tree. Through the door was a staircase that wrapped around the trunk. She led them up the stairs several floors high above the ground. Albert glanced out one of the windows to see Ethosis in its entirety. From here it looked even more mystical and serene than on the ground. The way the elves work with nature made it seem like they were one and the same. They soon came to a door that entered one of the spires, inside was a round common room with sofas, embroidered rugs, and a fireplace.

"That was not how I expected this to go," she said, spinning around to look at Albert and Luke catching them off guard. "But as I told you, Uthael is a good man."

"If you say so," Luke said unsure.

"What do you mean?" she asked.

"I don't know, something seems... off," replied Luke.

"I agree," said Albert. "Something just didn't seem right with him."

"So, you can sense it too. Strange how after only meeting him for a few seconds, you can tell there is something different about the king, yet my own people can't see it." Ashearah sighed, pointing to the door closest to the one they entered. "Albert that will be your room," she instructed. Pointing to the one next to the fireplace, "And Luke this room will be yours."

"What's the room in the middle for?" asked Albert.

"Royalty," she responded. "And the other door leads back into the palace. I have duties to attend to, but I will return shortly. They will expect you two to bathe and then food will be brought to you. Wait here till I return." Before she left, Ashearah turned to Albert. "Don't let anyone see the mark. I fear others might think it means you are here to harm us."

Albert and Luke went to explore their rooms, interested to see what they looked like. Both were identical with cream-colored walls, the outside wall curved with the shape of the spire. A large four-poster bed with dark red drapes sat against the curved wall and a large dresser with a mirror sat opposite. Lounge chairs dotted the room while a silver bathtub sat in front of draped archway portal that led out onto a balcony. All was positioned perfectly on a polished golden floor with a bright yellow rug with a silver border.

Shortly after they were done exploring their rooms, two elvan maids dressed in plain white servant uniforms entered the room from the door leading to the palace carrying steaming jugs of water. Both had hair intricately woven with silver lace down their backs, one's color was platinum with a slender face and the other golden with a more rounded face.

They sat in the common room around the fire pretending to talk, all the while betting on how many trips it would take the girls to fill the enormous tubs. Luke ended up winning in the end with a bet of nine times to Albert's twelve. When the tubs were filled, the maids bowed and left the room.

Excited to finally get clean, Albert leaped out of his seat as soon as the door was shut.

"What's your hurry?" Luke asked.

"Where I come from, we bathe daily," Albert told him. "I haven't felt comfortable since being here."

Luke snorted, "Al, it seems like a waste to bathe every day to me. I mean you're just going to get dirty the next day."

Albert rolled his eyes and entered his room excited about his bath.

Alone in his room, Albert started to undress when Ashearah's voice popped into his head reminding him to not let anyone see his mark. Quickly, he searched the room for anything he thought might be some type of camera. He didn't know what he was looking for but felt comfortable that no one was watching him. Closing the drapes on the archway, he once again started undressing. He was about to take off his underwear when he remembered that they were going to bring him a change of clothes. Not knowing if they were going to come barging in while he was bathing, he decided to leave his underwear on and hopped into the tub.

The water was the perfect temperature, hot but not too hot. It seemed to immediately soothe his aching muscles, cuts, scrapes, and bones. He slid down into the tub with just his nose out so he could breathe. Closing his eyes and, relaxing, he began to think about what had happened to him since he arrived in this world. He pictured in his mind all the animals and weird trees he had seen on his first day. He couldn't forget the bubble crab spraying mucus in his face. His thoughts then turned to Bernard, the nice but standoffish healer, and Nicolet, the caring, easily excitable woman who reminded him of his mother.

Albert reviewed their journey over the past week and a half and all the fun he and Luke had had. Albert thought of everything everyone had done for him since he was brought to Thu'hilen. If it wasn't for his friends, he wouldn't be here now. His thoughts then turned to his family back home. Tears filled his eyes as homesickness set in again. He began to think of all the things his parents had done for him throughout his life and how, since they had moved, he had treated them with resentment. Sniffing hard, he wiped away his tears. He vowed that when he got back, he was going to apologize.

Looking around the room, he still couldn't believe where he was. Ethosis was by far the best place he had been to yet. Everything seemed to have an essence of magic about it and all the buildings and structures' natural shapes made him feel at ease. Albert's previous concept of elves was nowhere near the mark. He had thought they would be tiny people like in the stories his mother read to him as a child. It was a surprise to him to find how much the men and women contrasted with each other.

His thoughts were interrupted when the maid came back into the room with clothes. Startled, he jumped, then quickly slid back down trying to cover the mark. The elvan maid set the change of clothes on the bed then came over and dipped her finger into the foot of the tub.

"I'll be back with some fresh water, my Lord." She bowed.

He was now glad he had the foresight to keep his underwear on.

She came back a moment later with another steaming jug of water bringing the tub back to the perfect temperature. Behind her came two male elvan servants carrying a full-length mirror. The servants placed the mirror next to the tub and dresser then left. The maid turned before exiting the room, asking if anything else was needed. "No," Albert squeaked, and the maid bowed, leaving the room and closing the door behind her.

Albert felt very intruded upon and hurried with his bath. The clothes they gave him to wear were made from fine linens and silks. The shirt was made from green silk and the pants were a nice, dark-brown cotton. The shoes they had provided, were of a smooth tan cloth that cradled his feet. He looked at himself in the mirror to see what he looked like. After deeming himself a wannabe elf, he entered the common room to find Luke sitting in front of the fire with a similar outfit except his shirt was red.

"How was *your* bath?" he asked, sitting down across from Luke.

"You mean besides the maid coming in to *refresh* my water, forcing me to grab the towel to cover myself," Luke said angrily. "It was pleasant though. I could get used to baths like that."

Albert laughed. "Yeah, that happened to me too, but I kept my underwear on just in case."

Luke looked at Albert feeling stupid. "Why didn't I think of that?"

Albert smirked at his misfortune. "So, you want to go on one of the balconies and look at the city?"

Luke shot out of his chair. "Sure."

They entered the closest, Luke's. From the balcony, they watched elves converse while sitting on wooden benches, or walking the streets through the city. A few large trees along the sidewalk hung signs above the doors, let them know which ones the shops were. "Elvan life seems kind of boring," said Albert.

Luke nodded in agreement. "Should we see what we can see from your balcony?"

There they saw below a blacksmith at his craft. They watched as he pounded on an elegant longsword, shaping it into the perfect, curved blade. Albert had soon noticed that all the elvan armor and weapons were very light and delicate, unlike Brom and Bowen's work. Though their work was elegant, it seemed bulky and solid, as if the wearer were meant to take the brunt of the damage. The elvan armor seemed more suitable for movement and agility.

The sounds of laughing kids turned their attention to a small group of children playing in the dimming light. They were chasing a fuzzy, blue, glowing ball that zoomed in and out of the trees. Albert and Luke watched as one kid leaped into the air, the ball flying just beyond his grasp. Another tripped, rolling to the ground as he chased it around a tree. Albert asked Luke what the little fuzzy ball was. Luke shrugged, "It must be a firebug or something."

"It is called a *wisp*," Ashearah said from behind them. "A legend states that if you catch one, you will be granted a wish."

Albert and Luke had not heard Ashearah enter and jumped.

"Don't do that!" Luke said, sharply.

Ashearah chuckled and smiled. "I'm sorry. I forget humans aren't used to the stillness of the elves."

"You can say that again." Luke retorted.

"Boys, tomorrow you will be encouraged to tour our city," informed Ashearah. "Please, enjoy all that it has to offer and make sure to take advantage of our hospitality. Humans haven't been in our city for many years. My people will be excited to show off their wares and trades."

"But we don't have any money," stated Albert.

"That will not matter. My people will be overjoyed to show off their expert works of art once again. Now, your supper is here. Have a good night's rest and tomorrow morning there will be someone here to guide you."

The next morning, Albert and Luke woke up to a new set of clothes much like yesterday's waiting for them. They exited to find Lilious sitting in the common room waiting for them. She sat at the table, a bowl of food in front of her. Seeing them enter, she put down her spoon, standing to greet them.

"I hope you don't mind," she said, gesturing to her plate. "You two took so long to wake, so I helped myself to some food."

"Eh, we'll let it slide, this time," said Luke sarcastically, as he sat down and dished some up.

Albert rolled his eyes and sat down, his stomach rumbling. "Luke's just kidding. We don't mind." He looked over the food on the table. Two covered wooden bowls and a pitcher of milk sat before him. Uncovering the bowls, he found a hot grain cereal and an assortment of fruits in the other. He scooped out two spoonsful of cereal into his bowl and got another bowl for his fruit. Then he grabbed the pitcher of milk, looking for a cup.

Lilious giggled, "Albert, you are supposed to mix them together." She tilted her bowl with the cereal and fruit toward him.

Albert, embarrassed, dumped everything into one bowl, stirring it together. "So, after breakfast, are we to just wait here till someone comes to show us around?" he said changing the subject.

"That is what I am here for," said Lilious, having finished a bite.

Albert's heart leapt at the news. Why was that? Sure, Lilious was pretty, but most girls were boring, and some were just outright annoying. He looked to Luke to see his reaction. He was busy dishing up seconds. *I guess he doesn't care. He'll probably have us just sneak away to explore the city ourselves.*

Without the rush of meeting the king, Ethosis could be taken in with all its glory. Though elves were about their daily lives, it seemed as if everything was done in serenity. No hurrying, rushing or loud noises. Everything was peacefully calm. This felt off to Albert and Luke, as if something was forcing it upon the city, instead of peace naturally occurring. Still, the harmony between the elves and nature seemed musical. Throughout the air, above the quiet conversations of the elves, an angelic singing could be sensed coming from the trees. Albert could feel that the very forest itself was caring for its inhabitants.

They visited master crafters to view their works and admire them. True to Ashearah's word, each artist proudly presented their finest accomplishments. A potter mesmerized them with a vase that, when spun in his hand, portrayed on its side a scene of two lovers dancing in the moonlight. A weaver demonstrated silken clothes that mirrored the wearers' surroundings, making them seem almost invisible. A blacksmith showed them a suit of armor that, when worn, made the person float above the ground. Each craftsman had a gift for Albert and Luke, a cup with the power to turn any liquid into pure water, cloaks to protect them from the coldest weather and boots that allowed the wearer to move as quietly as an elf.

Next, they visited an elderly man whose home was not what Albert and Luke were expecting. The tree itself was as if it had gone wild. The interior walls were rough, bulbous with tree limbs growing out of them. The man's furniture was old and worn. Some of it was carelessly strewn about. The main room was dimly lit by candles in nooks around the room. An elderly elvan man sat on a hand carved chair. He was hunched over to one side, absently staring at the floor. His head bald and his ears folded over where the cartilage had broken. The clothes he wore, once of the finest quality, were now riddled with holes.

"Why are we here?" asked Luke, kicking at a mouse that ran past his foot. "Other than to get rabies."

Albert looked around to find all sorts of rodents and small animals scurrying around the old elvan man's house.

"Not all the places we're going to today are for your enjoyment, Luke," replied Lilious. "One of my daily errands is to make sure Mr Edenthalas is doing well and getting taken care of."

"Well, it doesn't look like you are doing that great of a job," stated Luke. "This place is a mess, no offense," He corrected.

Lilious breathed in deeply, looked around, a smile on her face. Taking no heed to Luke's comment. "This tree is old, much like Mr Edenthalas. It and the animals that live here share a bond and take better care of him than I ever could."

Albert saw that what Lilious had said was true. The animals weren't just scurrying around for no reason. They brought him food, groomed him and did what they could to keep their home clean. Feeling sorry for Mr Edenthalas, Albert straightened some of the chairs and brushed some dirt and grime from off the end tables.

"Uh, Al, what are you doing?" asked Luke.

"Well," said Albert, situating an end table as best he could next to Mr Edenthalas. "Since we are here, might as well help out." Luke's shoulders dropped guiltily. He then hurried to help Albert move some of the furniture around. Soon the place began to look like an actual home. "There, Mr Edenthalas. Your home is good as new," comforted Albert, putting his hand on the old elf's shoulder.

Mr Edenthalas brought his head up and looked around the room. A smile crossed his face as he looked at the three kids standing before him. He gave a simple nod, then his head drooped, and the elf went back to staring blankly at the floor.

"Thank you, Albert," said Lilious, putting her arms around him. "We have not seen a smile cross his face in many years. I don't know how you did it, but somehow you reached him."

As Albert removed his hand from Mr Edenthalas' shoulder he discovered a small lizard had climbed onto his sleeve.

"Hey look, Al, another lizard admirer," commented Luke, amazed.

"What do you mean?" asked Lilious, puzzled.

"It seems the lizards of your world like me or something," responded Albert.

"Yeah, they even listen to what he says," added Luke.

Hmm, thought Lilious. "Take it as a sign of good luck and a gift from Mr Edenthalas."

"Cool," responded Albert, opening the flap to his knapsack. The small lizard, without any prompting, climbed from Albert's arm and into the sack.

They exited the house to stand under the glowing sun, basking in its warmth.

"I can't wait till my people are free from the evil that grips our forest," said Lilious, her face pointed toward the sun. "Then maybe more of my kind will venture to our forest, just as you two have."

With the mention of other elves, Albert and Luke suddenly remembered the group that came through Brookshire a few days ago.

"Lilious, have no other elves come to visit you?" asked Luke.

"No, why?" she asked as if confused.

"Because a group of elves came through Luke's town the other day on a mission to convince you and your people to come out of your forest," replied Albert.

"You two are the only ones that have passed our borders in many years," said Lilious. "Could they have gotten lost?"

"Nope," replied Luke. "It's a pretty easy journey from Brookshire to here. I mean, even Al and I were able to do it."

"I wonder if those Enokis got them?" wondered Albert.

"Enoki," spat Lilious. "Those foul creatures attack anything that enters our woods. I wish we could be rid of them."

"No, those elves had well-trained guards with them," informed Luke. "If we got past those Enokis, so did they. Lilious, do you have a prison or dungeon?"

"Yes, in the palace basement," she responded. "No one has been there for many years though. Why do you ask?"

"No reason, but I have a hunch," replied Luke.

Lilious, at the request of Luke, led the boys to the palace dungeon. A guard at the entrance stopped them, asking why they were there.

"My friends here would like to see our dungeon," said Lilious.

"Why would two human boys want to see our dungeons?" asked the guard, puzzled.

"Haven't you ever been a kid and wondered what a dungeon looks like?" said Luke.

The guard stood, a blank expression on his face. "Good point," he said, pulling the doors open. "Well, enjoy yourselves. There isn't much to see. These cells haven't been used in years."

The palace dungeon was one long tunnel made from packed dirt, stone, and giant tree roots. Four jail cells lined both walls, eight in total. No walls separated the cells, only iron bars. Diffused light filtered in from the roof from above. The three of them walked to the end finding each cell empty.

"What was the purpose of coming here?" asked Lilious.

"Huh," sighed Luke. "I could have sworn we would have found those elves imprisoned here. I mean, if Uthael is evil, which he seems, I thought he would have put them here."

"Maybe those Enokis really did get them," stated Albert.

They turned for the exit disappointed when Albert's bag began moving. As he opened the flap, the small lizard he had placed there scurried out and down his leg. The creature ran toward the back wall, licking the air with his tongue following a scent. There he began digging at the crack where the wall met the floor.

"Did I do something?" asked Albert. "Why is he trying to escape?"

Luke watched the lizard dig in a straight line across the floor. "I don't think he is trying to escape, Al," he said, running to the wall. Pulling out a dagger, with the back of the blade he began digging with the lizard. "I knew it."

"Knew what?" asked Albert, confused.

"There is a door here," stated Luke excitedly, continuing to dig out the hidden door.

"Stand back," Lilious commanded, raising a hand to the wall.

Luke quickly moved to stand beside Albert. He knew when a magic user was about to cast a spell. The lizard must have as well because it scurried back into Albert's pack.

"*Edro*," said Lilious, her eyes concentrating on the bit of wall concealing the door. At her command, cracks in the wall formed in the shape of a doorway as the stone wall silently slide backwards then moved to the side out of the way. Albert and Luke looked behind them to make sure the guard was not coming. Phew! All was clear.

Inside the newly discovered room, there was barely enough light to see. The small room had one cell in it. Stone walls formed the cell. An iron door with a small, barred window was its only means of entering or exiting. Albert, Luke, and Lilious peered through the window seeing ten sets of elvish eyes looking up at them.

"Please, help us!" cried one of the prisoners in a low shaky voice.

Chapter 13: Escape into the Night

"This is horrible," whispered Lilious. "Why did King Uthael have you thrown in here?"

"We did not get a chance to talk with your king, child," said an elvan man coming to the door. All they were able to make out of him in the dim light was his platinum hair and the purple of his clothes. "When we entered the forest, we were attacked by those mushroom creatures. When we awoke, we found ourselves here. Please let us out."

"How?" asked Albert. "There is no lock on this door."

"Are you kids all right in there?" called the guard from outside the dungeon.

Shoot! They were out of time.

"Guys, should we tell the guard?" asked Albert.

"No!" burst Luke. "If this is Uthael's doing, and I'm not saying it is, we could be thrown in there with them."

"Don't worry, we'll be back," Lilious informed the man in the cell. "My mother is the high priestess. She will get you out." She tried to leave, but Luke grabbed her by the arm.

"How do we know that it wasn't your mom who was controlling the Enoki and had them thrown in there?" accused Luke.

"Because my mother would never do such a horrible thing as this," flared Lilious, jerking her arm free. "Now come, before that guard catches us."

Sac, Lilious commanded as they exited the small prison chamber. The door slid closed behind them just before the guard came into the room to check on them.

"Have you three just been standing there the entire time?" he asked bewildered.

"Mmhmm," said Lilious, arms behind her back not making eye contact.

"Yep, we just wanted to see what it might be like to be an actual prisoner here," said Luke.

"Yep," said Albert trying not to look guilty as well.

"Okay, well if you are done pretending to be prisoners, I'll have to ask you to leave," informed the guard. "Unless you want to see what being a prisoner is really like?"

"Nope, I think we are good," Luke replied quickly, grabbing Albert and Lilious by the arm and hurrying them from the dungeon. When they were out of earshot from the guard and on the stairs, Luke brought them to a halt. "Okay, so who are we going to tell about this?"

"My mother, of course," responded Lilious, in an offended voice.

"I don't know," replied Luke. "Maybe we tell King Uthael about it. See what his reaction is?"

"Oh yes, Luke, tell the king," said Lilious. "And if it was him who had them thrown in there, he might have us killed to silence us."

"Whatever," replied Luke. "I'm not scared of him."

Luke, always trying to be like his father, thought Albert. Like he could take on an army.

"What do you think, Al? Who would you talk to?" asked Luke, leaving it up to him.

Oh, great! Now the pressure was on. He never did like being the deciding factor when two people argued. He didn't know if he could choose Ashearah, she had seemed nice, but he didn't know if she could be trusted. Albert also had no reason not to trust King Uthael, other than the pit in his stomach he got whenever his name was mentioned.

"Well, Albert," pestered Lilious. "Which is it going to be?"

Anxiety was setting in. Whom should he choose? Did he go with his friend or the girl who made his heart mysteriously jump every time her name was mentioned? Feeling the pressure, he blurted out the first name that came to mind, "Ashearah."

"I knew you would make the right choice, Albert," Lilious said, triumphantly. "You two head to your rooms and get cleaned up. Food should arrive shortly. I'll go tell my mother and we will visit you shortly." She turned, proud she had won, continuing up the stairs, head held high.

"You had to go with her, didn't you," said Luke, disappointed.

"I'm sorry, Luke, I panicked. I honestly didn't know who to choose, so I just blurted out the first name I thought of," replied Albert.

"Ahh, it's okay. At least we will find out whom we can trust," said Luke, pleased with the outcome. "Come on. I'm starving."

Back in the guest chambers, food was ready and waiting for them. Albert pulled the lizard out of his bag, placing it in a nearby ornamental tree before they rushed to the table to fill their plates full of fruits, vegetables, bread, and berries. They had just finished their first serving when the door opened. Ashearah and Lilious glided into the room coming to stand by the table.

"May we join you?" asked Ashearah, with a slight bow.

"Sure," responded Albert.

Luke put up his hand apologetically for Albert. "Yes, you may."

"Why thank you. Both of you," replied Ashearah.

"So, he does have manners after all," said Lilious, talking as if Luke wasn't in the room.

"Daughter, please behave," Ashearah said calmly as she dished up a small plate of food. "Lilious has told me of the grievous event that has befallen our elvan brethren. And I know what you are going to ask. The answer is, no. I cannot set them free, not yet that is. To do so would show our hand too early. I'm sure Uthael is the one holding them captive. A time will come when they shall be set free but now is not that time. I fear our king's choices are leading him down a dark path, one he might not be able to return from."

They ate in silence, contemplating the day's events. Albert, Luke and Lilious couldn't think of anything to talk about. Albert's head spun. What had started out as a journey to see the elves, was now turning into a rescue mission. Why was Uthael turning on his own kind? Was the constant threat of the darkness driving him mad? Would they have to challenge the king? Albert wished Warren were with them. He would know what to do.

"Albert, Luke." Ashearah broke the silence. "Tomorrow you will be fitted for clothes and instructed how to attend an elvan banquet. I feel during the festivities we might receive more answers. Now, let us bid you goodnight. We shall see you tomorrow for the feast."

Albert and Luke, left to themselves, moved to the chairs in front of the fire. They sat in silence, neither knowing what to say. Who would have thought their journey would turn out this way? Both didn't know if their lives would soon be in danger, but something inside told them they were heading in that direction.

"I wish your dad were here," said Albert, solemnly.

"Me too," replied Luke. "All my life I wanted to go on adventures like him, but I never really knew what that actually meant. I never thought my life would ever be in mortal peril."

Albert shook his head, trying to dismiss the mood. "Mortal peril? What are you talking about? We don't even know if we are in danger. This could all be a misunderstanding."

"You know what, Al, you're right. We are probably getting carried away," replied Luke. "Well, it's been a long day. I'm headed for bed."

"Me too," said Albert, standing from his chair with Luke. As they reached their rooms, the two looked at each other one more time before entering. Albert could see the worry on Luke's face matched his own. "Night, Luke," he said trying to dismiss the feeling.

"Good night, Al."

With the finality setting in, they got in their beds and stared at the ceiling. Both wanting to just go home. Tomorrow their lives would never be the same. Tomorrow the real adventure begins. No easy walk to Fort Valdrum. No escorted ride to Sanoran. The task of solving a hundred and fifty-year-old mystery lay before them.

The next morning, they awoke to a knock on their doors. The boys had found it hard to sleep. Wearily, they got out of bed answering the knock. Upon opening their doors, they were assaulted by elves with measuring devices. Forced to stand on pedestals, every inch of them was measured and then measured again. When they were done, the tailors left as quickly as they came.

At breakfast, three elvan gentlemen stood in the room awaiting. They began instructing them on everything they needed to know how to enter the room. How to walk appropriately toward the table. How to appropriately start a conversation. What type of conversations were permissible, and which were not.

They were taught how to properly sit at the table. How to dish their food onto their plate. Which utensil to use when and where. What foods to eat in what order. When it was appropriate to talk with food in your mouth and when it wasn't. If you had food in your mouth, you were supposed to cover your mouth so your conversation partner could not see what food you were chewing.

The only good thing about all this grooming was it didn't provide time to think about the events of last night. By feast time, Albert and Luke were exhausted. Their minds were numb from the constant barrage of instructions on how or how not to act at a royal dinner. Their clothes that had been made for them were of the highest quality, light-blue silk. The two just wanted this night over with. Finally, Ashearah entered the room dismissing their tutors.

"Now boys, before we go down, I must speak with you," said Ashearah, motioning for them to come closer. She lowered her voice to a whisper, "The king will want you to stay in these rooms tonight, but you mustn't. Who knows what he has planned? I would prefer you two left the city tonight."

"Tonight? Why?" asked Albert.

"Albert, the guard saw you, Luke and Lilious go into the secret prison chamber."

"Well that's not good," interrupted Luke.

"No, it is not," replied Ashearah. "I do not know if he knows what is in there, but King Uthael could not hide the fury on his face when he found out. Which is why, I want you two and Lilious to leave the city tonight. You will head to the mountains. They are sacred and off-limits. You will be safe there. Tonight, after the feast, wait for me on Albert's balcony. I will show you a secret passage out of the city which will put you at the mountain's base."

Albert and Luke nodded in agreement.

"Good. Now let us go."

Ashearah lead them out the door, descending the stairs that wrapped around the tree. At a set of double doors, a couple floors below their chambers, they could hear the clamor of voices and the playing of soft music. Inside was a rectangular foyer with green couches facing each other and another set double doors with servants waiting. As they drew near, the doors were opened for them, revealing a rectangular table large enough to seat a small village. The room had a comforting orange glow from the torches on the walls and smelled of all sorts of spices.

All the chairs had occupants except the three in the middle. As they entered, King Uthael stood and cheerfully introduced them to the rest of his guests gesturing to the open seats for them to sit. Ashearah bowed and moved to sit with Albert and Luke following. As they reached their seats, servants pulled their chairs out for them. It was nice having someone hold their chairs. Albert and Luke gladly sat down.

King Uthael thanked everyone for coming. "My friends, tonight I give this feast in honor of our new friends and allies, Albert and Luke."

Everyone at the table began looking around and clapping uncertainly.

"They have come here seeking us out, wondering if we were still alive when really we have been the ones hoping and seeking for an answer to see if the world outside our borders is still safe," announced King Uthael looking at the boys.

"These two boys have assured me that the world outside of our lands is free of this evil that plagues us. We have done it my friends; we have kept the evil from progressing past our forest. We have saved our fellow men."

Cheers and clapping rang throughout the hall.

Albert leaned over to Ashearah, whispering, "I thought you said King Uthael sealed the forest because he told everyone the danger was coming from the outside."

"He did, but it seems he is changing the story," she whispered back. "This doesn't make sense."

King Uthael raised his hand to calm the celebration. "With this new knowledge, we shall send an envoy out to our allies to request aid in defeating this evil. Therefore, I have chosen Malathis to be that envoy."

The guests clapped as a tall elvan with short, spikey platinum hair stood and bowed. The dark rings circling his cold eyes gave Albert the creeps. "I don't trust that guy," he said to Ashearah.

"And you shouldn't. He is King Uthael's personal attendant."

Malathis sat back down, and the clapping ceased.

"So, in honor of our two guests, let us raise our glasses and toast their arrival," finished King Uthael.

Everyone in the room raised a glass and with a signal, two doors at the back of the room opened. Servants with trays came hurrying out. Platters full of exotic fruits and vegetables were placed on the table for the diners. Albert looked around disappointed. He had had so many fruits and vegetables since being in Ethosis it was making him sick. If this was the only food they had at the feast, he had no choice but to go hungry.

As the last of the plates were brought out and set on the table, King Uthael stood: "To honor this night, an elder stag has given his life to celebrate this occasion." Servants then brought out large plates of cooked venison. Albert had never had venison before, and his eyes lit up. Maybe he wasn't going to go hungry tonight after all.

When everything was on the table, King Uthael gave the signal for everyone to eat. The venison was the first thing Albert went for. Not wanting to look odd in front of the elves, he scooped some weird looking potatoes, a sweet-smelling salad and some berries onto his plate as well. He looked over to find Luke's plate overflowing with food and gave him a questioning look.

"What?" Luke said. "I don't know how they do it, but elvan fruits and vegetables are the best tasting food you can ever eat."

"Aren't you tired of eating fruits and vegetables?"

"Nope," said Luke, shoving a spoonful of food into his mouth.

When Albert was done filling his plate, he looked at the other diners and felt embarrassed. Everyone except he and Luke had plates with perfectly proportioned amounts of food in their proper places. Sheepishly, he moved food around on his plate trying to make it look the best it could. Looking back to Luke he noticed he clearly wasn't carrying about manners stuffing his face with food.

Music began filling the room as conversations started. The popular topic was the evil that had taken over their forest and how they hoped it would soon be over. The gentleman next to Luke introduced himself as Galthinis and asked where he was from.

"Brookshire," replied Luke.

Hearing this, Galthinis' eyes lit up, "How is Guardian Dwayne?"

"He passed away many years ago," Luke informed him, going for another bite of food. "My dad is the guardian now."

Galthinis' eyes dimmed with the news. "It's a pity I never got to see him again. He and I used to be very close when I was a younger elf." With sadness in his voice he said, "I always remember traveling to Brookshire. Dwayne would teach me how to have fun and play in the dirt."

Luke imagined that farm life back home seemed very unrefined compared to elvan life. They continued their conversation about Brookshire while Albert spied on Ashearah's conversation with the gentleman sitting next to her. Apparently, he had picked up on how the king had changed the story as well. Elyon was the man's name. He whispered that his trust in the king had been waning. The king's recent remarks only fueled that distrust. "If we had been trying to contain this evil, then why has Sanoran not reported on our success?" he asked Ashearah.

"According to Albert and Luke, Sanoran was not occupied by elvan guards as we were led to believe, but by cowardly humans," Ashearah informed him.

This angered Elyon who leaned forward in his seat to ask Albert if it were true. Albert nodded. Elyon composed himself the best he could and sat in silence the rest of the feast. Ever so often, he would look at King Uthael with disgust.

When the feast was over and the plates were cleared, Elyon immediately stood, bowing to King Uthael then to Albert and Luke, and left the room. Conversations did not cease at the end of the meal;

people got up from the table, moving about talking to others. The table had been moved to one side of the room to let people move more freely about the space. Albert and Luke were swarmed with all sorts of questions about the world beyond Ethanan Forest. Luke answered to the best of his knowledge, trying to keep them from asking Albert. He had taken Ashearah's advice not letting anyone know about Albert's real origins.

Eventually King Uthael made his way over to Albert and Luke, "At last my two young friends, we get our chance to talk."

Albert and Luke stood petrified.

"So, my young friends, where was it you said you hail from?" he asked.

"Brookshire," Luke said, quickly. "Yep, my dad is the guardian there. He used to be a captain in King Altraeus' army but decided he wanted a simpler life."

"Fascinating Luke. And you, Albert?" Uthael asked.

Luke interrupted, "You know my Dad is the best warrior in all the land or, so I've been told. King Altraeus to this day still tries to bribe him to come back to his service."

"Interesting. Now, Albert, about where you were from?" he asked ignoring Luke. Albert had a feeling Uthael could tell he wasn't from Thu'hilen. He stood frozen, wondering what to say. *Should I lie and pretend he was from Brookshire as well?*

Ashearah hoping to save Albert stepped in, "Your Highness, don't you think it's about time for these two to retire. They have had a long day and a long journey."

King Uthael held up his hand, "They may be excused once Albert tells me where he is from."

Luke and Ashearah looked at Albert nervously. Albert smiled and chose to lie, "I'm from Brookshire, as well."

"Come now, Albert, tell the truth. I can tell when someone is lying," said King Uthael with a piercing stare.

Albert took a deep breath, "I'm from Waco."

"I've never heard of town called Waco. Where is it?"

"In the south," he responded, trying to be as close to the truth as he could.

"Really? What brought you here?"

"I wanted to venture to this forest."

"Why?"

"To solve the riddle if your people were still alive."

King Uthael glared at Albert determining whether his story was true or not. The stern look on his face turned back to a cheerful one. "Excellent. It's a good thing you did, now that you are here, we can finally prepare for the battle against this darkness."

He put his arms around Albert and Luke's shoulders clasping them. King Uthael thanked them for all that they had done for his people this day and moved onto another guest. When he was far enough away

Ashearah grabbed them by the hand and rushed them out of the room. Silently, they hurried up to the guest's spirecommonroom.

"Maybe we should get you two out of here now," Ashearah said, worried.

"Why? I think I covered pretty well," Albert said, proud of himself.

Ashearah smiled at him, "You did beautifully Albert, but I think King Uthael suspects something. He wouldn't dare cause a commotion with all his guests around, but as soon as they leave, who knows what will happen? Get your things ready. I will be back soon to retrieve you."

When she left, Albert and Luke hurriedly changed out of the clothes the king had given them. They packed their bags and secured their weapons. Luke rushed to Albert's room where they waited on the balcony.

A couple of hours went by and there was still no sign of Ashearah. A loud creak in one of the larger trees across from the balcony startled them. Leaping to their feet and drawing their weapons, Albert and Luke braced themselves for whatever was going to happen. Albert's eyes strained to see where the noise had come from. Through the branches came a griffon and its rider. With one flap of its giant wings, the two landed on the balcony. The creature was half-eagle, half-lion, with pearl-white feathers and neatly groomed, light-brown fur. Petrified, the two stood frozen not knowing what to do.

Chapter 14: Daratine Mountains

"Albert, Luke. Do not worry. It's me," whispered Ashearah from atop the bird.

Relieved, Albert asked, "What took so long?"

She apologized and told them she had been detained by some of the king's men while on her way to the stables. "Now there is no time to waste! Climb on and we will be gone from here!"

Albert and Luke quickly climbed on behind her holding on as best they could. Ashearah turned the griffon around and flicked the reins, the creature spread its wings and leaped into the air. The griffon glided through the trees to an opening on the edge of Ethosis. Albert and Luke found the flight exhilarating. The wind whooshed past them, and the ground speedily moved below them. Albert enjoyed the experience so much, he wished he had a griffon of his own.

Ashearah landed in a clearing. After they dismounted, she whispered something in elvish into the griffon's ear and the creature galloped off into the woods. Ashearah headed into the forest, ordering Albert and Luke to follow her. They walked several yards in silence to a hollowed-out tree. When they were a certain distance from the tree, Ashearah halted, making a weird chirping sound. A second later, a reply chirp came from inside the hollow. The signal given; she guided them into the tree where Lilious waited for them. The dim light of Lilious' lantern showed that she was now wearing light leather armor with a slender sword at her hip and a buckler on her back. A tunnel was at the back of the tree leading down into the earth.

"This passage will lead you to the base of the Daratrine Mountains," Ashearah told Albert and Luke. "But beware. It is like a labyrinth. There are many paths, so Lilious is here to guide you. She has been taught the fastest and safest way. Stick with her and you should have no trouble at all."

"You're not coming with us?" Albert asked, confused.

"I'm sorry Albert, I cannot. I must stay behind. If I disappeared as well, King Uthael might send men into the mountain looking for us, and we do not want that," she replied.

Albert and Luke agreed. Ashearah turned to Lilious, placing her hands on her shoulders speaking to her in elvish. Tears brimmed Lilious' eyes as she nodded in compliance. After taking a deep breath, Ashearah smiled and suggested they should get moving. Lilious wiped the water from her eyes and started down the passage ordering Albert and Luke to follow her. They looked to Ashearah who nodded for them to go. With a regretful sigh Albert and Luke followed Lilious down the hollow at her request.

Down in the tunnel Lilious took the lead with Albert and Luke following close behind.

"So, what was that all about?" asked Luke, tauntingly.

"She told me to try and keep you two alive," Lilious replied with a sneer. "Albert's important so I'll do everything in my power to make that so, but you... not so much." She huffed.

Luke snorted, "Like I need you to protect me."

"So, Lilious how long is it going to take us to get to the mountains?" Albert intervened trying to break up their squabbling before it got any worse.

"It should only take us a few hours, Albert," she said cheerily. "These caverns are empty for the most part. Though a few ground dwelling creatures have made this passage their home."

"Well it's a good thing we have you to show us the way," said Albert complimenting her.

Luke rolled his eyes at Albert's attempt to earn points with her. Albert pleaded with him to behave and eventually Luke gave in. After several minutes of walking Albert hurried to Lilious' side.

"So, what did your mom really tell you?" he asked, quietly.

Lilious looked back at Luke who pretended not to listen.

"She told me she might not be there when we got back. King Uthael is definitely going to be worried about your disappearance and he will undoubtedly know she had something to do with it," she said, solemnly.

"What does that mean?" he asked, guiltily.

"That tonight might be the last time I ever see my mother again," Lilious said trying to hold back tears.

Albert put his hand on her shoulder. "Don't worry. She will be all right." He smiled, trying to brighten the mood.

Lilious laughed reluctantly. "How do you know that?"

"I don't. I just have a feeling," he reassured her.

She smiled back at him, "Thank you, Albert."

"No problem."

To pass the time as they walked, Lilious asked Albert what their adventure had been like. He started by telling her about his first days in Thu'hilen, and about learning how to use a sword from Luke and Warren. He described his time at the Brookshire shops and the people he had met. She was awestruck when he told her about Dannon's house. Lilious had never met a wizard before, nor had she ever been in a house that was bigger on the inside than it was on the outside. To get Luke in on the conversation, Albert purposely told incorrect facts, which forced Luke to correct him. Eventually, Luke gave up trying to be stubborn and they laughed and joked while reminiscing about what had happened to them so far.

Lilious laughed in amazement. "Wow! You two have been through so many incredible situations for your age. All I've done is aid with the sentinel watches."

"How old are you?" Albert blurted out.

"Fourteen," she said, proudly.

Albert's heart sank a little to find she was two years older than him. He had hoped she was closer to his age and was about to make a comment about it when both Luke and Lilious stopped immediately signaling for silence.

"Do you see that light?" Luke asked.

"Yeah, and I can hear voices," Lilious replied.

Further down the tunnel, Albert could see flickering light coming from one of the offshoots. Quietly they drew their weapons, prepared for what could be coming ahead. Slowly, they inched towards the offshoot. Strange, high-pitched voices grew in volume as they drew closer. When they reached the offshoot, Lilious slowly looked around the corner to see where the light was coming from. To her disappointment, she saw a group of rodent-looking people digging around in the tunnel.

"Great, Kobolds." She cringed putting out her lamp.

"What are Kobolds?" Albert whispered.

"Rodent people," Luke informed him. "They are about half our size and very unpredictable."

Albert gave Luke a disgusted look.

"Maybe if we wait patiently, they will go back down the way they came," Lilious whispered.

"Only if we are lucky," replied Luke. "I don't really want to tangle with Kobolds."

Albert was growing worried. Luke was always ready to take on any challenge, and if he didn't want to fight with these rodent people, they must be bad. "What is so horrible about them?" he whispered.

"First of all, they are dirty fighters," Luke said. "They bite, kick, squirm, and will use whatever is in their hand as a weapon."

"If they get away to warn the rest of their pack, you could have every Kobold around coming down on you in seconds," Lilious finished.

"That doesn't sound good," Albert said, nervously.

"Oh, did I forget to mention that their bite is poisonous?" Luke interjected.

"Great."

They continued to peer breathlessly around the corner, hoping the Kobolds would turn and move away from them. As the rodent men grew closer, they pushed themselves against the wall trying to hide themselves.

"Do you two have on those boots the blacksmith gave you?" Lilious whispered.

Both the boys nodded.

"Good. Hold very still."

The creatures eventually made it to the main tunnel where they stopped, abruptly. Albert held his breath. He knew the Kobolds could sense their presence. To Albert, the creatures looked like humanoid rats, mice, and opossums, with torn and dirty pieces of cloth they had stitched together to make clothes. Most of them were carrying candles and some type of digging device.

The rodent men began sniffing the air and pointing their little candles towards the dark spots of the tunnel. Albert, Luke, and Lilious stood pushing themselves into the walls. Albert wished he could meld with the wall and just disappear. He didn't want to know what would happen if they found them. Turning his face, he chanced a look at his friends. Luke stood, stone-faced, probably wishing he was part of the wall as well. Lilious' eyes were closed, her lips were moving ever so slightly.

The Kobolds continued to sniff the air and search every inch of the tunnel. What Albert couldn't understand was, why hadn't they found them yet. Several times Kobold noses had come within inches of his own. When that happened, Albert had to keep himself from gagging. The smell of their breath was horrible. Eventually, the Kobolds gave up the search and headed into another tunnel.

When they were out of sight, Lilious relit her lamp, "Let's go, hurry." The three of them started jogging down the main tunnel with Lilious in the lead. After thirty minutes of intermittent jogging, Lilious stopped so they could catch their breath. Albert lay on the ground, his chest heaving. Never had he ran so much in his life, and he hoped he would never have to again. He looked at Luke who seemed only a little winded and then to Lilious who didn't seem tired at all.

"How did they not see us?" asked Albert, bewildered.

"Yeah, I thought we were goners," said Luke.

"Those boots you are wearing," replied Lilious. "They allow the wearer to move like elves, remember."

"How do boots hide you from Kobolds seeing you?" asked Luke.

"If elves stay very still, we can sort of disappear into the background," she replied. "I was hoping that wearing those boots would do the same thing."

"It seems like it worked," said Albert, thankful. "What were you saying back there?"

Lilious blushed. "I didn't want to put all my faith in those boots. So, I started asking the wind and earth elements to hide us."

"Well, whether it was the boots or the elements I'm glad those Kobold didn't see us," said Luke. "Shall we keep moving? I don't want those Kobolds to pick up our trail and follow us."

"Right. The tunnel ends just up ahead," Lilious informed.

The ground soon changed from dirt into stone. Steps ahead of them slowly spiraled upwards. Light from the moons pierced the darkness through cracks in the rocks. Albert stopped at one of the larger cracks to look. Through the hole he could see the Ethanan Forest spread out along the base of the mountains. It was clear that they were no longer under the forest but climbing a path leading up into the mountain.

The cracks between the rocks now gave enough light for Albert to see what it was they were climbing up. The walls were made from carved stone blocks and large boulders. It dawned on him that they were climbing a very old tower that the mountain had swallowed. Spots where windows once opened to the outside world, were now blocked by cave-ins. He was now wondering how this tower had been buried so far into the mountain. "Lilious, where are we?" he asked.

"In an old tower," she replied, bluntly.

"Well, I know that, but why is it here?" he replied.

Lilious chortled. "This was once part of the Lanoran Fortress. My mother told me long ago a ruthless necromancer lived here. He was a tyrannical ruler who enslaved and tortured the people. One day, the people revolted and sought the aid of a powerful wizard. He used his magic to erupt the mountain and bury Lanoran Fortress."

"Cool," Albert said, captivated.

"Some other parts of the fortress remain deep under the mountain, but they are very dangerous and are said to be haunted."

"How much longer?" Luke said, uninterested.

"The exit is just around the corner," she said, rolling her eyes at Luke. "We will travel up the side of the mountain from there."

At the next level of the tower, the wall opened to a cavern leading out into the moonlight. It was nice to be once again out into the cool night air instead of the damp staleness of the tunnel. All four moons were out, two high in the sky with one on the eastern horizon and one beginning to drop over the mountains. All four of their lights made the night bright and easily visible. Unfortunately, that meant they might be easily visible if someone was looking at the mountain for them.

Lilious left their lantern back in the cave, not wanting to give away their position. Where they exited had very little vegetation and jagged rocks protruding out of the mountainside. She led them up a path between the rocks to a cave close to the top.

"This is it," she said in an excited voice. "This is the hidden entrance to the wyvern colony."

Albert and Luke's eyes lit up with anticipation. They were finally nearing their goal and would soon find out what Albert's dream meant. Their excitement ceased when they got to the back of the cave and found nothing.

"What!" Albert said, disappointed.

Lilious giggled and shook her head in disbelief at their faith in her. She spoke a few words in elvish and the wall started folding in on itself revealing a doorway. Albert and Luke's excitement came back as they watched the magical door open. It opened to a small room lit with torches, much to their surprise. They walked inside finding crates stacked neatly around the room. Taking a quick look inside, they found different foods and other supplies.

"What's with all this food and equipment?" Luke asked.

"I don't know?" Lilious answered. "We all thought these caverns had been deserted."

While Luke and Lilious looked around Albert began hearing someone call his name.

"Do you guys hear that?" he asked, heading for the door.

"Albert, wait," Lilious urged. "We don't know whose supplies these are."

"I know but someone is calling my name."

"I don't hear anything," said Luke.

Albert grabbed the door, pulling it open to a well-lit hallway.

"Albert, what are you doing?" Luke said, horrified.

"I don't know, but something inside me is urging me forward, telling me I need to hurry," Albert replied.

"Well, fight it," Luke commanded.

"I would, but I don't want to."

Albert ventured down the hallway following the voice. Luke and Lilious hurried after him, trying to stop him. In the distance someone with a gravely voice could be heard shouting orders. By the time they had caught up with him, Albert had reached the end of the hall. Here it split into two halls with a hole cut out of the mountain overlooking the colony. Albert hurried to the opening, where he looked over a large cavern open to the sky above. A small city with big neon signs and lights had been built in the cavern with little green men and women busily working.

"Goblins!" Luke said, excited. "So that's who's living here now. I should have known."

"What are goblins doing in our mountain?" Lilious asked, disgusted. "Elves would never allow goblins to be in our forest let alone these sacred mountains."

"I don't think King Uthael cares," Luke snorted. "He is clearly evil."

"Agreed," said Albert and Lilious at the same time.

Albert could hear whoever it was calling his name from the corridor to their right.

"Come on this way," he said, pointing down one of the corridors.

"Wait. How do you know where you are going?" Lilious asked, annoyed.

"Because this is the way the voice is coming from," he responded.

"I don't think you should be following mysterious voices in your head," Luke stated, flatly.

Albert ignored him and continued down the hallway. Sighing, they hurried after him again. He led them down a twisting path leading deeper into the mountain. A few times they almost ran into a goblin busily working, but Lilious and Luke managed to pull Albert back and hide just in time to avoid getting caught. Luke was glad the elvan blacksmith had given them the boots that allowed them to step as lightly as an elf. The way Albert was tromping around, it was a wonder the whole colony didn't hear him. Albert continued to follow the voice until they reached an ornate, green, metal door. It was heavy, forcing him to use his entire strength to open it.

Inside was a large room with ornate stonework. Torches lined the walls, giving light to a gruesome sight. They saw several rows of tables with softball-sized eggs on them. The eggs were carefully situated on nests of straw. Each table had a wyvern chained to a rail system anchored to the ceiling caring for the eggs. Most of them were battered and beaten and all of them had their wings clipped. Whips and other torture tools hung from hooks on the walls, giving off a general feeling of sorrow and horror in Albert.

"This is awful," said Lilious aghast, her hands to her mouth.

"Seems like some kind of hatchery," commented Luke, investigating one of the tables. The wyverns watching over the eggs seemed not to notice him at all.

The voice in Albert's head was getting ever louder as it called to him, urging him onward. He followed the sound with Lilious in tow to a table, a couple aisles over and several rows back. There the wyvern watching over the eggs looked at Albert, walked over to one of the eggs, leaned down and nudged it with its nose.

Albert positioned himself in front of the egg, the voice pounding in his head. He looked at the egg knowing now where the voice was coming from. He hesitated, not knowing what to do or what was going to happen. Again, the wyvern on the table nudged the egg, coaxing him to touch it. Albert reached out to grab the egg, the mark on his arm moving as he did so. Panicked he stopped. The voice begged him to keep going.

"Albert, what's going on?" Lilious asked.

"The voice I've been hearing. It's coming from the egg. It wants me to pick it up."

"So, why'd you stop?"

"The mark on my arm moved as I reached out for the egg."

"Well, are you going to pick it up?"

Albert thought for a moment. "I think I have to."

He once again moved to pick up the egg. As he did, his mark unraveled, slithering down his arm toward his hand. When Albert wrapped his hand around the egg, the mark left his body, entering the egg. A flash of blinding light lit the room, forcing everyone to shield their eyes. When the light dissipated, they found the egg cracked open. In his hands asleep, lay a greenish-blue wyvern pup the size of a newborn puppy curled in a ball. Two small knobs for horns crowned its head. Tiny finlike ears fluttered against the side of the neck. The wyvern's wings ran the length of its body and its short tail curled in on itself. Dozens of little serrated teeth were visible as the creature slowly breathed in and out.

Albert was filled with excitement. Questions were finally starting to be answered. All they had to do now was escape back the way they came and tell Ashearah what was going on.

"Albert, what does this mean?" asked Lilious.

"I don't know, but we should get out of here," he replied.

Shortly after the pup hatched, the wyverns started swaying back and forth singing. "Uh, what are they doing?" asked Luke, who had been busy investigating the battered wyverns and how they were chained.

Albert replied, "I don't know, but if they don't stop, they are going attract someone's attention."

Luke, being closest to the door, could hear footsteps coming their way. "Too late," he said, dashing into the shadows to hide.

Chapter 15: Captured

Albert and Lilious looked around for some place to hide but were too slow. "Hey! Who'a you? What you doin' down here?" came a harsh, raspy voice behind them. They turned to see a goblin standing at the entrance to the hatchery. He had short, messy dark-green hair with clothing made from leather and wore a curved, wicked blade on his belt. Panicked, mumbled words fell from their lips as they tried to form sentences. The goblin rushed over to them. "What you doin' down here?" he asked, sternly. They looked around for Luke, but he had disappeared.

Albert was mumbling incoherent words when Lilious piped up. "We uh… are here to umm… check in on the eggs," she said, forcing a smile.

"You what?" the goblin gave her a questioning look. "Oh, no you don't. That's my job. Ain't no one takin' it from me."

"Well the uh—" Lilious struggled to come up with an answer.

"The king," Albert chimed in.

"Oh, yes, the king. He told me to come check in on them."

"Since when does the king send young elf maidens to check up on wyvern eggs? And when did you elves start associatin' with humans again?"

"Well, you see, the king uh… the king is umm… my father. Yes, the king is my father and he wanted me to learn about what is going on here, so he sent me up with Albert," she beamed.

"Who's Albert? The human?"

"Yes, he is uhh… my pet," Lilious exclaimed. The goblin looked at Albert and chuckled with approval.

Albert was about to protest being called a pet, but Lilious quickly gave him a sharp elbow to the side, flashing him a fierce look.

"All right, but you'll have to come with me to the Boss. Hav'ta confirm your story. All dealin' up here go through the Boss," said the goblin, eyeing Albert cradling something in his arms "What that you got in your arm, boy?" Albert held the pup close. Reluctant to let him see what was in his arms. "Come on. Show me or I'll have you off to the grinder right now."

Not wanting to find out what the 'Grinder' was he repositioned the wyvern in his arm so that the goblin could see it. The goblin gave a non-trusting look at Lilious.

"I, um… touched one of the eggs and it hatched," Albert blurted out. "I didn't mean to do anything I just wanted to see an egg close up."

"You ain't a wizard or sorcerer or anything are you?" the goblin stood on his tiptoes to look Albert square in the eye.

Albert bent back. The goblin smelt horrible, and his breath reeked of decay. "No Sir, I merely touched it," he choked.

The goblin searched Albert's eyes for any evidence that he might be lying. Appeased, he got down from his tiptoes. "I only ask because wyvern pups only hatch under certain conditions," he said eyeing Albert, who just shook his head, scared. "Okay well, hand it over, as well as that wretched piece of metal you got strapped to your waist and we will be on our way."

Albert, still reluctant to hand over the wyvern pup, handed his short sword to the goblin first. After seeing its workmanship, the goblin shook his head, calling it a dwarven piece of junk. Albert protested it was one of the finest swords he had ever seen. The goblin huffed and held out his other hand for the wyvern. Albert hesitated but slowly handed it over. When the goblin reached for the pup, sparks of lightning came from the wyvern, striking the goblin who winced in pain.

The goblin waved his hand in the air, trying to shake off the hurt. He threw his hand behind his back, trying to act as if it was nothing, "Yeah, well, you uhhh carry that thing till we get to the Boss. We'll see what he wants to do with it."

The goblin escorted the two up to the large cavern they had looked down upon earlier. As he guided them down the streets of the city, the other goblins stared wondering what was going on. Neon signs on buildings gave the city light, making Albert wonder how they were powered. The other goblins, intrigued by what was happening, followed as the hatchery keeper took them to the biggest building in the city.

The Boss' house looked as if it was put together from scraps of other buildings, windmills, and any other contraption they could get their hands on. A big neon sign centered in the middle of the house read, 'Gruttlik's'. A set of double metal doors at the top of metal stairs allowed one to enter the building. The inside of the house was a mess. Piles of junk lay in every corner with goblins searching through them. Paintings of the same goblin in different heroic situations covered the walls. Albert nodded as Lilious muttered, "I assume the goblin in the picture has to be Gruttlik." From the paintings' depiction, he was taller than most goblins with neatly combed black hair. In each picture he wore a different suit of exquisite armor.

In the main room of the house sat a throne made from pieces of metal railing with four large springs and a tattered cushion for a seat. Two steps led to the throne, allowing Gruttlik to sit. Albert and Lilious were ordered to stand in place until the Boss arrived. Obeying the order, they looked around to see the goblins from outside had followed them in, still wondering what was going on. The hatchery keeper disappeared and reappeared several minutes later with a goblin that looked similar the one from the paintings.

It wasn't any real surprise that Gruttlik had had his image improved for the paintings. He was taller than the rest, but not by much and his black hair was greasier and more matted to the side than combed. He wore black leather armor reminding Albert of someone from a biker gang in cartoons. Gruttlik had more wrinkles than the rest of the goblins as well. The goblin gave Albert the creeps. He had several scars on his face and beady red eyes. A long, crooked nose, and pointed ears, the left ear was missing half.

Gruttlik climbed his throne and sat down. His smile was a sneer. "Now, now, Zornic, what do we have here?"

"Boss, I found these two in the hatchery," Zornic announced. He grabbed Lilious, pulling her forward, "This one claims she is the king's daughter." Then grabbed Albert, "And this one says he touched a wyvern egg and it hatched."

Gruttlik, seeing the wyvern pup in Albert's arms, scowled. "Well, Well, Gerrick is not going to like this."

Albert and Lilious looked at each other, confused. Albert mouthed, "Who's Gerrick?" to Lilious who shrugged.

Gruttlik then turned to Lilious, "Now, missy, I know King Uthael, and I know he don't have any daughters. So, who are you?"

Lilious stood defiantly, not speaking. Gruttlik rolled his eyes and turned his attention back to Albert. "How about you, boy. Who are you?"

Albert, wanting to look brave in front of Lilious, kept silent.

"Don't want to talk huh? Well a couple days in the dungeons with no food or water ought to loosen those lips. If that don't work," Gruttlik flashed an evil smile. "Then it's the Grinder. Take them away and get rid of that thing." He pointed to the wyvern pup.

"Yes, Boss," said Zornic, who stopped, remembering the last time he tried to touch the wyvern. "Uh boss, the thing is, last time I tried to take the wyvern from the boy it shocked me."

Gruttlik rolled his eyes. "Fine! Get a cage and have the boy throw the thing in it. It'll stay in there till Gerrick gets here."

"Yes, Boss," Zornic bowed.

Zornic shoved Albert and Lilious forward, forcing them to walk out a side door. He led them down a hallway and out a door exiting the side of Gruttlik's house. They walked around the back of the house and down a tunnel to the dungeon. Here, there were three cells and more piles of junk strewn throughout the room.

Zornic pushed them into one of the cells, locking them in. He then searched one of the piles of junk to find a cage to put the wyvern in. A few minutes later, he returned with a small bird cage and opened their cell forcing Albert to put the pup inside. Once the wyvern was inside, Zornic locked their cell door and hung the cage across the room on a hook suspended from the ceiling. Satisfied, he chucked their gear into one of the piles and left the dungeon.

"Now what?" asked Lilious.

"I don't know, but I keep getting these strange images in my head."

She looked at him confused, "Like?"

"Well, first it was of dead small animals, and now of snow and things that are cold." Albert immediately thought of the wyvern pup and looked in its direction. It was whimpering and curled up into a ball.

"I think the images are coming from him?" Albert speculated.

"What do you mean?" Lilious asked.

"I think he is trying to communicate with me."

"Through images?"

"I guess."

The wyvern opened its eyes looking to see where its heat source had gone to find itself caged. It began frantically searching for a way out. Flashes of bars and cages entered Albert's mind.

"It's scared," he said. "I'm now getting images of its cage. It is trying to communicate with me."

"Well, you should try to communicate back," said Lilious. "Think of something comforting."

Albert thought about sitting on a couch with the wyvern in his lap petting it like he would a dog or cat. He also imagined being outside in his front yard playing with it on the lawn. The wyvern soon calmed down and cuddled with itself, though still whimpering.

"That seemed to do the trick," stated Lilious. "What did you think of?"

"I imagined myself playing with him on the front lawn of my house back home."

"That sounds... really childish and dorky," she laughed. "I'm sorry, I'm sorry," she said trying not to laugh any more.

Albert blushed with embarrassment, "Well, I am only twelve, so I guess I still am kind of a kid."

"A kid that has been on a grand adventure and will soon save a colony of wyverns," she said, encouraging him. "When we get out of here, that is."

"Well, Luke didn't get caught. He will get us out of here."

"I hope. So, what are you going to call your wyvern?"

Albert thought for a second, "I don't know." He looked over at the wyvern who picked up its head and looked back at him.

"It's like he can read my every thought," Albert said, amazed. The wyvern gave him a big smile and swayed happily.

Lilious giggled, "I believe he can."

"So, what's your name?" Albert asked the wyvern.

The wyvern pup shrugged its shoulders.

"Do you have a name?" he asked.

It shook its head, no.

"Okay then, what would you like to be called?"

An image of a raging fire came into his mind followed by the pup's wing.

"Raging Fire Wing?" he asked.

It shook its head and conjured up the image again.

"Fire Wing?" he tried.

Shaking its head again it conjured up the image but this time focusing on the intensity of the fire.

"Rage Wing?" Albert guessed once again.

Getting it right the wyvern smiled proudly.

"Rage Wing, huh?" He thought for a minute. "It is a cool name, but it does seem a little…" Albert trailed off thinking how he was going to tell him it didn't sound like a real name.

"Cumbersome," piped Lilious coming to Albert's aide.

"Yeah, cumbersome," Albert repeated, thanking Lilious for bailing him out. "What about the name, 'Umber'. It sounds cool too." He didn't know where that name had come from, but it felt right.

The wyvern thought about it for a minute then smiled and bobbed up and down in agreement.

"Well then, Umber, it is," Albert said, satisfied.

Lilious looked at Umber, "It's finally a pleasure to meet you, Umber. I am Lilious."

Umber smiled proudly hearing his new name.

"Now all we have to do is wait for Luke to come rescue us," Albert said, disheartened. He and Lilious slumped to the ground, leaning against each other.

Several hours later, Luke had found his way to the dungeon. He found Albert and Lilious asleep against the bars of the cell. Grabbing a pipe from the floor, Luke tapped the cell bar by Albert's head. He woke up with a shot wondering what was happening. Seeing Luke's face brought much-needed relief to Albert as he smiled at his friend. Umber chirped in his cage, feeling Albert's excitement.

"Hey Al. What's with Wyvie back there?" said Luke.

Umber's chirps turned to a low growl.

"Way to hurt Umber's feelings Luke," Albert teased.

"Who's Umber and how do you know I hurt his feelings?" he asked.

"Umber is Wyvie, as you called him, and we are mentally linked, I think. We know what each other is thinking and feeling."

"Cool," said Luke. "I wish I was mentally linked to an animal." He looked at Lilious whose eyes were still closed. "Wow, is she asleep!"

Lilious still lay there, "I'm not sleeping I'm just trying to ignore you."

Luke grabbed the key off the wall, "Yeah, yeah. Let's hurry and get you guys out of here before anyone comes in."

He had just opened the cell when the jailor walked in, "Now what do we have here? Another prisoner for the Grinder."

Luke panicked for a second then remembered his mother's lessons about goblins. "How much gold for you to just walk away and pretend you didn't see anything?" he asked.

The goblin looked at him wearily, "How much you got?"

"Six gold."

"Seven, and I didn't see nuttin," The goblin smiled greedily.

"Done." Luke pulled out a bag of gold that Albert didn't know about. He handed seven gold pieces to the jailor. Once the jailor had his gold, he walked out of the dungeon whistling happily.

Luke laughed to himself, "Goblins."

"I didn't think we had any money!" said Albert. "Where did that come from?"

"Of course, I had money on me, Al," replied Luke. "My parents taught me to always be prepared for situations like these."

As soon as they were free, Lilious quickly grabbed their gear from the pile of junk as Albert scooped up Umber. His bag back in his possession, he reached in for some jerky and gave it to the wyvern pup who wasted no time snatching the meat from Albert's hands finishing it in a couple bites.

"He's been starving since he hatched," Albert exclaimed.

"We should move though. Someone else could show up soon," said Lilious.

Luke urged, "Lilious is right, we need to go. Follow me. I know the way out."

Albert nodded, and they followed Luke out of the dungeon. He led them down a different hallway than the one they had taken to the dungeon. This one seemed to circle the city instead of heading straight through it. As they moved along the goblin tunnels, Luke apologized for taking so long to rescue them. "I wanted to investigate more of the hallways and tunnels to get a better idea of what was going on," he said. "I found something that might be of interest. All the wyvern eggs are taken to a room on the lower levels where they are put into crates to be taken somewhere. It took me a bit to find where they were holding you, so I bribed a goblin, with a few silver to see if he knew where the crates were going." Luke shook his head, "He didn't have a clue and no one else here knows either."

"Not even Gruttlik?" Albert asked.

"Not even him," Luke responded. "All they were hired to do was keep the wyverns under control and get their eggs ready for transportation."

"Wonder if King Uthael knows?" Lilious wondered.

"Maybe. We'll have to ask him when we get back."

Before they knew it, they were back in the supply room where they had first entered. Thanks to Luke's guidance they easily avoided every goblin patrol that roamed the halls. Exiting through the secret door, they were glad to finally be out of the goblin caves. With the noon day sun high above them, they decided it would be better to wait till nightfall before traveling down the mountain. Exhausted, they ate what little food they had, then curled up on the dirt floor, falling asleep almost instantly. The last thing Albert could remember before falling asleep was Umber crawling out of his knapsack and cuddling beside him.

Chapter 16: Secrets Revealed

Albert woke to Luke shaking him awake. Night had fallen with two of the moons in the sky, one of them waning. It was a blessing the moons weren't giving off much light, making them less visible. Glad no one had found them while they slept, Albert, Luke and Lilious gathered their things. Albert put Umber back in his knapsack, and they started down the mountain. Reaching the secret passage took less time than it had been on the way up. There, they found Lilious' lamp and with a word of magic, the lamp was alight. Ready for the dark tunnels, they started down the tower.

Albert's decision to put Umber in his pack wasn't making it easier for him to move. The wyvern constantly jostled around, making it awkward for him to run. Making matters worse, his pack also seemed to be getting heavier. Looking inside, he found Umber had eaten what food he could find and was now more than twice the size of when he first hatched.

"Whoa!" commented Albert, as they ran down the stairs of the tower.

"What?" Luke and Lilious said in unison afraid something was wrong.

"It's just Umber. He is growing really fast."

When they looked inside Albert's bag, they were surprised to find Umber now the size of a terrier.

"Growing fast is an understatement!" Luke exclaimed.

Umber smiled up at them, then climbed out of the bag and jumped down to the floor.

"He says he will run with us," Albert stated. "Apparently, he didn't want to wear me out by carrying him the whole way, so he ate what he needed to grow and run on his own."

"Well isn't that thoughtful of him!" said Lilious, cheerfully.

Umber grinned at her, proud of himself.

"Yes, it is," Luke said, hurriedly. "Don't you think we should be going now?" he reminded them.

Umber looked up with a quick nod then started running down the steps of the tower.

"At least someone agrees with me," Luke smiled, running after him.

Albert and Lilious followed down the stairs, close behind. They were at the bottom of the tower within minutes. Halfway through the tunnel they stopped to rest for food and water. Lilious and Luke splitting their food with Albert. "Where should we go once back in Ethosis?" asked Albert.

"Obviously, my house," suggested Lilious.

"I don't think so," said Luke. "If the king did suspect your mother, he most likely has people waiting there for us to return. I think we should bypass the city and head straight for Sanoran. My dad will probably still be there waiting to hear from us. I suggest we go, get him, come back and free your mom. Then we go back to the colony and show those goblins who's boss."

"We don't have time to go back to Sanoran," Lilious protested. "If the goblins don't already know we are missing, they will soon. Then, who knows what will happen to the wyverns? We need help now!"

"So, then what do you suggest we do?" Luke thundered.

Lilious sat, stumped, trying hard to not show that she was scared. Luke waited for her answer.

"I don't know," she finally admitted. "What do you think we should do, Albert?"

Albert looked back and forth at them, feeling the pressure. "Ugh, why do I always have to be the deciding factor." He then looked at Umber in communication. "Really, you think?" he said out loud. Umber nodded his head.

"Um, Al, do you want to clue us in at what is going on?" said Luke, confused.

"Oh right, sorry. Umber was wondering what Sanoran was and how far. I told him and he thinks we should try both," said Albert.

"What?" said Luke.

"Okay so, we'll go to Lilious' house. Luke, you sneak up and look inside while Umber searches the area around the house. If we spot the king's men there, we will head to Sanoran and get your dad. Agreed?"

Luke and Lilious thought about the plan for a minute, then agreed with the compromise. Their break done and plan settled, they continued down the tunnel, rushing faster than before. When they reached the tree hollow, it was still night outside. Lilious put out the lamp, leaving it there. Sneaking through the forest and into the city would be easier without it. None of the sentinels seemed to be on their usual patrols. While this made it easy to get back into the city, it was a signal to them that something wasn't right. They were sure at any moment ambushers were going to pop out and capture them.

When they reached the city, they found that the usual guards were missing there as well. Peeking into the houses, they found their inhabitants asleep in their beds. Everything seemed to be fine, so why weren't there any guards? Lilious' house finally came into view. Following through with their plan, Lilious and Albert hid behind her neighbor's house. They watched as Luke snuck through the shadows; Umber climbed high enough up the house to try flying over. Albert worried about Umber, though. He had never flown before and Albert worried if he was ready. The wyvern's unsure response made him feel even worse. When he was near the top of the tree, Umber spread his wings flapping them a few times to practice, trying to get it right.

"Are you sure he is ready for this?" Lilious whispered, concerned.

"No, but he says he can do it," said Albert, unsure.

Albert could tell by the look on her face, his lack of confidence worried her more. They watched as Umber leapt into the air, spreading his wings, gliding over to Lilious' house. He teetered and wobbled as he went. A couple times they feared he was going to come crashing down to the ground. Thankfully, he made it to the other side, grabbed tightly onto a branch and stayed there for a while to recover.

"Is he Okay?" Lilious asked.

"Yes, but a little shaken. Gliding over to your house was more difficult than he thought it would be," he responded.

"Great," she said, nervously. "Hopefully, he doesn't have to fly back over here."

Both Albert and Umber froze, not having thought that far ahead. "Yeah, let's hope," said Albert, shakily.

Luke was now at the front door of the house. As he grabbed for the door handle, he found it locked. Slowly, he pulled out his tool kit and began picking the lock on the door. He found the elvish lock was a little more difficult than usual. Eventually, the door unlocked, opening just enough so he could sneak into the house.

Inside everything was quiet. Feeling a little more confident, Luke moved through the house quickly. Nothing in the main room was out of place and no one was lying in wait to spring a trap. Silently he moved up the stairs to the upper level. Like most of the houses, the stairs followed the trunk of the tree. On the upper floor were four bedrooms. He glided to the first door, slinking inside. From what he could see in the dark, the room was a prayer room with celestial ornaments of moons and stars hanging from the ceiling and a prayer rug on the floor. Seeing no place to hide in the room Luke returned to the outer hall.

The next room was a broom closet filled with cleaning items. Luke quickly looked through the room, finding no one. The other two rooms were Lilious' and Ashearah's. Both were very regal in design yet plain and empty, concealing no one in them. Convinced there was no one in the house, he quietly hurried down to the window, waving that everything was clear.

"There's Luke," said Lilious. "Has Umber seen anything?" she asked Albert.

While Lilious was watching for Luke, Albert had been concentrating on the images Umber had been giving him.

"Umber hasn't seen anything. I think we're good," Albert said, confidently.

"Okay, let's sneak over," replied Lilious, confident.

"Right. I'll tell Umber just to climb down the side of the house."

Albert and Lilious quickly darted across the street to meet Umber at the door. Slipping inside, they found Luke lounging in one of the chairs. Tired, Albert found a seat of his own and flopped down in it as Umber climbed into his lap. Lilious, still worried that they might be in trouble, urged them to get back up. Suddenly, all the lights in the house flashed into life as elvan guards came storming into the house. Within seconds all three were being restrained with Umber being scooped up into a bag.

"You are all under arrest, by order of the king," informed a guard with long golden hair, wearing the thick leather armor of a captain.

Albert, Luke, and Lilious fought against their captors, trying to break free when one of the guards came crashing through the front door onto the floor.

"Are you sure about that?" came a familiar voice.

Albert and Luke's eyes lit up, recognizing the voice. Warren stepped into the room battle axe lazily on his shoulder.

"Now, by order of King Altraeus, as the guardian of Brookshire, I order you to let the children go," Warren said with authority.

The guard scoffed at Warren, "Ha, this is not Brookshire, this is Ethosis, and we do not recognize your king's authority here. Besides, there is one of you and seven of us. What makes you think we will listen to you?"

A yelp from another guard directed everyone's attention to the back of the room. Ashearah was standing behind the guard a knife at his throat.

"High Priestess Ashearah!" the guard spat. "You finally show yourself, traitor."

"I'm not the traitor, Elsin," said Ashearah, coldly. "That would be our king. Now if I were you, I would obey Warren's orders."

"And why is that?" Elsin said, shrewdly.

"Because I've already seen him take out fifteen of the king's men by himself. You and your men wouldn't stand a chance," she said with a smile.

Elsin looked at Warren standing calmly as if the battle had already been won.

"Let them go," Elsin sighed.

Elsin's men unhanded Albert, Luke, Lilious and let Umber out of the sack. Upon being free Umber quickly scurried over between Albert's leg hissing at his former captor.

"Before we go, Ashearah, tell me why you have betrayed your king," Elsin said.

Ashearah walked over to Umber, scooping him up into her arms. "For this, Elsin," she said, happily.

Elsin eyed Umber warily. "And what is that?"

Ashearah laughed. "Are you too young to know what a wyvern looks like? Here is one right before your eyes?"

Elsin's eyes widened, "But King Uthael, said the evil that plagues these lands destroyed all the wyverns."

"I thought so too, but it seems they are not yet extinct," she said pleased. "It would seem these three have some new information for us, Albert would you tell us what is happening up in our mountains?"

"Goblins," Luke said confidently.

"She asked Albert, Luke," Warren said, reprimanding his son. Luke shied away from his father apologizing.

"Goblins!" Elsin echoed. "How did those filthy creatures get in our mountain?"

"Ask King Uthael," Lilious said, spitefully. "He's been working with them, and a man named Gerrick."

Elsin looked shocked. His world as well as his devotion to his king were being shattered.

"When we got to the wyvern colony, we found that goblins had taken over the place," Albert informed them. "They have the wyverns imprisoned there and their eggs are being taken somewhere."

"Why would our king do this?" Elsin asked. "As a child, I was always taught that the wyverns were our greatest friends and allies." Pointing to Umber he said, "Is that one of the ones who were imprisoned? Did you free it before you left?"

"No," Albert answered. "I was marked by a wyvern about a week ago, and Umber hatched when I touched his egg."

"So, you are a Dragoon then," Warren said, with a huge smile.

Albert shrugged, "I guess so."

Elsin was stunned. "A Dragoon? None of their order has been seen for generations. I've always wished to see a wyvern. May I look at him?"

Albert and Umber looked at each other communicating, "He said you may, but don't try anything funny or you will regret it."

Elsin stepped closer, eyeing Umber. "Now, I understand your actions High Priestess. But what do we do now?"

"Then you are with us, Elsin?" Ashearah asked, confidently.

"I am, my Priestess," he responded.

"Good. Meet us tomorrow morning behind Elyon's house. There we shall plan King Uthael's surrender, hopefully without a fight."

Elsin saluted Ashearah and he and his men left her house. Ashearah looked at the broken and disarrayed state of her home. She spoke a word of magic and the room arranged itself back together. Appeased with her house back in order, she turned to her daughter whose eyes were brimming with tears. Ashearah walked to her, throwing her arms around Lilious, speaking in elvish.

Luke walked over to Warren nonchalantly, "So, what happened to you?"

"Ahh, the people of Sanoran attacked me when they found you guys had slipped past the gate into the forest," said Warren, casually.

"And?" Luke asked.

"It was like fighting a bunch of children, those cowards," Warren spat. "Not even the mercenaries they hired put up much of a challenge."

"So, why did you come into the forest?" Albert butted in.

"We will talk about that later. We should get back to our hideout. More of the King's men could be on their way," he suggested.

"You guys have a hideout?" asked Luke, surprised.

"Warren is right, let us make haste," replied Ashearah.

Quietly they snuck out of Ashearah's house and across the street. They stealthily made their way behind the house Albert and Lilious had hid behind. There they moved silently through the city where Ashearah revealed a secret door at the base of a home. The basement was cold and dark with only the light from a fireplace at the back of the room. The ceiling was the gnarled roots of the tree twisting their way downwards, forming walls. Shelves with food storage lined the walls with five cots huddled around the fireplace for warmth.

"Whose house is this?" asked Luke.

"Elyon's," replied Lilious. Albert and Luke gave her a questioning look.

"Elyon, is no friend of the king!" Ashearah informed them. "When he found out I was going into hiding he offered this basement as a place for me to stay."

Now, safely inside Elyon's basement, Albert turned to Warren, "So, why did you come into the forest?"

"Leegahr," Warren laughed. "He was afraid I was going to kill him, and he started confessing everything. He told me King Uthael had sealed the forest imprisoning his people. I knew I had to get here as quickly as I could."

"If Warren hadn't shown up when he did, I would most likely be in the palace dungeon right now with my elvan brethren," said Ashearah.

"You're welcome," Warren said.

"I owe you an apology, Luke," she continued. "When you said your father really was the greatest warrior in the land, I did not believe it. But, after watching him beat so many of the king's men so easily, it is hard not to believe."

Luke smiled proudly.

Warren shrugged, "Well, I don't know if I'm the greatest."

"Nonetheless. If you hadn't taken out Malathis and his men, I do not think I would be here to see my daughter again," Ashearah said, thankfully.

Warren shrugged again as if it was something he did daily. "So, you three, what transpired in the mountains?" asked Asherah. They took turns telling Ashearah and Warren everything that had happened since they parted at the tree hollow: their encounter with the Kobolds, the hatchery, and getting captured. Albert went into detail about hearing Umber calling him when he entered the colony. How his mark transferred itself into the egg when he touched it.

Albert and Lilious shared how they got captured by a goblin named Zornic and taken to the goblin boss,

Gruttlik. At the mention of Gruttlik's name, Warren snorted.

"Do you know him?" asked Albert.

"Know him?" said Warren. "I've been trying to get my hands on that sleaze for years. Somehow, he always manages to evade me. But that doesn't matter, continue."

Ashearah and Warren were both genuinely intrigued when Albert told them how he and Umber communicate. Everyone had always wondered how the Dragoons and their wyverns worked together. Since they have not been seen for hundreds of years, it had been a mystery.

"Albert, you should start honing the ability to communicate telepathically," suggested Ashearah. "It would make sense that once your minds are truly in sync, there would be no need for communication at all. More like one person, always knowing what the other is feeling, thinking, and what action to perform next."

When they were done with their tale, everyone agreed it was imperative that they rescue the wyvern colony when King Uthael was dealt with. Warren then suggested they all get some rest for the next day's events. Exhausted from getting very little sleep over the past few days, Albert welcomed one of the cots. He dropped all his gear on the floor, not caring where it landed, as he dragged his feet to the middle cot. Plopping down, he kicked off his boots and lay on his belly staring at the fire. Umber seized the opportunity, quickly jumped on Albert settling down comfortably between his legs. Luke and Lilious were not too far behind him, flopping down in the cots on either side of him. It wasn't long before the three of them were asleep.

Ashearah stood over Albert, looking down upon him, "If not for this young boy, who knows how long my people would continue to be prisoners to King Uthael? I do not know what power brought him here to our world, but I thank them."

"That is what has me worried," said Warren.

Ashearah looked questioningly at him.

"I feel a strange force is behind all of this," said Warren, concerned. "If it wasn't for Albert, we never would have found out about your people."

"So, why are you worried?"

"Something like this should have never happened to your people or the wyverns. World portals no longer function. So, if one was created to bring Albert to our world, there may be a danger we don't know about."

"But what is that danger?"

"That's what I intend to find out, and Albert seems to be the key."

"So, it would seem. Also, who is this Gerrick and what is he doing with wyvern eggs?"

Warren shook his head. "We should get some rest. We have a long day tomorrow. Dethroning a king and removing goblins from a mountain is no easy task."

Ashearah bid Warren goodnight and went to her daughter, whispering into her sleeping ear, "Sleep well, my daughter. I am so glad we are together once again." Lilious smiled, mumbling in her sleep. Ashearah then got into the cot next to her. Warren knelt between Albert and Luke, laying his hands on their shoulders, proud of all that they had accomplished. Umber sensing Warren's presence crawled over and nudged his hand. Warren smiled, scratching the pup under his chin.

"Get some sleep, my little friend," he said warmly. "We have a busy day tomorrow and we are going to need your help."

Umber nodded, curling into Albert's side. Warren stood looking over his companions, new and old. Excitement and gratitude filled him. The long-lost elves were finally going to be free to join the world once again and now there was a hope that the Dragoons might be reborn. Eager to see what the future brought he fell asleep in his cot, imagining how Nicolet would act when they arrived home with a wyvern in their midst.

Chapter 17: King Uthael

By midday everyone was awake, and a plan was in place. Albert, with Ashearah, Luke, and Lilious would enter through the palace's main entrance, while Elsin would sneak Warren and Umber in through one of the escape tunnels. Albert thought it best to send Umber with Warren so they could communicate telepathically. Albert figured this also allowed them to hide their knowledge of the wyvern imprisonment and of him being a Dragoon.

As they set out, Albert felt like he was part of a spy group planning some elaborate scheme, excitement flowed through him. Exiting Elyon's house, the two groups split heading on their planned paths. If everything went according to plan, there would be no fighting or bloodshed, that's if they didn't run into any trouble along the way.

Warren and Elsin headed into the forest. The rest of them headed toward the palace. The main road was strangely quiet, the usual traffic absent. The shops were closed as well, and no tradesmen were at their craft. Something was going on and it seemed the elvan people knew it. As they walked down the street and up the palace steps, Albert kept checking the windows of the houses and shops. No faces peeked out and every house seemed to be empty.

When they reached the palace, Ashearah opened the magnificent golden doors. Inside, the entire city seemed to be in attendance, filling the great hall. Most of the Ethosis people were on the upper balcony. Those on the main floor seated a few feet away from the throne were those that had attended the feast. King Uthael was on his throne with Malathis at his side. As they entered the palace, guards encircled them, taking them captive.

"Ahh, High Priestess Ashearah, you've finally decided to show yourself, have you?" said King Uthael, with a smile. "I sensed there was a plot to overthrow me. It saddens me to think you were the one behind it."

Ashearah stood silent.

"And it would seem you have beguiled our guests into aiding you," he continued. "What lies has she told you boys to gain your trust?"

"No lies," replied Luke.

"I see," sighed Uthael. "Then our hopes of being free were all for naught." He stood looking at his people. "It would seem the outside world isn't as free as we thought. Clearly, she has brought these two thieves into our kingdom attempting to ruin us."

The crowd booed and accused Ashearah of being a traitor.

"Tell us again, your Highness. How did you regain your youth?" Ashearah cried in a loud voice. "I, as do many of you here, remember an old and wise king at the end of his days. Then, suddenly, you were mysteriously young and healthy again. How did you do it?"

The crowd grew quiet as Uthael looked at her shrewdly, "I apparently need to educate you again on this matter. I knew of this impending darkness and used the power of the elves to renew myself."

"Yes, something no elvan has ever been able to do, though most would give everything they have to be able to do what you did," she replied, calmly. "Most of you are too young to remember when our friends the wyverns would play in our woods. It wasn't till our suddenly changed king tried to fend off this darkness, that they started disappearing."

"And you think I had something to do with that?" asked King Uthael, appalled.

"Yes," Ashearah responded.

Uthael barked at her claim, "What proof do you have?"

"I have sent my daughter, along with Albert and Luke, up into the Daratrine Mountains to investigate what has happened to our friends," she replied.

"Treason," came a voice from the crowd. Galthanis stepped out into the hall, "It is against our laws to venture into those mountains. Yet you sent not one but two human boys up there."

The crowd again burst into an outrage. King Uthael raised his hand, calling for silence.

"And, what did your two treacherous spies find up there?" he asked.

"It only became law to not venture into those mountains after this darkness had encircled our land," she said. "The boys found that goblins had imprisoned the wyverns of the Daratrine Mountains, by order of our king."

The crowd roared in anger, calling Ashearah a liar.

King Uthael raised his hand again, quieting them. "More false words from these heretics. Where is your proof?"

Ashearah stood silent. Except for Umber she had no proof and without him here she didn't know what to do.

"I have your proof right here," piped Luke, smugly. He stepped out past the guards into the hall a scroll in his hand.

Albert moved to his side confused. "What are you doing?"

"Don't worry, Al, I got this," he whispered. Loudly, Luke shouted, "I have here in my hand a letter signed by the king himself."

One of the guards grabbed the scroll out of his hand and opened it. As he looked over the letter his eyes widened; his mouth dropped. "The boy tells the truth. It is written in the king's handwriting and signed by the king himself."

The crowd began to murmur like a swarm of bees.

"What proof do they have that this has anything to do with goblins?" Galthanis asked.

The guard turned the scroll to the crowd. The words were written in a language Albert had never seen before.

"It is written in goblin," replied the guard.

Murmurs grew in intensity and spread through the crowd. King Uthael nervously moved back down onto his throne.

"I have heard enough of this," Malathis yelled, drawing his bow and pointing it at Ashearah. "Ashearah, you are a liar and a traitor. You have used these children to spread your propaganda to turn our people against their king. And for that, you will pay the price."

The pwang of a bowstring rang through the hall. Malathis screamed in pain, dropping his bow to the ground an arrow protruding through his forearm. Everyone turned to find Elsin standing in front of an open doorway, bow in hand. Quickly, some of the palace guards rushed towards him. Warren burst from the door behind Elsin, followed by Umber, quickly disarming the guards who had acted. More rushed over trying to swarm them. Umber leaped into the air, landing on one guard's head. He kicked off from him onto another, disorienting them as he went. This left easy targets for Warren and Elsin to disarm. Speedily, Umber flitted over to Albert's side.

Having Umber back relaxed Albert. He was sure that once the crowd had seen him, everyone would join their side. At the sight of a wyvern, the crowd gasped in awe. Ashearah excused herself from the guards, walking into the center of the room ahead of Albert and Luke.

"Many of you might be too young to remember a wyvern," she said calmly. "But here is your proof of our tale. King Uthael warned us that this evil was coming from outside our borders," she continued. "So, we put a magical seal around our forest in an effort to keep it out. For countless years, we believed it was working, only to find that when Albert and Luke arrived, King Uthael began changing his story."

Lilious said in a loud voice moving to her mother's side. "I have seen how the wyverns have been treated, battered, beaten and in chains!"

"Lili and I were even imprisoned there until Luke came and rescued us," Albert declared, Lilious blushing in embarrassment at the nickname he had given her.

The crowd turned on Uthael, demanding an explanation. The king looked around the room at his subjects. "What would you know of trying to protect this kingdom!" he said forcefully. "What would any of you know!"

His countenance and face had changed, transforming slightly demonic.

"You haven't protected us from anything!" said Ashearah. "You have merely made us prisoners in our own home."

King Uthael scoffed, "I did what I had to do."

"What you did was wrong. And you have betrayed our greatest allies and oldest friends," she sharply accused, pointing at Umber.

The crowd shouted, calling King Uthael the traitor and demanding his removal from the throne. Uthael looked around the room, a devilish smile on his face. As his eyes came to Albert and Umber his smile turned to anger. "I should have killed you myself when you entered my woods, instead of sending those pathetic Enokis after you," he hissed at Albert. "That is a mistake I will remedy this instant."

With inhuman speed, King Uthael leaped from the dais, running toward Albert. Warren ran to stop him, but the possessed king was too fast. Ashearah also rushed forward to intercept him, but a wave of King Uthael's hand sent her flying off to the side. Fear gripped Albert as he nervously tried to unsheathe his sword. Umber, feeling Albert's fear, bolted forward toward Uthael jumping in the air, head down like a ram.

As Umber and Uthael collided, a bright flash of light exploded between them. King Uthael was blasted backward and smashed into a column. He lay there motionless, groaning in pain. Recovered from the flash, Warren hurried over to the king and put an axe to his throat.

"Make no attempt to move, your Highness," he warned.

The crowd was silent. They sat motionless, waiting to see what would happen next.

"That was amazing," said Warren. "How did you two do it?"

Albert shrugged and looked at Umber who was just as surprised.

"Well, anyway, go help Ashearah," suggested Warren.

Nodding Albert and Umber along with Luke and Lilious rushed to Ashearah's aid. Helping her to her feet. Ashearah made her way to King Uthael. He lay still whimpering in pain. His face, strangely, both old and young.

"What's happening?" asked Luke.

"I don't know?" said Ashearah, confused.

Lilious noticed the pendant Uthael always wore around his neck was cracked and broken. "His pendant. It was fractured during the fight."

Ashearah reached for the pendant with one hand to examine it. As she touched the necklace, a dark, ice-cold presence emanated from it, burning her hand. Carefully, she took it off from around his neck using her sleeves to avoid its touch. She smashed it on the ground using all her strength. Immediately, the rest of Uthael's face began to age rapidly, returning to his former self.

"Ashearah is that you?" said Uthael, through dim eyes. He reached up with an old, wrinkled hand to touch her face. "How can this be? You are but a child. Not this beautiful woman I see before me."

Ashereah's eyes brimmed with tears, as she caressed his hand. "My King, I am not a little girl any more."

King Uthael looked at her confused.

"You have been under a spell for many years, Your Highness," she said to him softly.

Tears streamed down his face as he covered it in shame. Ashearah looked at her, newly freed, noble king with both tears of joy and sadness. She was glad that he was finally once again himself and free of the curse. She stood and turned to Elsin.

"Take the king to his bed chamber and send your best men to meet me at the stables."

"Yes, High Priestess," he replied, with a salute. "Calfuray and her squad will meet you there." He signaled for two of the palace guards to help King Uthael out a door behind the throne.

"Good," she said, turning to Warren. "We need to get to the mountain quickly."

"Right," said Warren, excited. He put his hands on Albert and Luke's shoulders. "Do you think you are ready to fight goblins?" he asked with a smile.

Albert looked up at him nervously while Luke shot him a grin, twirling his daggers. "I can't wait."

"High Priestess," Galthanis interrupted. "What is going on? What about King Uthael and the kingdom?"

Ashearah looked at the crowd of worried and confused elves. "My people, our king is again ours and free of the curse that has kept him and us trapped for these many years. But alas, he has not the strength to lead us now and I must travel to the Daratrine Mountains to force out the goblins who have taken up residency there. Galthanis, Elyon, and the other council members will lead until I get back."

The crowd clapped and cheered in response. Galthanis bowed in thanks to Ashearah, then joined Elyon and the other council members. Her strength recovered, Ashearah led Albert and the rest of his companions out of the palace, heading for the stables.

Chapter 18: Ambush

Ashearah led the group through the city toward the stables. A little outside of the city, a small metal ball sailed through the air, landing at Ashearah's feet. Warren immediately recognized it as a grenade and kicked it hard into the air away from them.

"Take cover!" he shouted turning his back in the direction in which he kicked the weapon.

Everyone turned to shield themselves. The ball was on its descent when it exploded, sending fire, smoke, and shrapnel through the air. Tiny bits of debris pelted them, searing their skin and clothes where it landed. Seconds later, numerous goblins jumped out from behind trees, weapons drawn, rushing towards them.

"Luke, Albert, Umber, to me," Warren ordered drawing both his one-handed war axes.

Albert and Luke quickly rushed to Warren's side drawing their weapons as they moved with Umber close behind. Ashearah and Lilious were already back-to-back, swords drawn, ready for battle. Goblins swarmed them from all sides, leaving no way to escape. Warren moved quickly to dispatch the foe in front of him, then maneuvered in front of Albert or Luke, trying to keep multiple goblins from them. Luke took every chance he got to step out from around his father to join the ruckus. Albert and Umber, stayed back, trying to protect Warren's flank.

Albert had just fended off a goblin when he noticed that Warren and Luke had moved away from him. Albert and Umber were now on their own with three goblins heading their way. A lump formed in Albert's throat as fear began to overtake him. Never having faced more than one opponent before, he was beginning to panic. Sensing his fear, Umber jumped in front of him, roaring as loud as he could at the goblins. Unsure of what was happening, the goblins stopped, confused. Seeing Umber challenge the three goblins, reminded Albert he wasn't alone. With new confidence, Albert rushed forward, sword ready.

Reaching the first, Albert brought his sword down hard against his first opponent. The goblin moved to block but wasn't quick enough and Albert hit his sword away. Before he could strike again, one of the other goblins slashed at Albert, forcing him to dodge away. Umber was quick to take Albert's place though, leaping up onto his first opponent and sinking his teeth into the goblin's shoulder, before leaping away. The goblin howled in pain before dropping back retreating from the fight.

Recovering quickly, Albert pressed the attack on the second goblin while Umber leaped after the third. Fighting one-on-one was much easier, he soon had the upper hand, forcing his opponent backward. Fear almost overcame him when out the corner of his eye he saw Umber get slashed by his opponent's sword. He wanted to run to his wyvern's side, but Umber's tough dragon hide had protected him. The sword merely scraped against his scales causing no harm. Umber got to his feet and lunged for the goblin's leg, biting down hard into the calf.

Relieved Umber was safe, Albert returned to his attack. A few perfectly-timed strikes of his sword left the goblin wounded in multiple places, forcing him to limp away. Albert hurried to Umber who was still clamped down hard onto the last goblin's leg. The goblin, grunting in pain, was too busy trying to pull Umber from his leg to see Albert barreling toward him. Albert lowered his shoulder, preparing to plow into the Goblin's side. As Albert was about to make contact, Umber let go. Albert and the goblin went tumbling to the ground. Albert jumped to his feet, ready to strike.

The goblin got to his feet. "That's it. I'm done," choked the goblin. "They ain't payin' me enough for this," he said as he hobbled off into the forest.

Soon the rest of the goblins began fleeing into the forest themselves. The battle had been won just in time for the city guard to appear.

"Tend to the wounded," commanded Ashearah. "And when you have rounded up the rest, throw them all in the dungeon till my return." The guards saluted and set off, leaving Albert and his group to continue.

The stable was the only building in the city not constructed from a tree. It had a large pitched green wooden tile roof with ornate swooping eves. The barn doors opened to a main aisle with stalls housing hippogriffs. Upon seeing the animals, Warren stopped, looking nervous.

"Is everything all right?" Ashearah asked concerned.

"Uhh... yeah," Warren responded. "I uhhh... just thought when you said stable, we would be riding horses."

"Horses would take too long," She replied. "Hippogriffs will be much faster."

"I uhh... just don't trust animals that are half one thing and half another."

Luke chuckled to himself, Albert and Lilious both wondered what was so funny.

"Dad is afraid of flying," he whispered to them.

Albert was shocked to hear that a man who ran headlong into battle against multiple foes was afraid of a small thing like flying. Lilious stifled a laugh, finding it a bit funny herself. Warren looked at them suspiciously. Luke and Lilious tried to control their giggling while Albert tried not to look surprised.

Hearing voices, an old, grey-haired elvan exited his office to meet them. His long ears pointed straight back instead of upwards, and he walked slightly hunched over, using a cane to assist him. Seeing Ashearah, his eyes lit up, his pace quickening to meet her.

"Ashearah, my dear, it is so great to see you."

"Uncle Baltheo! It is good to see you," she smiled.

"Hello, Uncle Baltheo," Lilious chimed in.

"My, my," said Baltheo straining his eyes to look at Lilious. "Lilious, my dear, you are more beautiful each time I see you." Baltheo turned his attention back to Ashearah. "My dear niece, is it true what I am hearing? Have you really been branded a traitor?"

Ashearah shook her head. "No, my dear uncle. I have not."

"Oh, that is good to hear. You never can believe rumors, can you? Now, Ashearah, what can I do for you?"

"I'm here because we need ten hippogriffs saddled and ready."

Baltheo looked at them confused, "But I only see five here and a giant lizard creature."

Umber snorted at him, offended.

"Uncle, Umber is a wyvern, and we have five other people on their way."

"Oh, is it now?" he said looking at Umber. "It's been a while since I've seen one." Baltheo leaned down and scratched Umber on his head. "Guess I forgot what they looked like. Well, he's a good-looking lizard, isn't he?"

Umber snorted again at being called a lizard.

"All right, my dear, give me a few minutes and I'll have those hippogriffs saddled and ready."

Albert and Luke laughed in disbelief that Baltheo could do anything in a few minutes, let alone saddle ten hippogriffs. Baltheo whistled, and three teenage stable hands appeared standing at attention. Albert and Luke both turned embarrassed. Baltheo kindly gave them their orders to saddle the hippogriffs. The three nodded and scurried off to accomplish their task.

"Um, Ashearah?" Albert said trying to get her attention.

"Yes, Albert?" she responded politely.

"When you picked up Luke and me from the balcony, you used a griffon," he paused. "Why are we now riding hippogriffs?"

Ashearah smiled, "I used a griffon to sneak you out of the palace, because they are better suited for stealth. Hippogriffs however are much faster fliers, and we have little time."

"Oh, can I still ride one?" Albert asked innocently.

"We'll just stick to hippogriffs, maybe you can ride one after all this is over."

Albert sighed, smiled, and nodded his head.

While the stable hands got everything ready, Ashearah and Lilious conversed with Baltheo, catching up on their lives. Warren looked at the hippogriffs uneasy. Albert, Luke, and Umber climbed up one of the stall doors to look at the hippogriff inside. The front half of the creature was an eagle with head and neck feathers that were black, brown, and gold. Its torso and wing feathers were tan and red. The back half was that of a bay horse with shiny brown hair that was white just above the hooves, its tail a dark black that faded into a light brown. When the hippogriff saw Umber, it screeched, raising its neck feathers and plumage.

"I don't think it likes you, Umber," Luke said.

Umber climbed onto the rail of the door and stood up on his hind legs staring into the hippogriff's eyes. The two stared at each other for several seconds, neither breaking eye contact. A few times the hippogriff tried to peck Umber, but he quickly leaped into the air to dodge its attempts and pecked it on the head instead. Finally, the hippogriff submitted, lowering its head and eyes. Pleased, Umber jumped into the stall with the hippogriff, nestling himself into its neck feathers. The creature twisted its neck back playfully, nipping at Umber.

"Mr. Baltheo?" said Albert.

Baltheo looked over from his conversation. "Yes, my dear boy?"

"Can I ride this one?" he asked.

Baltheo slowly walked over to the stall and looked in.

"Looks like Adalhard has a new friend," he said with a smile. "Are you sure want to ride this one? He's good in a fight but not the fastest, and he's stubborn to boot."

"I'm sure," smiled Albert.

"Yeah, Umber will keep it in line," laughed Luke.

Baltheo nodded, calling over one of the stable hands to get Adalhard ready to go. A couple more minutes and all the hippogriffs were saddled. Calfuray and her men arrived just after the hippogriffs had been walked outside awaiting their riders.

Now that they were all gathered, Warren, Ashearah, and Calfuray began planning. They had Albert, Luke and Lilious describe to them the layout of the Wyvern Colony and roughly how long it would take to get from room to room. Once they understood the layout, their plan starting forming. Luke would lead Calfuray, along with two of her men, in through the secret entrance. From there, he would take them down to the hatchery and any other place where wyverns were being kept prisoners. They would then make their way up to the main city.

While they were freeing the wyverns, the rest of them would wait several minutes before dropping down into the goblin city from above. The two archers would find a perch to shoot arrows at the goblins while the rest would attack them from the ground. They hoped to surprise them on two fronts to keep the goblins distracted.

"Can I suggest something?" Albert interjected.

"Of course, Albert, what is it?" Ashearah said kindly.

"Since Umber and I are linked or whatever, why doesn't he go with Luke to rescue the wyverns? That way I can know what's going on."

"That's a brilliant idea, Albert," said Warren. "That way we can also know if they run into trouble. Then we can provide a distraction sooner rather than later."

"All right then, Umber will go with Luke and Calfuray," Ashearah said pleased.

Now that the plan was ready, everyone began mounting their hippogriffs, except Albert. He had never gotten up on a horse by himself in his life let alone a hippogriff. He attempted to climb on top of Adalhard but failed. Lilious, saw Albert struggle and delicately walked over to him and asked if he needed help.

Albert blushed. "Yes, please," he whispered.

"Okay, Albert. First, you will want to grab the horn," she instructed. "Since you are on the left side, you will want to take your left foot and put it in the stirrup. Now just swing your right leg over as you pull yourself up onto the saddle."

It took him a couple of tries, but he got up on the saddle and smiled down at her.

"See," said Lilious smiling back. "That wasn't so hard."

"Nope. Thanks, now what do I do."

"Okay grab the reins, but don't pull on them. Just hold them firm in your hands but leave some slack."

Albert did as she said.

"Okay, good. Now, when we take off, don't worry about kicking him to go. He will follow everyone's lead. Just brace yourself and hold on with your feet not your knees, or else he will kick. Got it?"

Albert nodded nervously. Believing he would be fine Lilious got back up on her hippogriff. Umber hopped his way up onto Albert's lap wedging himself in.

"Umber, aren't you going to fly?" asked Warren.

Umber looked away.

"He doesn't yet know how to fly properly," Albert said. "He's only done it once and it wasn't the greatest performance."

Warren trotted his hippogriff over to Albert and Umber, "Of course he can fly. He just needs a few more tries is all."

Inspired by Warren's confidence, Umber jumped down from Adalhard. Determinedly, he ran at full speed, then jumped into the air and began flapping his wings rapidly. He twisted and turned in the air before falling back to the ground. He attempted to fly again and again.

"Umber," Ashearah called, getting his attention.

He looked over at her.

"Like this," she heeled her hippogriff into a gallop. The creature got up to speed, and spread its wings, angling them upward. In one fluid motion, the hippogriff pushed off the ground while flapping its enormous wings, taking flight. Ashearah soared high into the sky before circling back down for a landing.

Umber was excited to try again. He galloped at full speed and, like the hippogriff, spread his wings, angling upward. Then, with almost one fluid motion, Umber pushed off from the ground flapping his wings as hard as he could. Shakily, he glided along a few feet above the ground, almost crashing a few times. With courage, he pulled his head up, flapping his wings harder. Slowly he rose into the air. He was soon above the tree line, circling the party below.

After a couple more passes, he descended, landing in the middle of the group. Everyone clapped and cheered him on. Feeling more confident, he practiced a few more leaps into the air and circled just above their heads.

Now that everyone was mounted and Umber was capable of flying, Ashearah ordered the group into formation and kicked her hippogriff off into the air. One by one everyone followed her lead. When it came to be Albert's turn he did as Lilious had told him, bracing himself and tightening up his grip on Adalhard with his feet. Following the other hippogriffs, Adalhard galloped a few paces, spread his wings, and leaped hard, jumping into the air while flapping his wings. Albert was jostled a little during the takeoff, but once in the air, everything was fine, and the amazing sensation of flying came back to him.

Ashearah was right, the trip to the mountain was much quicker flying. Albert watched as the trees rushed underneath him. The rich, thick Ethanan forest soon thinned, uncovering the rocky rugged terrain of the Daratrine Mountains. He could see the tip of a fortress tower peeking its way out of the mountain, recognizing it as Lanoran Fortress. What had taken them hours to walk only took them minutes on a hippogriff.

When they reached the cave with the secret entrance, Luke, Umber and Calfuray broke off from the group, landing near the cave. The other group's flight to the cavern opening only took another minute more. Albert could see the opening fifty yards away when Ashearah quickly descended, the rest of them following her. As soon as they landed, Warren and Ashearah slid from their mounts effortlessly, each of them running off in different direction to scout out the area. Albert, Lilious and the Calfuray's men waited where they had landed until they returned.

Several minutes later, Ashearah returned. Warren reappeared seconds after her.

"I tied up a guard who was asleep," she informed them.

"I got two," Warren said. "They were playing some sort of game."

"Some watchmen," one of Calfuray's men replied, rolling his eyes.

"Indeed. They will not be bothering us," Ashearah laughed.

They moved to the ridge of the cavern opening above the city and waited in silence. Albert sat on top of Adalhard, concentrated on what Umber was seeing.

Luke, Umber, and Calfuray, along with her two men snuck silently into the goblin's storage room. Calfuray moved to peer out the door leading into the colony. Through the crack in the door, she could see someone coming their way. Lining themselves up against the wall they waited silently as two goblins walked into the room. One of the elves pushed the door closed behind them. The goblins turned to see three elves and a young human with weapons pointed at them.

Both goblins threw their hands in the air. "We don't want any trouble. We'll go quietly," said one of the goblins.

Eyeing some rope hanging from the wall, Calfuray ordered one of her men to bind them. After they were bound, she nodded her head to the soldier who gave both goblins a swift blow to the back of the head with the hilt of his sword.

"Goblins are slippery creatures," she said to Luke. "I figure it's best if they are bound and knocked out. We don't want them getting free and warning everyone."

Luke shrugged. "Hey, you don't have to explain yourself to me. I don't care what you do with a couple of goblins." He cracked open the door to peek out finding the balcony area vacant. "Okay, we can go."

He led them down the hall, he, Albert, and Lilious has previously used to reach the hatchery. Two goblins now guarded the door, he was surprised they had decided to beef up security. Excited to finally be able to use his throwing knives, Luke lodged a knife in each of the goblin's thighs. Before the guards could even cry out in pain, Calfuray and one of her men bolted over, knocking them out.

"Well done, young Luke," Calfuray whispered.

"Thanks," he whispered back with a smile. "I practice at home all the time."

Inside the hatchery, seven more goblins stood guard. Five of the guards drew swords and charged them while the other two notched arrows to their bows ready to fire. Luke, Calfuray, and her men tried to keep in constant motion as they fought, so as to not be a sitting target. Umber jumped around trying to land on the goblin that came running toward him. One elf stood still for too long, giving a goblin archer a clear shot. Just as he let loose his arrow, one of the chained wyverns stood on its hind legs in its path. The arrow splintered off the wyvern's hide. Angrily the goblin notched another arrow and let it fly. Again, another wyvern moved in front of the arrow's path. One of the old wyverns close to an archer crouched down ready to spew flames. Unfortunately, the only thing that came out was a big puff of black smoke.

The goblin laughed. "You almost gave me a scare there you old salamander."

Mad from the goblin's taunt, the wyvern sucked in another huge breath trying one more time. Sparks flew from its mouth, dousing the goblin in embers. The goblin danced around trying to brush off them before they burned further into his clothing. Turning around, worry began to build up as he saw a fire burning in the old wyvern's dim eyes. As the wyvern took another breath, the goblin quickly shot off an arrow, trying to stop him. The arrow bounced off as flames spewed forth out of its mouth. Jumping out of the way, the archer barely missed getting scorched alive. Taking the cue, the rest of the wyverns had their try at breathing fire. Soon, flame spouts shot everywhere in the back of the hatchery, as one dragon after another tried to hit their goblin targets.

A random flame spurt nearly hit Luke. He yelled loudly, "Whoa!" Everyone turned in the direction of the wyverns, ready to jump out of the way just in case. With the goblins in the back crouched together shouting in surrender, the flame spouts stopped. Luke, Calfuray, her men and the goblins stood in silence, afraid if anyone made a sound, the old half-blind wyverns would turn them into a matchstick. Umber jumped on top one of the tables coming to his fellow wyvern. The two touched horns conversing by a series of chirps and barks.

Slowly, one of the goblins tried to move toward the door. A wyvern turned toward him mouth open a stream of flames bellowing up out of its throat. The goblin ducked throwing his arms overs his head for protection.

"I wonder," said Luke, as he slowly moved away from the goblin near him. He breathed a sigh of relief when none of the wyverns reacted. Another goblin moved. Again, the closest wyvern hunched down ready to unleash a bolt of fire. Luke walked over to Umber tapping him on the back.

"Are we good, Wyvie?" he asked.

Umber turned with a smile, his entire body bobbing up and down, yes.

Calfuray turned to the nearest goblin. "Who bears the keys to these wyverns' chains?"

"Why would we tell you?" the goblin said defiantly.

"Because if you don't, we will let them turn you to cinders," she said.

"I have them right here," said another goblin, eagerly holding the keys up in the air.

"Luke, would you mind?" Calfuray asked politely.

"Don't mind if I do," said Luke confidently. Moving over to the goblin he grabbed the keys and then went around the room unlocking the wyverns' collars. The wyverns free, the goblins were ushered to a corner with the wyverns set to watch over them.

"Don't worry, filth. After we have freed the rest of our friends and dealt with your ilk, we will be back to deal with you," Calfuray snarled as she turned to head to the door.

"Wait," complained a goblin. "You aren't going to just leave us here with these ember belchers, are you?"

"I wouldn't be worried," laughed Luke. "You only imprisoned them, tortured them, and cut off their wings. Why would they want to hurt you?" he said as he shut the door.

The rescuers continued to sneak through the halls, Luke leading them down paths he found unused from his last visit. The elves marveled at the once glorious mosaics that lined the now dilapidated walls. Saddened at the state of the wyverns and their home, Calfuray and her men cursed the goblins that had let the sacred halls turn to ruin. They were near the rookery when Luke stopped them. They ducked into a nearby tunnel.

"Okay," he said. "This path will put us out right in the rookery."

"Good," said Calfuray.

"It's kind of a tight squeeze even for me though," he warned.

The two elvan soldiers looked at each other worried.

"We'll manage," Calfuray assured him. "We need to hurry. I'm sure Ashearah and the others are anxious to attack by now."

"Let's go then," said Luke. "You ready to go free the rest of your kind, Umber?"

Umber looked up at him giving him a serious nod.

The tunnel was in serious disrepair. They climbed over large boulders that had fallen from the ceiling. Some parts of the tunnel had caved in almost entirely, forcing them to crawl. Very little light led them on their way, causing them to move slowly, the air dusty and hard to breathe. Soon, light could be seen in front of them. As the light grew brighter, the tunnel kept getting narrower and narrower. Calfuray's men eventually had to remove their armor to proceed.

By the time they made it to the end of the tunnel, they were forced to crawl on their bellies inch by agonizing inch. Calfuray and her men were beginning to realize that Luke wasn't kidding when he said it was going to be a tight squeeze. They let out a sigh of relief when he announced they were at the end.

"Okay, here is where it gets tricky," Luke said. "As soon as we exit, everyone will know, so we have to be quick."

Calfuray and her men nodded that they were ready. Luke waited until the guard moved past, then made his move. Speedily, he pulled himself out of the hole, dropping to the ground, followed by Umber. The two moved fast to take out the guard who had just passed by. Not long after, Calfuray and her men were out of the hole. Without anywhere to hide, they had to find out fast how to free the wyverns, hoping for their aid.

The rookery was carved into a gigantic multi-tiered cavern. Each tier was supported by beautiful columns with dragons of all different types carved into them. Arched doorways ran along the walls, leading into homes that were blocked by iron gates. Levers controlling the gates were stuck to the wall every several feet. Ramps allowed access to the different levels of the rookery.

It didn't take long for them to get noticed. Dozens of goblins armed from head to toe ran to them, demanding they stop. Luke, Umber, and their group pressed onward, pulling the levers as they went to open the gates. It wasn't long till they were surrounded and forced to fight. Luke and Umber worked together taking down one goblin after another while Calfuray and her men quickly dealt with those that were behind them. Realizing they were losing the fight; a goblin took off running for a red button on the wall.

"Luke!" shouted Calfuray. "He is going to warn them!"

Luke looked to see the guard nearing the button. Quickly he pulled out a throwing knife, flinging it through the air. The goblin was too far away for his aim and his knife hit the button instead. Bells began to clang all throughout the rookery, continuing out into the whole colony.

Luke moaned aloud in disappointment.

"Don't worry, Luke." Calfuray tried to comfort him. "It's up to Ashearah and Warren now. Let's just hope they cause enough confusion so that we don't get outnumbered."

Luckily for them, the goblins weren't the only ones alerted to the noise. One by one, the caged wyverns began coming out of their cells.

Chapter 19: Gruttlik's Weapon

"Great," burst Albert.

"What?" asked Warren, anxiously interrupting.

"Someone sounded an alarm," he replied.

"That's our cue," Ashearah said, spurring her hippogriff into a gallop, plummeting into the opening.

Albert and the others followed her over the edge and down into the cavern. They dove down toward the city below, the cold air rushing past them. As they drew near, the two archers broke away, finding a ledge from which to launch their arrows. Pulling up hard, they landed in the middle of the goblin city. On the ground, goblins scurried, grabbing weapons to answer the call to arms. Warren, Ashearah and Lilious dismounted within seconds of landing, drew their weapons, ready to attack.

Their plan was working. Confused, the goblins didn't know where the danger was. Some merely screamed in fright and ran back to their homes. Albert's usual paralyzing fear had vanished. His decision to dismount came too late for Adalhard though. The bird turned its head, grabbed him by the shirt, and pulled him to the ground hard before he could join the fight.

Lilious laughed shaking her head helping Albert to his feet, "Baltheo told you he was more of fighter than a flier."

"Yeah, yeah," replied Albert, drawing his sword.

Fighting goblins was a lot like sparring with Luke. The difficult part was, there were a lot more of them. He was glad Warren had concentrated on parrying and disarming in their instructions. It was all he could do against the horde of goblins attacking him. Luckily, he had three skilled warriors at his side who had no problem fighting multiple enemies at once.

Every chance he got to take a breath, he watched Warren moving swiftly through enemies, every step and swing perfectly timed and placed. With every swing of an axe, a goblin was either disarmed or knocked unconscious. Ashearah and Lilious, each armed with a sword and a buckler fought in unison, their movements mirroring each other. Albert could tell they had been training for years together. Their combination of sword strikes, and spells intertwined perfectly with each other.

He was so mesmerized by their fighting that he did not notice the goblin about to smash him in the head with a hammer. Fear gripped him as he tried to lift his sword to defend himself but knew he could not do it in time. The goblin's face grimaced as it suddenly slumped to the floor, an arrow in its back. Albert looked to see an elf shaking his head in dismay before aiming for another goblin.

Albert felt stupid. He needed to stop admiring his friends and concentrate on his own battles. Taking a deep breath to clear his mind, he moved close to Adalhard. The goblins were trying to keep their distance from the hippogriff. Staying close to him meant safety. The goblins in the city weren't nearly as difficult to fight as the ones that had ambushed them. Most were common workers wearing clothes, rather than armor. They used whatever weapon was closest to them at the time. Most were sloppy and unskilled, giving up quickly and retreating.

Confidence growing, he inched away from the group. With each skirmish he got into, his skill with the sword was improving. He also could now recognize the best times to take advantage of an opponent's mistake.

One goblin overswung. Albert used this as an opportunity to spin the goblin around, kick him from behind and send him head over heels. Another, thrust his sword toward him at the wrong moment, allowing Albert to grab his arm to pull the goblin forward. As it fell forward, Albert brought his knee up into the goblin's stomach. The little green man slumped over unable to get back up. With every opponent defeated Albert felt more confident. As more goblins fell, their comrades began to flee in fear. Glad that the battle would soon be over, Albert pulled back close to Ashearah and Lilious.

"Well they are fleeing as you predicted," Ashearah noted.

"I told you they would. Now let's go deal with Gruttlik," Warren said, scornfully.

"Yes, but first, I would like an update on our other party," said Ashearah, concerned.

Albert concentrated on what Umber was seeing. "They are all right," he said, thankfully. "It seems we were able to stop a lot of reinforcements from reaching them. They are headed this way now, with forces of their own."

"Good," said Warren, pleased, heading toward Gruttlik's house.

"Stay up there and cover us," shouted Ashearah, to the two archers.

The group walked up the steps of the house and opened the door. No guards attacked them. Cautiously, they continued. Warren laughed in disgust at the pictures of Gruttlik on the wall. Opening the doors to the main chamber, they found the goblin sitting on his throne. To one side of the throne was a caged wyvern. Albert immediately recognized it as the same wyvern who marked him when he first got to Thu'hilen.

Seeing Warren walk into the room, Gruttlik jumped out of his chair, a grin on his face.

"Warren, you... you old scoundrel you." He slapped his knee. "I should have known it would be you trashing up my city. And it looks like you've got my escapees with you."

"Well you know, Gruttlik, once I heard you were in town, I just had to come pay you a visit," Warren replied, taking a step forward.

Gruttlik held up a hand. "That's far enough, Warren." He clicked his fingers together. Up above on each side of the chamber, the walls fell away to reveal six multibarreled guns pointed right at them.

Albert and the others stood afraid of what was going to happen next.

"How do you like my latest creations?" Gruttlik chortled. "I call them my motor-powered revolving multibarreled boomsticks. Oh yeah, they fire hundreds of rounds a minute."

"You made machine guns," Albert replied, flatly.

Gruttlik looked at him. "Machine gun? I like the sound of that. Thanks, kid, I'll take that as my own. So, do you have any last words?"

"Do you know any protection spells?" Warren whispered to Ashearah.

"Not any powerful enough," she whispered back. "You?"

"Sorry, Bernard and I haven't gotten that far yet," he replied.

"Guys, don't worry," Albert whispered back.

Ashearah looked at him confused.

"What do you mean, don't worry? Those things are going to tear us apart," cried Lilious.

"We just have to buy a little more time," replied Albert. He turned to speak loudly, "What are you and this Gerrick doing with all those wyvern eggs?" he asked Gruttlik.

"Albert, what are you doing?" whispered Warren.

"Buying us some time," Albert responded.

"Why do you want to know?" Gruttlik replied.

"Because, I happen to be a Dragoon and it's my business to know," Albert replied.

"A Dragoon?" Gruttlik laughed. "You ain't no Dragoon. Where's your wyvern?"

"Oh, he's around here somewhere," said Albert, coolly.

"Yeah, sure," replied Gruttlik, rolling his eyes. "There ain't been no Dragoons for hundreds of years."

"I am too a Dragoon. You saw me holding my wyvern when you captured me."

"That don't prove anything. I'm tired of this. Warren, our little battles were fun, but... I have to kill you now," said Gruttlik, a little disappointed. "Boys! Show them what you got." He smirked.

Everyone, except Albert, quickly searched for cover. Albert stood, arms folded, looking around as if he were bored.

"Uhh, boys. I said fire," yelled Gruttlik, annoyed. When the guns still didn't go off Gruttlik yelled louder at his men in rage. "*Fire!*" Frustrated, he looked up to see a dozen wyverns staring back down at him, mouths filled with flame and smoke poised to spit fire at any moment. Gruttlik backed up to his throne and grabbed the cage with the wyvern in it.

"Back off," he spat. "None of you is willing to hurt your dear King Sunchaser, are you?"

The wyvern cage however, swung freely in his hands. Gruttlik looked down to see it empty. Sunchaser was missing. Dropping the cage, he nervously backed up to his throne.

"Give it up, Gruttlik," Warren demanded. "You have nowhere to go."

"You know, Warren, as much as I love our little back and forths, I should be going," he said, pushing a button on his chair that collapsed the seat.

Warren leapt forward dropping his one-handed axes and sliding out his two-handed battle-ax. His swing barely missing Gruttlik's head as he fell into the escape hatch. Warren growled in anger.

"I almost had him, that little weasel."

Ashearah put a hand on his arm trying to calm him. "My friend, it is all right. The battle is won. We have freed the wyverns."

"You are right," he said, taking a deep breath. "By the way, how did that wyvern escape from his cage?" asked Warren, confused.

"You didn't see?" Albert laughed. "I guess you all were too distracted trying to find a place to hide. Luke snuck in and freed Sunchaser when no one was looking."

Luke strutted into the room, Umber beside him. "Did someone say my name? You should have seen the looks on your faces when he ordered them to fire on you," he laughed.

"Did you know about this all along, Albert?" asked Warren, surprised.

"Yes Sir," he said with a big grin.

"We were about to come storming through the door behind you," began Luke, jumping in. "But suddenly Wyvie here went crazy, trying to find another way in. He must have seen those big cannons through Albert. We figured something must be wrong. It didn't take us long to find out. At the first corner we rounded, we heard Albert's voice echoing down a stairwell. We headed up finding that upper balcony. It only took seconds to take care of the goblins manning the cannons. I looked down into the room and eyed the caged wyvern. I figured whoever was in that cage must be important, so I snuck down and used the distraction of the guns not firing to free him."

Warren smacked his son on the back, proud of his craftiness. Umber, excited to be reunited with Albert, leaped onto his shoulder perching there. The wyverns, along with Calfuray and her men, filled the room rejoicing in their hard-fought victory. Everyone made room as Sunchaser walked to Albert and his friends.

"By the way, where is Gruttlik?" Luke asked.

"Ah, the weasel escaped through some sort of secret hatch in his chair," Warren replied.

"I think I know where he is going," Luke responded, rushing for the front door. "Come on. If we hurry, we might be able to catch him."

"Sweet," cheered Albert. "Let's go, Umber," he said as he chased after Luke.

"Wait, you two," Warren yelled after them.

Ashearah put her hand on his shoulder, "Go, my friend. We will take care of things here."

Nodding, Warren ran after Luke, Albert, and Umber.

Chapter 20: Gerrick

They headed for a tunnel to the right of the house. After jogging for several minutes down a freshly carved hallway, they entered the room where the eggs were kept for transporting. The staging room looked different from the rest of the colony. Recently dug, there were no carvings or engravings on its walls.

"Where is everything?" Luke wondered, finding the room empty.

"There," pointed Warren, to a tunnel leading out the back of the room. "Let's see where that takes us."

Slowly they walked, weapons drawn, ready for an ambush. Albert, Luke, and Umber followed close behind, prepared for anything. They followed the dimly lit tunnel farther and farther into the mountain. Eventually, it began opening into another large room with the back blown out, open to the outside. Even from where they were standing, they could see a ship floated on the ocean just offshore in the distance.

"Now we know how they were getting the eggs out of the mountain without anyone knowing!" said Warren. Several wagons carrying large crates being pulled by mules were making their way to the shore. Gruttlik and a hooded man in a dark cloak with rune symbols covering it stood in the middle of the room conversing.

"I bet that is Gerrick," said Albert, pointing at the strange man.

"Gerrick!" Warren shouted.

The cloaked man and Gruttlik looked up. Gerrick's skin was a light red with what looked like small scales in places. His hair was a deeper red. Bronze eyes peered at them curious to who had interrupted their work.

"I order you to surrender and relinquish those wyvern eggs back to their rightful owners," Warren demanded. His shouting had alerted several goblins, who were now rallying around Gerrick.

"Continue moving the cargo to the ship," ordered Gerrick, calmly. "I will deal with this."

"Pardon me, my Lord, but the tales of Warren don't do him justice. I'm afraid you are going to need us," said Gruttlik, stopping his men from leaving.

Gerrick's eyes flashed with excitement at hearing Warren's name. "Ah, so you are Warren? It is a pleasure to meet you. My associate here talks of you incessantly. Sadly, after today, your righteous do-gooder days will be over."

"Any associate of Gruttlik is an enemy of the king," Warren replied, with authority.

"Yes, well, King Altraeus has many enemies, inside and outside of his court," Gerrick continued to smirk. "And plenty of them would love to see you dead."

"What are you doing with those eggs and why did you bring me here?" burst Albert before Warren could reply.

"Ahh, so you must be Albert, Thu'hilen's newest Dragoon," said Gerrick, pleased. "You and I have a great destiny, boy. Come with me. Together we will save this world and bring about a peace that shall reign indefinitely." He held out his hand, urging Albert to join him.

Albert stood confused. Wasn't Gerrick supposed to be the bad guy? I mean, he and King Uthael did enslave the wyverns and trick the elves into being prisoners in their own city. How was Gerrick going to save the world and bring about peace? Why did he need him, Albert, to do it?

Warren stepped in front of Albert, shielding him. "Enough of this," he demanded. "I don't know what game you are playing, but I will not allow you to try and trick Albert, pretending to be his friend with some fictitious destiny you share. Surrender now or your neck meets my axe."

Gerrick laughed. "You will see soon enough. Soon a great evil that sleeps in the depths of our world will be freed. This boy and myself are the only ones that can stop it. And if the boy won't come with me willingly, then I shall have to take him by force." Gerrick raised his hands and pointed them toward Warren in a claw like manner.

"Get behind me!" Warren shouted.

Everyone ducked behind Warren as lightning bolts shot forth out of Gerrick's hands. The bolts streaked towards Warren as he swung his war axes in an upward-arcing motion, the bolts of lightning deflected off his blades striking the ceiling above him. Pieces of rubble burst out from where the lightning hit, forcing Albert, Luke, and Umber to cover their heads. Warren stood unphased as pieces of ceiling pounced off his armor. Gerrick's smirk turned into sneer when he saw Warren standing untouched.

"You've come prepared, I see," Gerrick said, irritated.

"I've spent my entire life in battles and wars," Warren said. "You thought I wouldn't?"

Gerrick tilted his head toward Gruttlik. "I'll deal with the brute. Bring me Albert and the wyvern alive. Kill the other brat."

Warren stood ready, "Don't let Gruttlik fool you, boys. He is a better fighter than you would think. Take out his guards first, then focus on him. They are going to try and separate you. Don't let them. Take them down together. I won't be there to help you on this one. Don't be scared. You two can do this. Albert, follow Luke's orders, and Luke, trust yourself. You know what you're doing. Umber, take care of them."

Albert and Luke nervously nodded their heads. Getting out of the way, Albert and Umber followed Luke as he suggested they head close to the wall.

With the whisper of magic, two swords appeared in Gerrick's hands. Rushing forward, Gerrick began his attack on Warren. Warren calmly and coolly evaded, dodged and deflected Gerrick's attacks. Frustrated, Gerrick began casting small spells making it harder for Warren to fight. Warren began finding it difficult to counter Gerrick's assault. He was being forced to deflect away small streaks of lighting or fire and tiny gusts of wind that cut like a razor's edge.

After receiving several small gashes and wounds from Gerrick's spells Warren realized he was going to have to put everything he had into this fight. He deflected a slash upward, which led into a thrust he deflected to the side. This left Gerrick open, giving Warren the opportunity for a head-butt. Gerrick stepped backwards dazed. He tried to recover but wasn't quick enough. Warren was on the assault unleashing, blow after blow. It was all Gerrick could do to stay on his feet. Flashes of steel cut through the air. A whirlwind of attacks assailed him. Gerrick was not able to deflect or parry every blow. Blood flowed from gashes on his arms, legs and torso.

Gerrick jumped back out of the fight. Before Warren could close the gap, he threw up his hands shouting a word of magic. A burst of air flew from his hands, sending Warren flying backwards and onto his back, his war axes ripped from his hands, scattering on the ground. With the momentum of the spell, Warren rolled backwards onto his feet. Without missing a beat, he whipped out his two-handed battle axe ready for Gerrick who was almost at him. Gerrick brought both swords down over his head hoping to overpower Warren. Warren threw up his axe locking weapons with Gerrick.

"If you thought I was good with two axes, Gerrick, you haven't seen anything yet," Warren said.

Pushing Gerrick back, Warren went into his next assault. He kept Gerrick at a good distance with wide sweeps and could tell Gerrick was growing nervous and impatient. Warren was almost as quick with his two-handed battle axe as with his one-handed axes. Gerrick couldn't get an opportunity to close the gap to attack. The mage tried casting a few spells, but with no effect. The space between them gave Warren plenty of time to deflect them. Warren could see more beads of sweet trickling down Gerrick's face and knew the mage couldn't last much longer.

***

Albert, Luke, and Umber stuck close to the wall, making it hard for Gruttlik and his men to split them up. One of the guards pressed the attack, targeting Albert first. Albert deflected his thrust away leaving the goblin open for an attack from Luke. Taking advantage of the opportunity, Luke lunged in with one of his daggers, cutting into the goblins side. Injured, the goblin backed away fleeing.

"You fools," Gruttlik grunted. "Don't attack one at a time. These kids ain't wimps."

The other four guards pressed the attack. Umber used his speed to maneuver around one of the goblins jumping onto his back. Sinking his claws into holes in the goblins armor, he bit down on the goblin's neck. The goblin shrieked in pain crumpling to the ground, while the other three guards kept up their assault. Albert and Luke tried to focus on one guard at a time, but they kept close to one another. Taking a risk, Luke feinted an attack, leaving himself open. One of the goblins fell for it, swinging his sword from the side. Luke ducked under the attack, letting the goblin's sword slice through the air. His risk had paid off, enabling him to drive a dagger hard into the goblin's thigh.

Albert, noticing Luke's second attacker was forced to dodge his comrade's swing, pushed off from the goblin he was facing, forcing the goblin backward. Moving quickly, he swung his sword downward at the off-balance guard slicing his arm. Luke relieved his dagger from the other goblin, spinning around Albert, and going after his former opponent. With those two guards out of the fight, Albert, Luke, and Umber teamed up on the final guard. Attacking from all three sides, the guard finally went down in surrender.

"Warren has taught you two well," Gruttlik complemented them, taking his shield from his back and drawing his sword.

Albert, Luke, and Umber circled Gruttlik preparing to attack. Umber came from behind, trying to jump on his back. At the same time Albert rushed him from the front. Spinning, Gruttlik deflected Albert's attack and smashed Umber mid-air with his shield. Umber sailed through the air skidding to the ground unconscious.

"It's okay," said Albert, trying to control himself from freaking out. "He's just knocked out."

Luke took a deep breath. "All right, Albert, follow my lead."

Luke moved in, jabbing both daggers forward. Gruttlik blocked with his shield allowing Luke's daggers to sink deep into the wood. With Luke's daggers locked up, the goblin attacked him in a downward arc with his sword. Before he could make contact, Albert was there locking swords with Gruttlik. Gruttlik was now trying to overpower both boys at the same time. Luke used all his strength to force Gruttlik backward. Albert, guessing what Luke was trying to do, stepped on one of the goblin's feet. This kept the goblin from steeping backward and keeping himself on his feet. Gruttlik lost balance and crashed to the ground losing his shield to Luke, whose daggers were still lodged deep into its wood.

Albert pressed the attack, forcing Gruttlik to crawl backward on the ground trying to parry his attacks. Strike after strike, Albert was wearing Gruttlik down. Swinging as hard as he could, Albert knocked Gruttlik's sword from his hand. He stood breathing heavily, sword high in the air. Albert delayed for a moment, wondering if he should bring his sword down to finish Gruttlik off. Before he could decide, Gruttlik fished something from of his pocket and threw it to the ground. A blinding light filled the area, forcing Albert to shield his eyes. It took several moments for Albert's vision to come back. When it finally did, Gruttlik was gone.

***

Warren deflected both of Gerrick's blades and kicked him hard in the stomach. The mage rolled backward onto the ground. Before Gerrick could catch his breath, Warren smacked him across the jaw with the hilt of his axe. Towering over Gerrick, He could see the fear in his eyes. Warren gripped his battle-ax firmly in his hand ready to strike. A bright light flashed through the room, causing Warren to shield his eyes. Gerrick was able to shield his eyes from the flash with his arm. He could either continue the fight with Warren and hope the distraction could give him the upper hand, or he could escape and live another day.

Gerrick used the distraction to limp to the exit at the back of the cavern. With what little strength he had left, Gerrick pointed to the ceiling, casting a spell. Warren recovered from the flash in time to see the mage work his magic. The ceiling shook and large chunks of rock broke free, falling to the ground.

"Luke! Albert! We need to get out of here," he shouted. "Back through the tunnel."

Luke, still trying to pry his daggers from the shield, scooped it up to take it with him as he made for the tunnel. Albert hurried to Umber scooping him off the ground chasing after Luke. Warren collected his axes waited for the two at the entrance to make sure they made it safely. They ran, pushing themselves to the very brink of collapsing as the tunnel crumpled behind them. Once back in the staging room, Albert and Luke fell to the floor gasping for breath. Warren took a few deep breaths of his own, shouldered his axes, and patted the boys on their back.

"Great job, you two," he said with a smile. "I couldn't be prouder. Now come on. We got to get back to the colony." He took off at a light jog toward the hall leading to the wyvern colony. Albert and Luke groaned, as they wearily pushed themselves to their feet and followed Warren.

Chapter 21: Sunchaser

When the group made it back to the colony Umber had regained consciousness. Albert briefly explained that Gruttlik's shield had knocked him out, Gruttlik and Gerrick had managed to escape, and that they couldn't pursue them, because Gerrick had brought down the cavern while fleeing. Disappointed that he couldn't have been of more help, Umber curled into Albert, apologetic.

"No need bud," Albert consoled him. "The important part is the wyverns are free."

What goblins were left were sitting outside of Gruttlik's mansion guarded by both wyverns and elves. Calfuray ran to them, a look of concern on her face. Albert and his friends were battered, bruised, and were covered with a thick layer of dirt.

"What happened?" she asked. "Are you all right?"

"Yeah, we're fine," Warren replied looking disappointed. "Gerrick and Gruttlik got away. Are those the goblins that surrendered?"

Calfuray nodded her head.

"What are you going to do with them?" Albert asked.

"This lot, along with the ones in the palace dungeon, will help clear out this city. When they are done, they are free to leave this mountain and our forest," she replied.

"That's awfully nice of you," said Luke, disappointed their punishment wasn't more severe.

Calfuray chortled. "We are not a vengeful people, my friend. Oh, Ashearah and Sunchaser would like to speak with you. They are up above, just outside the opening." She ordered one of her men to bring them their hippogriffs.

"Ugh," sighed Warren, disgusted with flying again. Albert and Luke laughed to each other at Warren's discomfort.

Mounting their hippogriffs, they soared into the air. Umber rode with Albert, as he was still weak from being knocked out. They climbed high into the air out of the cavern's opening. Ashearah, Lilious, and Sunchaser were seen conversing on a large boulder a little way from the opening. Descending, they discovered a great platform built on top of the mountain. Ashearah, Lilious, and Sunchaser approached them as they dismounted. Statues of wyverns with crowns atop their heads circled the parameter of the platform.

"Welcome back," announced Ashearah. "By all that shaking a few minutes ago, I'm going to guess things didn't go well."

"We all lived and that's what matters," said Warren, trying to be positive.

"I'm guessing Gruttlik got away," she replied.

"Gerrick too," added Albert.

"Gerrick was there?" Ashearah said surprised.

"Sure was," replied Luke. "My dad sent him running for his life, though."

"Luke is exaggerating," said Warren. "It was a close call. I hate to admit, it but Gerrick is probably a better fighter than I am. If he had expected us to be there, the encounter would have gone another way."

"It sounds like this puzzle is far from being solved," sighed Ashearah.

"At least my people are free, and Gerrick has been scared out of these lands," added Sunchaser, his voice soothing and majestic. "Let us focus on that happiness instead of the grimness of Gerrick."

Albert drew back dumbfounded, "You can talk?"

"I can speak most of the tongues of men, young Dragoon," Sunchaser replied. "I am pleased to be able to finally meet you, Albert," he said cheerfully. "Thank you all, for what you have done. If it were not for you three, our peoples would still be slaves to Gerrick and his pawns."

Warren bowed before Sunchaser. "It was my pleasure, Your Highness." Albert and Luke bowed after seeing Warren bow.

Sunchaser chuckled. "You do not need to bow. You are the heroes of Daratrine. Stories will be told of your heroics for generations."

Huge smiles crossed Albert and Luke's faces. The thought of being heroes and having stories told of them began to inflate their egos.

"Heroes of Daratrine," smiled Luke, pleased at the sound.

"I wonder if people will bow to us as we walk by?" asked Albert.

"Remember, you two, true heroes take accolades with a bit of humility," reminded Warren.

Lilious nudged them on the shoulder, "Children."

Albert nudged her back, "You are one of those heroes as well."

Her eyes brightened and a smirk flashed across her face. Lilious quickly composed herself before anyone could see.

"Now. Albert, I am sure you have plenty of questions for me," Sunchaser continued. "What would you like to know?"

"Why me?" he asked a little too quickly. "If you didn't bring me here, who did? And the darkness from my dream have we stopped it or are we too late?"

Sunchaser looked at him caringly and answered. "Sadly, I don't know who brought you to Thu'hilen. Why you? I cannot say. I was instructed by my father before Gerrick had him executed, that a boy would arrive in our world on a certain date. He told me this boy would free our people and destroy the evil that was destined to consume our world. I was instructed to mark you as the first in a new line of Dragoons. I had to bribe a goblin to release me on that day so I could be there to meet you in the forest. I so badly wanted to talk to you and let you know what was happening, but I could not risk being gone from the colony too long. Who knows what Gruttlik would have done to my people if he had found out I was missing? I am sorry I left you there in the forest, though I'm glad to see you were found and taken care of." He turned and bowed to Warren.

"It was nothing," shrugged Warren.

"Nonetheless. The world is indebted to you, Warren, for taking care of our young Dragoon."

"So, are you going to teach me how to be a Dragoon?" Albert asked timidly.

Sunchaser's eyes dropped. "Unfortunately, I cannot. The Dragoon disappeared well before my time. Besides, the Daratrine Wyverns were never used in the marking and training of a Dragoon. The Kadala Wyverns were the ones who lived closest to the secret Dragoon monastery of Nian. They were the ones who knew the arts to train a Dragoon, and they disappeared at the same time as well. I'm sorry but I'm afraid you may be on your own, but I will help in any way that I can."

"Do you think maybe Gerrick has them secretly imprisoned just like you guys were?" asked Luke.

"It is possible, but if he does… I don't think it will be that way much longer. I'm afraid he may get rid of them now that you have discovered what he is doing," Sunchaser replied solemnly.

"So, if the Kadala Wyverns were the only ones that could mark people as Dragoons?" wondered Albert. "How were you able to mark me?"

"I never said the Kadala Wyverns were the *only* ones that could mark a person to become a Dragoon," Sunchaser politely corrected. "Kadala is the birthplace of the wyverns. So the Dragoons decided to make their monastery there?"

"Then how did you get here?" asked Warren.

Sunchaser looked over to Warren. "My father told me, many years before the Dragoons disappeared, there was a plan to establish three other Dragoon monasteries, one in the west, one in the south and one in the east. These mountains were chosen along with the elves of the forest as the western monastery. The swamps of Zolin for the monastery in the south. The cliffs of Baerll were chosen in the east for the last."

"Great!" said Luke, excitedly. "Two more wyvern colonies to go set free."

"That might not be necessary, Luke," replied Sunchaser. "My father never knew whether the other two colonies were every created or not. I'm afraid me and my people might be the last of our kind."

Everyone grew silent as the thought saddened their minds.

"Lilious and I must get back to our kingdom. With Uthael back to his rightful self, who knows how much longer he'll last?" Ashearah announced. "Calfuray and her men will stay behind to help, and we shall send others, King Sunchaser."

Sunchaser bowed in appreciation.

"We'll come too," Warren added. "Who knows if Uthael had back up plans in store, just in case something like this happened."

"Thank you, my friends," Ashaerah bowed. "Your assistance is greatly appreciated, and you are welcome to stay with the elves as long as you like."

As they prepared to leave, Sunchaser asked if he could have a moment alone with Albert and Umber. The three walked to the edge of the platform overlooking the Ethanan forest and into the Great Plains.

"You two are the first human and wyvern pairing in a long time, as I have said before," Sunchaser said with reverence. "From the moment you touched that egg, Albert, you two became one. As such, neither of you can live without the other. If one of you were to die so would the other."

Albert and Umber looked at each other fearful.

"Do not be discouraged, my young friends," said Sunchaser. "For my father told me that the bond between the two is strong, one being able to preserve the other. How long that moment is I do not know, but if you are always by each other's side, you need not worry."

"So, if I was to get injured really bad, Umber could keep me alive?" Albert asked mystified.

"In a sense."

"Cool," he and Umber looked at each with shared excitement.

"Now as you grow together and your bond becomes stronger, you two will notice changes happening to you. Some may be good. Some may be bad. Having no experience being a Dragoon's companion I cannot know for sure. Now you'd best be going. I have a feeling more news awaits you in the chambers of the Elvan King."

"Thanks, Sunchaser," Albert said. "Umber and I will most likely be staying with Warren and Luke for a while. You should come to visit."

"Indeed, I will. Now your friends are waiting for you."

Albert bowed and began to turn away when Umber jumped out of his arms. He bowed low to the ground. Albert felt his grief that he would be leaving his people so shortly after having freed them.

"It's okay Umber. If you want to stay with your people for a while, you can," Albert informed him.

Sunchaser shook his head, putting a paw on Umber's shoulder. "Go, my son. There will be plenty of time to be with your people when all this is over."

Emboldened, Umber nodded with a smile and ran back to Albert, claiming his perch on Albert's shoulder.

"Albert, one more thing," Sunchaser said, stopping them. "Listen to Umber. He and you may not know it yet, but he is wise beyond his years. Out of all the pups that could have bonded with you, he was the one willing to sacrifice his free will to become a Dragoon's companion. As a Dragoon, you will soon be able to control not only him but other dragons. May you use this power wisely."

With that thought in his mind, they waved goodbye. Mounting their hippogriff, they took to the sky. Flying back to Ethosis was a lot more enjoyable than to the wyvern colony. Albert wasn't worrying the entire trip about fighting goblins and enjoyed the serenity of the cool breeze flowing over them. They cheered on Umber as he practiced twists, turns, corkscrews and barrel rolls in the air, feeling more confident in his flying. As they looked down, they saw that the forest was already starting to recover from the curse King Uthael had placed on the land. The dark, overgrown moss that covered leaves and shadowed the forest floor was receding. As the light broke through the trees, its rays brought new life to the forest as Ethanan's wildlife began returning.

Chapter 22: Long Live the Queen

Ashearah's destination was the grassy area in front of the palace. As they began their descent, the elvan people began cheering their return. Elsin was there waiting to greet them, his face sullen, like someone ready to give bad news.

"High Priestess Ashearah," he said, concern in his voice. "You must all come quickly."

"What is it, Elsin?" replied Ashearah.

"It's King Uthael. His strength is failing him. I believe he will not be with us much longer."

"Let us make haste, then."

The group slid from their hippogriffs to rush after Elsin into the palace. He led them through the main hall to a door behind the throne. Inside the room was circular with no exits. Two palace guards stood watch and elvish writing formed a large circle on the floor. When they were all in the room, the two guards closed the door. Ashearah asked everyone to stand within the circle. When she spoke a phrase in elvish, the words on the floor illuminated. A bright light lit the room. When the light vanished, the door behind them was now in front of them. They entered the king's royal chambers. On the bed in front of them lay a now ancient and frail Uthael.

An elvan nurse dressed in white was by his side attending to him. Everyone hurried to Uthael's bedside.

"How much longer do we have?" asked Ashearah.

"His strength is fading fast," replied the nurse. "He will slip into the next life at any moment."

Ashearah kneeled by his side, taking his hand in hers, "My King."

King Uthael opened his eyes. His iris' white and cloudy. Looking around aimlessly he tried speaking her name. The nurse put a glass of water to his mouth, allowing him to take a few sips, wetting his throat. "Forgive me, my child. Forgive me. Forgive me. Forgive me," begged Uthael.

Ashearah squeezed his hand gently, "Please, Your Highness, speak no more of this. You have been forgiven of everything." Tears brimmed Uthael's eyes.

"My King, we need to know. Where is Gerrick?" At the mention of Gerrick's name, scorn covered King Uthael's face. He pressed his mouth tightly closed.

"Please Your Highness. You have to tell us where he is," Albert pleaded.

Uthael looked around, confused, "Who is that?"

"This is Albert, My Lord," informed Ashearah. "He is the first Dragoon to be born in centuries."

Uthael croaked a laugh. "Gerrick told me someone might try to come into the forest wanting to explore the mountain looking for wyverns. I'm glad the boy succeeded, and our people are free once more." A smile beamed across his face but faded to a grimace. "I despise Gerrick for deceiving me. For forcing me to hurt the people I care for the most."

"Then please King Uthael, tell me where he is so we can stop him," Albert pleaded again.

King Uthael's face grew woeful. "I don't know where he is."

Everyone in the room sighed in disappointment. More tears streaked down Uthael's face.

"My King, what is the matter?" asked Ashaerah.

Uthael's hand searched the air. "The boy. Where is the boy?"

"Here." Ashearah grabbed Albert's hand placing it in Uthael's.

Uthael's hand was cold, and thin and reminded Albert of his great-grandmother's just before she had passed away. Tears continued to stream down Uthael's face as words came between sobs.

"My dear boy, I am so sorry..." he cried. "I should have been here to welcome you... with open arms... celebrating your arrival. Taking you up to the mountain myself— so, you could be paired with a wyvern." Uthael erupted into violent coughing. His nursemaid hurried to his side asking everyone to leave. Uthael threw up his hand, dismissing her. "I must still apologize," he heaved.

"Please, please, forgive me my dear boy," he continued. "I instead sent those nasty Enokis after you, threw a fake party to try to gain your confidence, and planned to kill you in your sleep." He took a deep, agonizing breath. "I am so thankful for Ashearah. If it were not for her, we would all still be prisoners to Gerrick and his trickery."

Ashearah, with tears in her eyes, put a loving hand on Uthael's leg, "I only wanted the kind, loving, and wise king I knew as a child back."

Uthael grabbed her hand, stroking her wrist with his thumb. "I am so sorry everyone. Many years ago, I saw in my dreams visions of darkness encompassing the land. Desperate to find a way to counteract this evil, I took council from Gerrick. He told me he could help me fight this darkness. He gave me a medallion that he said would give me back my strength. Little did I know that it would twist my mind and turn me into his pawn."

"About the darkness?" Albert asked. "In my dream, I saw the darkness emanating from this forest and out into the world. I've been wondering, was I having that dream because I was supposed to stop that from happening, or has it already happened?"

"I'm afraid, dear Albert, that this darkness you see in your dream has already spread across all of Thu'hilen," Uthael informed them grimly. "I regret the part I played in bringing this darkness upon us. Will you ever forgive me, young Dragoon?" he pleaded.

Albert smiled. "Of course. It wasn't your fault. Gerrick had control of your mind."

Uthael smiled peacefully. "The innocence of youth. How I wish we could all be so forgiving. Young Dragoon, do not let fear guide your actions, for if you do it will lead to your destruction as it did mine. Fear led me into accepting Gerrick's help, and in turn, the evil that I wanted to prevent."

Tired of speaking, King Uthael began to cough violently. Fearing the worst, his nurse asked everyone to leave so she could treat him again. Albert and the rest of his friends walked back to the door they entered through, taking one last look at King Uthael. His nurse had her hands placed over him casting a spell. She was trying to bring him back, but Albert could tell she was losing the battle.

They were again back in the main hall. Ashearah had stayed behind in the King's chamber to be with Uthael in his last moments.

"What will happen after he dies?" asked Albert, turning to Lilious.

"Does he have any children that will take his throne?" asked Luke.

"No. No children," she replied. "Though we do not decide the right to rule through birthright. The council agrees on who should lead next, then they petition the people for their agreement."

Fifteen minutes passed before Ashearah walked into the hall. The council had gathered, awaiting the news. "King Uthael has slipped through the veil of this life and into the next. May his ancestors see him to the evergreen hills," she announced. A moment of silence covered the hall as her people mourned his passing.

After the appropriate time had passed, she met with Albert and the others.

"Are you all right?" asked Albert.

"I will be," she answered. "My friends, I know you are probably eager to start your journey home, but we would be honored if you would be our guests for a few more days."

"Sure," replied Albert and Luke enthusiastically. Warren shook his head chuckling.

"Thank you," she bowed. "In two days, there will be a ceremony to honor King Uthael. My people and I would be most grateful if you would attend."

"We would be more than happy to attend," Warren said, bowing.

"Thank you." Ashearah bowed in return. "Lilious, would you escort them upstairs to the guest rooms?"

Lilious bowed to her mother then led them out of the great hall. As they ascended the stairs to their rooms, Albert, Luke, and Lilious excitedly talked about their day, Luke and Lilious arguing who sent more goblins running for their lives. Umber had found a new perch on Warren's shoulder, the two marveling at the elvan architecture and craftsmanship.

Reaching the common room, Lilious instructed them which room would be whose. "Albert, your room will be on the right and Luke…"

"Will be on the left," reminded Luke. "We know already."

Lilious rolled her eyes, annoyed. "Warren, you will have the room in the middle."

He nodded his head, then plodded to one of the sofas easing himself down, exhausted from his fight with Gerrick.

"Warren?" Lilious said, getting his attention. "Would you like me to get a healer?"

He looked at her confused, then looked down at himself in tatters. Years of training and fighting in battle had taught him how to ignore pain. "Thank you," he said with a long sigh.

Lilious bowed. "You three ought to get cleaned up," she told Albert, Luke, and Umber. "I will be back in a little bit to get you for dinner."

The two boys and the wyvern joined Warren on the sofas. A few minutes later, maids came to fill the baths in their rooms, while elvan healers, treated their wounds. Some of Warren's were deep and the elves kept muttering to themselves in disbelief, wondering how Warren was still alive. The baths ready and wounds mended, they headed to their rooms.

"Oh yeah, don't forget a towel," reminded Albert, before shutting his door.

Warren looked after him befuddled as Luke loudly thanked him for reminding him.

Albert and Umber were the first to make it back to the common room. Tying one of his socks into a ball, Albert tossed it high into the air for Umber to fly up and catch it mid-flight. Luke was the next to make his way into the room and joined in. It was a lot harder for Umber when Luke threw the sock. Not being able to read his thoughts, the wyvern had to predict where it would be thrown by watching Luke's eye movements. When Lilious returned, they greeted her, then went back to their game with Umber.

"Is Warren not out yet?" she asked.

"Nope," replied Luke.

"Guess I'll just have a seat then," she said sitting on one of the sofas.

A few minutes later, Warren exited his room giving Albert and Luke a dirty look. "Thanks for telling me about the *Refresher*."

"Albert did tell you to keep your towel close by," Luke laughed.

Warren rolled his eyes.

Lilious stood, "Are we ready to go down?"

"I think we are now," replied Warren.

When they entered the dining chamber, Ashearah and the rest of the high council greeted them. All ten council members thanked them individually for the service they had rendered to Ethosis. Ashearah guided Albert and his friends to the head of the table where six seats sat empty beside the grand chair that used to be Uthael's, a bell was rung, and servants began bringing in the food.

From the very start, this feast was drastically different from the last. The emotion in the room was cheerful. Beautiful music played in the background as those who remembered Uthael, before the curse, toasted the great king he was. At one point, Albert, Luke, and Lilious were asked to recount their journey into the mountain. As the feast came to an end, Galthanis stood, calling for everyone's attention.

"Friends, this may not be the appropriate time, but with the passing of King Uthael we are now leaderless," he said mournfully. "The council and I have been deliberating this day since his passing, and we, as well as the rest of the Ethosis, people have come to a consensus." Galthanis turned and looked at Ashearah. "High Priestess Ashearah, we offer you the right and privilege of leading our people, if you would accept it." He bowed to her as he finished. The rest of the council stood, turned, and bowed to her as well.

Ashearah looked around the room with a shocked expression. Taking a deep breath, she stood, "Though I do not feel worthy of this calling, I would be honored to lead our people with the council at my side."

Everyone in the room cheered, some hailing her name.

Ashearah held her hand in the air, calling for silence. "My first act, if the council would allow me after the burial ceremony for the King, is to order the immediate dispelling of the barrier around our forest."

"I think our people would want nothing more," Galthanis smiled.

"I think so too," she smiled back. "Our people need to go out and join the world once again."

The room broke into cheers. Elves congratulated her with a bow. Music again filled the room, this time with boisterous melodies and singing.

Soon the party moved into the great hall where the elves of Ethosis were already dancing in celebration. The elves' behavior surprised Albert and Luke. Since they had been in Ethosis they had not seen one elf so much as give a smile. Until now, they had assumed all elves were stuffy and had no fun.

Albert, Luke, Umber, and Warren stood off to the side watching as the elves danced on the floor. Neither one of them was up for dancing. Several elvan women approached Warren inquiring if he would dance. Each time, he smiled politely, pointing to his wedding ring, "I'm sorry. I'm already taken." Albert and Luke laughed each time a girl got shot down by Warren. Both knew it wasn't because he was married that he wasn't dancing, but like them, he didn't like dancing either. After a couple of minutes they watched as Ashearah and Lilious walked over.

"And, why aren't the Heroes of Ethosis out celebrating?" said Ashearah staring them down.

"Because neither of us like dancing," Luke laughed.

"Is that right?" she said with a raised brow. "Well then, as queen, I order each of you to dance with me."

All three of them chuckled.

"And if we don't?" asked Albert.

"Then I will have each of you thrown in the dungeon until you can learn to lighten up." She grinned menacingly. She held out her arm waiting for someone to take it.

"I guess I'll be the first to suffer," Warren said jokingly, taking her arm.

Ashearah scoffed sarcastically and the two headed out onto the dance floor. Lilious then walked up to Albert holding out her arm.

"Albert care to join me?" she asked politely.

His face went red as butterflies filled his stomach.

"S-s-s-sure," he stammered taking her arm. Luke laughed at Albert as Albert nervously walked out onto the floor with Lilious.

"Well Wyvie," said Luke, looking down at Umber. "Shall we?" Umber bobbed up and down in place with excitement then jumped out onto the dance floor with Luke following behind him.

Albert nervously danced with Lilious. The only girl he had ever danced with was his mother, to classic rock in their living room back at home. He stepped on her feet several times. "I'm sorry," Albert apologized. "I'm not very good at this."

Lilious giggled, "Don't worry Albert, you are doing very well."

When the song ended, everyone switched partners. Ashearah took Albert's hand as Lilious took Luke's. Warren stood off to the side with Umber on his shoulder.

Dancing with Ashearah reminded Albert a lot of his mother. Tears brimmed his eyes as thoughts of his family flooded his mind. Ashearah looked at him concerned.

"Albert, my dear, are you all right?" she asked.

He wiped his eyes trying to clear away the tears. "Yeah, I'm fine," he said. "Dancing with you just reminds me of my mother. I just wonder if I will ever get home."

Ashearah gave Albert a hug. "Don't be sad, Albert," she said lovingly. "You will see your family again. I have seen it."

He looked at her hopeful. She smiled back at him.

"Besides, look around. You have a family here that will always be by your side."

Albert looked at his friends. He remembered all they had done for him. He remembered the promise they made to help him get back home. A rush of joy filled him. Feeling better, Albert picked up the pace as they danced, enjoying himself. When the song finished Albert and Ashearah bowed to each other, thanking one another for the dance. It was now Luke's turn to dance with the new queen as Albert went to stand next to Warren. Umber knowing Albert was headed over, took to the air soaring over to his shoulder, his tail wrapping around to the other.

"So, Albert, how does it feel to dance with a queen?" Warren asked with a teasing grin.

"Better than be trying to be killed by a king," he joked back.

Warren laughed heartily. "You get used to that part. The people trying to kill you I mean."

Albert looked at him worried.

"Albert, I'm joking," Warren said. "Besides, I'll always be there to keep you safe. Plus, Luke wouldn't let you go anywhere without him."

It wasn't long before the party died down and people began to retire for the night. Ashearah and Lilious escorted Albert, Luke, Warren, and Umber to their suite. Gathering in the sofas around the fire the friends talked about the events of the past couple of days. Albert, Luke, and Lilious rehearsed in more detail about their journey through the tunnel and them narrowly escaping getting caught by Kobolds. They reminisced about sneaking around the goblin tunnels, seeing the hatchery, getting themselves captured, and escaping. Warren, with a big grin on his face, was excited to hear about their narrow escapes and near misses. Ashearah on the other hand was more apprehensive, letting out gasps here and there.

It was close to midnight when Ashearah and Lilious stood to leave. "Well, we must bid you three good night," said Ashearah.

Warren stood with a yawn, "I guess it is rather late. Besides, you three kids look like you can hardly stay awake."

"Nah, we're fine," said Luke, rubbing his eyes.

"Sure, you are," replied Warren, helping Luke to his feet. "Come on, son. Let's get some sleep. Albert, you too."

Albert got to his feet holding Umber with one arm. "Well, good night then everyone."

"Good night. We will see you in the morning," said Ashearah opening the door to exit.

"Good night. Oh, and Albert. Thank you," said Lilious before leaving.

"What was that all about?" asked Warren, puzzled.

"I think it was because I told her I would find a way to help Ashearah when she thought she would never see her again," replied Albert.

"That was a big promise," said Warren. "I don't know if, at your age, I would have been able to make one like that."

"I couldn't just let her sit there and worry about her mother, could I?" responded Albert.

"No. No, you couldn't," replied Warren. "Good night, Albert. Good night, Luke," he bid before entering his room.

"Good night, Al," said Luke. "I'm glad you talked me into going on this journey. It was worth it." Luke closed the door to his room, leaving Albert and Umber alone in the common room.

Albert stood, one hand on the door to his room, the other holding Umber. They watched as the last flame flickered out of existence. As he turned the door handle, a servant girl entered the common room, a pitcher in her hand. Albert watched as she doused the fire, making sure it was out. As she turned to leave, she stopped, noticing him watching her.

"Thank you master Albert and master Umber," she bowed, before hurrying out of the room.

Slightly embarrassed, Albert went into his room. He wasn't used to being thanked for something he didn't really do. Hopefully, it wouldn't be like this the rest of the time they were in Ethosis. Two more days, then it was back out after Gerrick. Albert was bummed he hadn't figured out who brought him here and he wasn't able to go home yet. A part of him was glad though. He had gained some amazing new friends, especially Umber, and he couldn't imagine a life without them now. He was wishing to find a way to combine his two worlds. Pushing that from his mind, he flopped down on the bed, Umber by his side, and fell asleep.

Chapter 23: Journey Back

Albert woke to beams of sunlight shining on his face. Umber was still curled at his side. As he reached down to pet him, Umber leaned upward, reading his thoughts. Albert laughed to himself. Would he ever surprise him? Umber turned his head and, with a sleepy smile, shook his head, no. Albert stretched, got out of bed, put on his clothes, and then exited the room.

The two entered the main chamber, finding Warren and Luke sitting around the fireplace eating breakfast. The smell of pastries and honey glazed ham filled the air. Their stomachs rumbled with hunger. Umber couldn't wait. He flew just a few inches above the ground, landing next to the serving table. He reached up with his neck and grabbed several large slices of ham. The wyvern dropped them on the floor and began devouring them. Albert was embarrassed. Umber feeling his thoughts, reached back up, snagged a plate, and placed the meat on it before continuing. Warren and Luke chuckled at the site.

"Morning," said Albert, sitting down and grabbing a plate full of food.

No one spoke as the four shoveled food into their mouths. It had been a couple days since they had a good breakfast, and they weren't going to pass it up. A knock on the main door rang through the air as Lilious strolled in.

"Good morning, everyone," she said happily. "May I join you?"

"Of course," replied Warren before shoveling more food into his mouth.

Lilious grabbed a plate. She filled it with fruits and hot cereal before sitting down.

"So, what are we doing today?" asked Albert enthusiastically after gulping down a large mouthful.

"Today, we perform King Uthael's burial ceremony," responded Lilious, with reverence.

Oops. Albert had forgotten that was today because they had been so busy the day before hanging around Ethosis, receiving yet more gifts and making trips back and forth to the wyvern colony.

"I'm sorry," replied Albert, ashamed. "I should have remembered."

"No need to apologize," responded Lilious. "Elves do not view death as most do. We celebrate it, for we know they have passed onto a better life, one without pain or sorrow."

"Sounds like a view we should all adopt," said Warren, respectfully.

"Thank you." Lilious bowed. "When we are done eating, clothes will be brought up for the ceremony."

When they finished eating, a maid entered the common room carrying funeral garments. Albert, Luke, and Warren grabbed their clothing and headed to the rooms to change. The garments were of pure white with gold and silver trimmings. When they returned to the common room Lilious had gone leaving the maid to usher them to the great hall.

The entire city had gathered filling the main floor. Ashearah was sitting on the throne with Lilious standing at her side, both were in elegant white and gold dresses. A majestic casket sat in the middle of the hall with King Uthael laying peacefully inside. Albert, Umber, and their friends were instructed to stand by the dais next to the high council.

A member started the ceremony. He walked around the casket crumbling herbs and sprinkled fluid over Uthael as he went along chanting in elvish. When he was done, another council member did the routine with a different foliage and a different fluid. This continued till all the council members had completed their part of the ritual. When done, Ashearah stood holding her arms in the air. In elvish, she praised their king and blessed him with peace and happiness as he traveled into the next life.

When she was done with the ritual, ceremonial guards surrounded Uthael's casket. The guards lifted it onto their shoulders and carried the casket out the front of the palace with Ashearah, Lilious, and the council following. Albert, Luke, Warren, and Umber were ushered in behind them continuing the precession with the rest of the city following behind. They traveled around the back of the palace and out of the city to an old oak tree slightly smaller than the great tree that housed the palace itself. There, the guards set the casket at its base. All watched as the tree came to life. It groaned and creaked as it lifted off the ground. Tree roots rose from the dirt enveloping the casket and taking it into the tree itself. Within moments, the casket disappeared into the depths of the tree and the old oak returned to its original state.

Once the ceremony was over, everyone returned to the palace. There in the great hall, another grand feast began, this one to celebrate the choosing of a new leader. By the end, Albert, Luke, and Umber had eaten more food than they should have and felt they were about to burst. They stumbled back to the rooms, heading to bed. Albert lay in bed disappointed he had to leave tomorrow. However, he was excited to discover where they were going next.

They met in Ashearah's private meeting chamber the next morning to discuss what the next step was.

"So, why are we here?" asked Luke, intrigued.

Warren put his hand on Luke's shoulder giving it a bit of squeeze. "Try to show a little more respect please, Luke."

Luke's face stiffened as he tried to ignore the slight pain from his father's grasp. "What?" he said with disbelief. "A few days ago, before she was a queen, she was our friend."

Warren began to retort when Ashearah interrupted. "It's okay, Luke is right. I am your friend before I am a queen."

"See," Luke said shrugging off his dad's grip.

Albert spoke next. "Yeah, like Luke said, why are we here?"

"We were wondering what you planned to do next?" Elyon spoke.

"Oh, that's easy," responded Albert. "Go after Gerrick of course."

"Hold on there, Albert," Warren jumped in. Albert looked at him confused and defeated. "We have no idea where he went. We are going to need King Altraeus' help. My plan was to head to Fort Valdrum, there we would inform Captain Reno of the situation. I will ask him to send a message on to Port Junon to send out ships in search of Gerrick."

"So, we aren't headed out after Gerrick then?" Albert asked, disappointed.

"I'm afraid not, Albert," Warren said trying to console him. "We will head back to Brookshire. There we will discuss what our next move is."

Albert stood depressed, his hopes of getting home were moving further and further into the future.

"Take heart young Dragoon," Ashearah said cheerfully. "You will find out where Gerrick is soon enough. Until then relax, enjoy your time, and be a kid."

"Which brings us to why we asked you here," spoke Galthanis. "We would like to send an envoy of men with you to Fort Valdrum to help us get out into the world once again. If you would be so willing."

"We would be more than happy to help you restore the relations you once had in this world," Warren smiled.

Ashearah clapped her hands together. "Fantastic. Then Galthanis, Lilious and an escort will accompany you on your journey home."

"Lilious?" Albert said a little too excited.

"Why not?" Lilious responded laughing at his eagerness. "I've always wanted to see outside these woods and who better to show me than my friends?"

"Are you sure about this Ashearah?" Warren asked.

"I am," she replied hesitantly.

"Well, if that's your choice," he said surprised. "I know a couple old wizards who would love to come meet you. I will have one of them set up a Kryon crystal in your city, if that is okay?"

"A Kryon crystal?" Ashearah looked confused.

"It's a small crystal that is buried in the ground. Once its activated, certain mages can tune into it to teleport themselves or others."

"Then Lilious would be able to travel home instantly?" she asked enthusiastically.

"Yep."

"Very well then. We shall have a Kryon crystal placed at the center of our city."

With everything settled they went back to their rooms for their bags. Before noon, the group was ready to head out. Saying their goodbyes, they headed toward Sanoran. The road back was much more pleasant this time around. Ethanan was back to a place of peace and solitude. At Sanoran they found elves busy repairing the city. Leegahr was still magistrate of the little town with a new elvan assistant, who strongly *encouraged* what decisions he should make.

West road to Fort Valdrum was quiet and uneventful the entire way. The next two days to reach the fort was spent by Albert and Luke telling Lilious all their mishaps along the road. Lilious and the other elves were mesmerized with the vastness of the Great Plains. Most of them never had seen such open space before. To Albert it seemed to excite them as much as frighten. At the fort, citizens were surprised at elves in their city. The fort was built well after King Uthael had imprisoned the elves in their own forest. Gerard immediately escorted them to the garrison for a meeting with Captain Reno.

"I agree wholeheartedly, old friend," stated Captain Reno, after hearing about Gerrick's escape. "The search for this Gerrick can't be delayed any longer. I will send two copies of a letter immediately, one to Port Junon and one to Tiranos. We'll find him."

"Thank you, Captain," replied Warren.

"It is my pleasure," said Reno, holding out his hand.

Warren grasped it firmly. "Take good care of our friends." He motioned to Galthanis.

"We will," smiled the captain. "And Warren. If you need anything." His gaze switched to Albert. "My men and I will be there."

"Thank you," replied Albert. Great! Another admirer praised him for something he didn't really do.

"Well, Galthanis, this is where we part ways for now," said Warren, biding the elves farewell.

"Till we meet again," replied Galthanis. "Farewell, Albert. Ethosis will be expecting your quick return."

"Bye Gal. I'm sure Ashearah will find some reason for me to return," responded Albert.

They bid the rest of the elves farewell leaving them in Captain Reno's care. It only took Albert and his friends another day-and-a-half to get back to Brookshire. As they entered the town, the people ran up to Warren, cheering his return. They were glad he was back, and that Mayor Dryden was no longer solely in charge. The crowd swarmed them with questions. What the lizard creature was that was riding with Albert? Where did the elvan girl come from? What of the Ethosis elves? Was she an Ethosian?

"Everybody, please," shouted Warren. "You will get your answers later, so please allow us to retire home and get cleaned up. Unless you want to spend time in jail?"

The crowd stood, confused, trying to remember if their town even had a jail. Taking advantage of the confusion, Albert and his group pressed on home. Riding to the stables around back of the house, they unloaded their gear and turned out their horses. Leaving the barn, Warren picked up a few pebbles from the ground throwing, them at the back door. Albert, Lilious, and Umber looked at Luke confused. He just smiled and shrugged, "It's just their thing."

"Gemma, come quickly. Your father and the boys are home," called Nicolet, smiling as she came out the door. She walked to greet them when she spotted Umber skirting along the ground. Her eyes grew large with excitement at the site of the wyvern.

"Uh oh, Umber. Better run for cover," warned Albert.

Umber looked up at him confused. Before he could blink, Nicolet had run over and scooped him up. She began investigating every inch of him commenting on everything that she loved. Warren rolled his eyes, putting his arm around her and kissing her on the forehead. After she had had her fill of examining Umber, she gave her son and Albert warm hugs welcoming them back.

"Thank you for coming home in one piece," said Nicolet.

Gemma soon came running out of the house, jumping into her father's arms. He held her close, "I missed you too, Gemma." After getting down, she gave Luke a quick hug than punched him in the arm.

"I'm mad at you," she stated. "You left me behind."

He nudged her back, "You wouldn't have survived the journey, anyway."

Gemma stuck her tongue out at her brother then, turning to Albert, she blushed. "Glad you made it back safely, Albert."

"Um, thanks," said Albert, awkwardly. "This is Umber," he said trying to get the attention off him.

Umber leaped into Gemma's arms with a couple of licks on her face. She giggled, holding Umber like she would a puppy. "And who is she?" asked Gemma, motioning to Lilious who had barely acknowledged her before.

Lilious stepped forward next to Albert and Luke with a bow and introduced herself. "I am Lilious, daughter of Queen Ashearah of the Ethosis elves."

Nicolet took her hand gently, "I am Nicolet, Warren's wife and the mother of Luke and Gemma. I am so excited to meet an Ethosis elf." Her eyes were bright with cheer.

"But what are you doing here?" Gemma rudely stated.

Ignoring Gemma's attitude, Lilious continued, "I am here to experience the outside world and Albert is going to show me," she said linking arms with Albert's.

"Okay, I guess you can tag along with us," replied Gemma, feigning disinterest. "Come on, Umber. Let's go inside." She turned and strode inside, Umber still in her arms.

Nicolet shook her head with a laugh. "Come on, dinner is ready. I want to hear all about your adventure."

"It's not over yet," replied Warren, concerned.